THE CHINESE BELL MURDERS

JUDGE DEE

Collection of the National Palace Museum
Taiwan, Republic of China

THE
CHINESE BELL MURDERS

ROBERT VAN GULIK

With an Introduction
by
DONALD F. LACH

THE UNIVERSITY OF CHICAGO PRESS
Chicago and London

The University of Chicago Press, Chicago 60637
The University of Chicago Press, Ltd., London

© 1958 by Robert van Gulik
© 1977 by The University of Chicago
All rights reserved. Published 1977
Printed in the United States of America

01 00 99 98 97 96 95 94 93   9 10 11 12 13 14
ISBN: 0-226-84862-0
LCN: 77-80378

The Chinese Bell Murders is published by arrangement
with Harper & Row, Publishers, Inc.

CONTENTS

DRAMATIS PERSONAE

*It should be noted that in China the surname – here
printed in capitals – precedes the personal name*

Main Characters

DEE Jen-djieh, newly appointed magistrate of Poo-yang, a
town district in Kiangsu Province. Referred to as 'Judge
Dee' or 'the judge.'

HOONG Liang, Judge Dee's trusted adviser and Sergeant
of the tribunal. Referred to as 'Sergeant Hoong' or 'the
sergeant.'

MA Joong
CHIAO Tai } the three lieutenants of Judge Dee.
TAO Gan

Persons connected with 'The Rape Murder in Half Moon Street'

HSIAO Foo-han, a butcher, father of the murdered girl.
Referred to as 'Butcher Hsiao.'

PURE JADE, his daughter, victim of the rape murder.

LOONG, a tailor living opposite Butcher Hsiao.

WANG Hsien-djoong, a Candidate of Literature.

YANG Poo, his friend.

GAO, warden of the quarter where the murder occurred.

HWANG San, a vagabond.

Persons connected with 'The Secret of the Buddhist Temple'

'Spiritual Virtue,' abbot of the Temple of Boundless Mercy.
'Complete Enlightenment,' former abbot of the same
temple.

BAO, a retired General.

WAN, a retired judge of the Provincial Court.

LING, master of the Guild of Goldsmiths.

WEN, master of the Guild of Carpenters.

Persons connected with 'The Mysterious Skeleton'

Mrs LIANG, *née* OU-YANG, widow of a wealthy Cantonese merchant.

LIANG Hoong, her son, killed by brigands.

LIANG Ko-fa, her grandson.

LIN Fan, a wealthy merchant from Canton.

Others

SHENG Pa, counsellor of the Beggars' Guild.

PAN, magistrate of the district Woo-yee.

LO, magistrate of the district Chin-hwa.

APRICOT, a prostitute of Chin-hwa.

BLUE JADE, her sister.

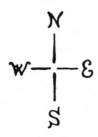

Sketch Map of Poo-yang

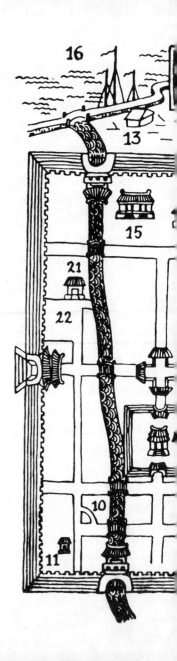

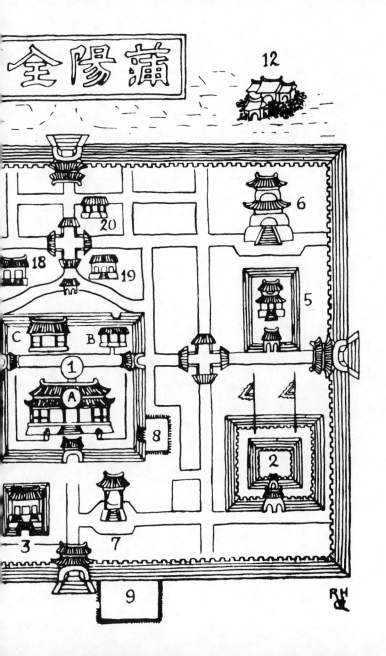

INTRODUCTION

Years ago when looking for English materials on life in traditional China, I found the novels, commentaries, and reflections of Lin Yu-tang, Pearl Buck, and Alice Tisdale Hobart very enlightening. Their perceptions, written in charming prose, gently introduced the readers of the 1930s to Chinese society, with its gentry, peasants, and businessmen of the port cities. These writers also translated sensitively certain pieces of popular Chinese literature. Materials of such caliber and character became exceedingly difficult to find in the years following the Second World War, since most Western observers of China, as well as the Chinese themselves, had become obsessed with efforts to explain the decline and fall of the Nationalist government and the rise of the Communists to power. So it was with a sense of relief and satisfaction that readers of the 1950s welcomed the appearance of Robert Hans van Gulik's Judge Dee detective novels, in which imperial China is depicted as a living, identifiable culture rather than as a characterless pawn in the international power game. Because it is no longer possible to recapture the old China by visiting the new, the Dee stories continue to be one of the best available means of recovering a bit of the everyday life of the past.

The career of Van Gulik was a varicolored tapestry woven of threads from the skeins of scholarship, diplomacy, and art. The son of a medical officer of the Netherlands army of Indonesia, he was born in 1910 in Zutphen in Holland's province of Gelderland. Between the ages of three to twelve he lived as a colonial in Indonesia. Upon his family's return to Holland in 1922, young Robert was enrolled in the classical gymnasium

I

(secondary school) at Nijmegen, where his considerable talents for language were quickly recognized. Through C. C. Uhlenbeck, a linguist of Amsterdam University, he was introduced at this early age to the study of Sanskrit and to the language of the Blackfoot Indians of America. In his spare time, he took private lessons in Chinese, his first tutor being a Chinese student of agriculture in Wageningen.

In 1934 Van Gulik attended the University of Leyden, one of Europe's major centers for East Asian studies. Here he worked at Chinese and Japanese systematically but without relinquishing his earlier interest in other Asian languages and literatures. For example, in 1932 he published a Dutch translation of an ancient Indian play written by Kālidasā (ca. A.D. 400). His doctoral dissertation on the horse cult of China, Japan, India, and Tibet, defended at Utrecht in 1934, was published in 1935 by Brill, the publisher of Leyden who specializes in Asian materials. In the meantime Van Gulik also wrote articles for Dutch periodicals on Chinese, Indian, and Indonesian topics; in these articles he first displayed his love for the ancient ways of Asia and his resigned acceptance of the changes taking place.

With his university studies behind him, Van Gulik entered the foreign service of the Netherlands in 1935. His first assignment took him to the legation at Tokyo, where he had an opportunity in off hours to pursue his private scholarly studies. Most of his subjects of inquiry were chosen with reference to the preoccupations of the traditional Chinese literati. His investigations were limited in scope, though rarely in depth, by the time restrictions under which he worked. Like a traditional Chinese gentleman, he himself collected rare books, small objets d'art, scroll paintings, and musical instruments. He also scrutinized his treasures with a scholarship and a connoisseurship that won the respect of leading Oriental collectors. He translated a famous Chinese text by Mi Fu on ink stones, the valued objects on which the calligrapher prepares his ink for writing. He was

2

himself a talented calligrapher, a rare achievement for a Westerner. He played the ancient Chinese lute (*ch'in*) and wrote two monographs about it based on Chinese sources. Most of his publications in these peaceful and seminal years were issued in Peking and Tokyo and won appreciation from both Asian and European scholars.

The holocaust of the Second World War brought an abrupt end to Van Gulik's first Tokyo sojourn. Evacuated in 1942 with other Allied diplomats, he was sent to Chungking as secretary of the Netherlands mission to China. At this remote post he published in 1944 an edition of a rare Chinese work about the Ch'an master Tung-kao, a Buddhist monk who was loyal to the Ming cause in the days of its defeat. He remained in China until the end of the European war in 1945, then returned to The Hague until 1947. The following two years he spent as Councillor of the Dutch embassy in Washington, but in 1949 he finally returned to Japan for a four-year tour of duty.

In 1940 Van Gulik had run across an anonymous eighteenth-century Chinese detective novel that entranced him. Thereafter the vagaries of war and its aftermath cut him off from many of his sources and deprived him of much of his leisure, but he managed to spend odds and ends of free time in studying Chinese popular literature, especially detective and courtroom stories. He prepared an English translation of a traditional detective tale which he published at Tokyo in a limited edition in 1949 under the title *Dee Goong An*. This story in three episodes was the first of the publications through which the Western world learned of the exploits of Judge Dee, one of China's traditional detective heroes.

Van Gulik's fascination with Judge Dee, an exemplar of the imperial magistrate and of the Confucian scholar, led him to further investigations of Chinese jurisprudence and detection. In 1956 he published his English translation of a thirteenth-century case manual called *T'ang-yin pi-shih*.

Van Gulik's engrossment with detective literature was soon paralleled by an interest in Chinese erotic literature and art, especially in that of the Ming dynasty (1368–1644). Dalliances with courtesans and concubines were often as much a part of the Chinese gentleman's life as the collecting of ink stones or the playing of the *ch'in*. To demonstrate this point, Van Gulik, always a connoisseur of Chinese pictorial art, published at Tokyo in 1951 a private edition in fifty copies of erotic color prints of the Ming era along with a handwritten essay on the history of Chinese sex life from 206 B.C. to A.D. 1644. While extramarital sex and the popular novel were generally considered off-limits for the Confucian scholar-gentleman, it is clear that many such men relished illicit sex and enjoyed and wrote novels surreptitiously. Through a number of works Van Gulik showed that although the gentlemen of traditional China often gave lip-service to high moral standards, they displayed in their personal lives the moral weakness of people everywhere.

While the erotica published by Van Gulik circulated only to a select audience, his numerous translations and adaptations of Chinese detective stories made Judge Dee famous in the West, especially during the 1950s. Whether posted in New Delhi, The Hague, or Kuala Lumpur, Van Gulik continued to turn out the Judge Dee stories, to a total of at least seventeen. His final diplomatic appointment brought him back to Tokyo in 1965 as the ambassador of the Netherlands to Japan, a post that he had long coveted. Two years later, while on home leave, Van Gulik put down his writing-brush for the last time.

Throughout his relatively short life, Van Gulik found time in the midst of his busy diplomatic career to inquire into an amazing variety of esoteric subjects and to publish his findings. He did not focus upon the great political, social, or economic problems of China, though he was certainly aware of their significance, in touch with the latest scholarly debates, and cognizant of contemporary political events. He did not specialize in a particular period, or even in literature alone, but ranged in his quests from Chinese classical antiquity (ca. 1200 B.C.–A.D. 200) to the end of the Ch'ing dynasty (A.D. 1644–1911). His interest was limited to traditional China rather than to the twentieth-century country with its postimperial and revolutionary struggles. He sought out the "little topics" usually favored by dilettantes and amateurs of arts and letters. To the investigation of these previously unstudied byways he brought his considerable talents as linguist, historian, and connoisseur. While many of his scholarly works appealed to a limited public, his researches into the novel, jurisprudence and crime detection, and erotica were brought to Western popular audiences through his stories about the exploits of Judge Dee, the Sherlock Holmes of China.

Until the present century, the popular Chinese novel was not studied seriously by scholars either in China or in the West. It was in the era between the two world wars that intensive study of Chinese popular literature began. In the aftermath of the Chinese revolution of 1911–12 and of the disruptions brought on by the First World War, the new literati of Republican China sought to establish the spoken language (*pai-hua*) as the general language in order to help modernize the country. The leaders of this radical literary renaissance—Hu Shih, Lu Hsün, and Ts'ai Yüan-p'ei—began to revive the popular literature of the past in the hope of showing that the spoken language had been, and so might be to a greater extent in the future, a sturdy vehicle of literary expression. Because they were also eager to provide new reading matter for the masses, they looked to the past for appealing tales, intricate plots, and moral examples which could be reissued or refurbished for the public. As recently as 1975, Chinese archeologists uncovered in Hupeh Province a cache of bamboo books from the Ch'in dynasty (221–207 B.C.) which reportedly include materials on crime and detection as well as popular accounts of the magistrate as detective. Thus the search for the origins of the crime novel is being continued.

The Japanese literati, who were not as prejudiced against popular literature as their Chinese contemporaries, had long collected Chinese popular dramas and stories and had sometimes adapted them to Japanese tastes before publishing new editions. Western scholars, especially the French school of sinologues exemplified in our century by Paul Pelliot, had studied Chinese legend and story before the reforming scholars of the Chinese Republic became alert to their importance as mediums of political instruction and propaganda. In the 1930's the Chinese Communists likewise became aware of the significance of popular drama for propaganda; nor have they lost that awareness since taking over the government in 1949.

Van Gulik, a product of the European sinological school dominated by Pelliot, shared that school's enthusiasm for comparative studies and exotic subjects. For this breed of scholars, the smallest and most esoteric topics became broadly meaningful through the extraordinary linguistic, literary, and artistic analyses and perceptions of the investigator. In short, the subject was given importance, substance, and relevance by the imaginative powers and talents of the researcher. When Van Gulik first arrived in Japan in 1935, he was quick to see that its artistic collections and libraries were rich in the materials of Chinese popular culture. As an imaginative scholar with limited time at his disposal, Van Gulik immediately realized that he could produce fascinating studies of the culture of the Chinese gentry through intensive study of the objects which those privileged people collected and the customs they observed.

The Chinese crime or courtroom novel was a later form of one of the main genres of the colloquial narrative tradition— the detective story. From the time of the Sung dynasty (A.D. 960-1279), and probably much earlier, the common people delighted in listening to the tales of the storytellers who performed in the bazaars or on the streets of cities and towns. One of the popular detective heroes of the storytellers was Judge Dee (Ti Jen-chieh), a historical personage and statesman of the T'ang court who lived from A.D. 630 to 700. He and other magistrates, especially Pao Cheng (A.D. 999–1062), were celebrated by storytellers, dramatists, and novelists. In the process the historical deeds of the judge became the basis for legendary accomplishments in detection, unswervingly right conduct, and superhuman insight. The judge-detective became the central figure of a stereotype that permeated all forms of popular literature.

The hero of the traditional Chinese detective novel is normally a local magistrate. The story is usually told in colloquial language from the point of view of the working magistrate, who acts as detective, inquisitor, judge, and public avenger. It ordinarily involves a number of crimes, for the magistrate rarely had the leisure or opportunity to deal with one crime at a time. The crimes normally occur early in the story and are often interrelated. Usually the plays or stories are not didactic, and involve crimes against the person rather than misdeeds against society. The crime is always a specific infraction of statute law, ordinarily murder or rape or both. The judge acts as the instrument of the state or the emperor in establishing the facts of the case, capturing the criminal, and meting out the punishments prescribed by law. There is almost no place in the traditional stories for the judge personally to exercise discretion, extend mercy, or play favorites. The judge exemplifies courage, sagacity, honesty, impartiality, and severity; he possesses a flair for detection which is sometimes aided by superhuman insights or by knowledge conveyed to him by ghosts directly from the netherworld. Humor and lightness are rarely associated with the judge, though his subordinates sometimes become involved in clownish escapades.

The judge, always a middle-aged male of the literary class, is disdainful of luxury, protective of the weak or wronged, and above corruption and flattery. The criminal, especially the murderer, is usually cold-blooded and irredeemably evil, requires several beatings to confess, and deserves the awful punishments prescribed by law. The criminal may be of any age or class and of either sex. Tartars, Mongols, Taoists, and Buddhists are almost always cast as miscreants. The victim ordinarily belongs to the artisan class, as did most of the audience.

A rudimentary theme of social justice runs through the stories. In imperial China the administration of justice aimed at retribution and the redress of wrongs; a magistrate dutifully and correctly performs these functions as he keeps the affairs of this earth in harmony with the will of Heaven. All trials were held in the courtroom and could be viewed by the public. The prosecuting judge had to question the accused in open court and never in private. While the judge himself was thought to recognize guilt or innocence intuitively and immediately, he was required to prove his case in public and had to force a confession from the accused. All the proceedings were carefully written down for the record, and the accused had to verify the accuracy of the transcript by signing it. Because criminals were often sly, the judge was sometimes confused, though never more than momentarily. Although most of the investigation was conducted by bailiffs, the judge, in the interests of efficiency or justice would sometimes make a personal investigation. The public, both in the street and in the courtroom, criticized or praised the activities and decisions of the judge. If the people suspected the judge of corruption, favoritism, or wrong-headedness, public protests and disorders were expected to follow. If a magistrate's superiors became convinced of his wrongdoing, he was dismissed and punished; if a public protest was adjudged wrong and seditious, an entire district would be punished.

When Van Gulik published his first translation of a Judge Dee story in 1949, he suggested that a modern writer of detective stories might try his hand at a novel in the Chinese mode for the day's readers. Because nobody accepted this challenge, Van Gulik decided to undertake the task himself, even though he had no previous experience in writing fiction. Originally he intended to show the reading public of Japan and China how much better the traditional stories were than those translated from Western originals then being sold in the stalls of Tokyo and Shanghai. He wrote his first two novels in English as working drafts for versions that he intended ultimately to publish in Japanese and Chinese. When his Western friends exhibited enthusiasm for this new type of detective story, he decided to continue writing in English, another foreign language in which he had become highly proficient.

The giant step from scholarly research and translation to imaginative writing was one that Van Gulik made decisively and successfully. His former involvement with unfrequented paths of scholarly research proved to be splendid preparation for his leap into the writing of atmospheric Chinese detective stories. Now it was no longer necessary to stick to precise historical facts and texts; accuracy of background and realistic portrayal of life in traditional China had become paramount. While using Judge Dee as a stock character, Van Gulik could draw freely upon the plots, stories, and data offered by the whole body of Chinese literature. And to these he could easily add fascinating and titillating embellishments from his own scholarly researches and reading. He also enlivened the novels with his own imaginary maps and with his drawings of Chinese scenes based on sixteenth-century pictorial block prints.

Van Gulik's earlier Judge Dee stories, prepared between 1950 and 1958, are closer to Chinese originals than are those he wrote subsequently. Five in number, these early novels include *The Chinese Bell Murders* and *The Chinese Nail Murders* now reproduced in new editions. Van Gulik wrote the *Bell Murders* in Tokyo during 1950 as the first of his efforts; the *Nail Murders* he wrote in Beirut in 1956. He ordinarily chose his plots and characters while relaxing from official duties, and laid out the preliminary topography as he prepared a map of an imaginary city. In the *Bell Murders* all three plots were taken directly from Chinese stories; in the other Judge Dee books Van Gulik himself supplied most of the themes and plots. Once the actual writing began, it normally took him about six weeks to complete a novel.

From the beginning Van Gulik was aware of the limitations of traditional Chinese prose fiction. Stories of murder, adultery, mystery, and violence were sure to appeal to a Western audience which never seemed to be sated by such offerings. But other features of Chinese colloquial fiction were not likely to be so well received. The criminal's identity was ordinarily revealed at the beginning of Chinese stories; out of deference to Western custom Van Gulik puts the solution near the end. Chinese materials were too often drawn from unfamiliar customs and beliefs, and Chinese authors too often content to solve a puzzling mystery by calling for supernatural knowledge or intervention. Where Westerners would expect morals to be drawn or motivations clarified, the Chinese authors rarely made these matters explicit. Character portrayal in Chinese novels was often limited to depiction of social types. Practically no effort was made to analyze or develop individual character and to evaluate the influence of environment or background upon it.

Judge Dee himself, as depicted in the Chinese stories, was a character utterly foreign to Westerners. To make him more credible Van Gulik sought to make him more human. Occasionally he smiles, becomes excited in the presence of an attractive woman, or feels unsure of himself and his decisions. Van Gulik also plays down Dee's strict Confucian view of the world, which included an unshakable faith in the superiority of everything Chinese and a disdain for all foreigners, a steadfast belief in all aspects of filial piety, a matter-of-fact attitude toward torture, and an unrelenting hostility to Buddhism and Taoism.

While he could not completely ignore these traditional attributes, Van Gulik preferred to soften his Judge's attitudes and to add to his human dimension by making him a devoted family man, a connoisseur of arts and letters, and a deeply religious person. Normally the Judge also tries to solve crimes rationally and without intervention at critical moments from the netherworld.

While consciously adapting his stories to the Western audience, Van Gulik preserved extraordinarily well the way of life of imperial China. The reader will appreciate the part played in that society by family when Dee chastizes the father for not watching more closely over the virtue of his daughter. He will come to understand the role of the student, his privileges and responsibilities to society, and the relation of education to morality. He will also learn from Dee that Buddhist monks typically lust for women and are crafty in politics, that Tartars are untrustworthy and, like Taoists, given to black magic, and that southerners differ greatly from northerners in spoken language and customs. The smallest items—ink stones, nails in a Tartar shoe, the gongs of Taoist monks, door knobs—are brought into the stories at strategic points in the plot to give Van Gulik the opportunity to enlighten the Western reader about these strange objects and their functions. No foreign reader can escape a feeling for the importance in China of the written language and of written records and documents; for the prevalence of social corporations unfamiliar to Westerners, such as the Beggar's Guild; or for the exaggerated concern with proper ceremony and polite forms of address. The seamy side of life is also exposed by reference to the sale of female children into slavery and by the prevalence of prostitution. Asides on foreign trade, on the imperial salt monopoly, on "squeeze" or petty bribery, and on cooking add to the realism of the stories. The role of women is depicted as limited to homemaking, sex, handicrafts, and childrearing.

The Judge Dee stories should not be taken as completely accurate depictions of life in imperial China. For one thing, they are anachronistic. The historical Judge Dee lived in the seventh century, but most of the Chinese stories about him were written down in the sixteenth to nineteenth centuries and reflect the standards and practices current then. Van Gulik based his adaptations on these later collections. Although he was a close student of the Ming and Ch'ing dynasties, the Dutch scholar's experiences with life in China were limited to a few brief visits and to several years' stay during the Second World War. He idealizes the China which existed before the empire had been shaken by the disruptive influences of the West and Japan. He sees imperial China most often from the viewpoint of the Confucian gentry for whose way of life he had respect and affection.

Still, these stories, for all their limitations and biases, provide relatively accurate portrayals of certain aspects of everyday life in imperial China. Van Gulik's personal observations were made in a pre-Communist era when the old ways were still followed in the villages and towns and when the magistrate was still dominant in local affairs. Highly sensitive to the stuff of everyday life, Van Gulik was not an ordinary observer of the Chinese scene. From his studies and his experience with the highest echelons of government he acquired qualifications for understanding traditional China that are no longer part of the equipment of specialists. No amount of reading in classical texts, gazeteers, dynastic histories, or diplomatic documents will by itself provide depth of understanding about the basic workings of life in traditional China. For the Westerner, direct translations of Chinese popular tales are often too foreign in nature and leave references to common matters too frequently unexplained for full comprehension. The insights and elucidations offered by Van Gulik provide the Westerner with a painless and pleasant introduction to premodern China and with an understanding of how different, yet sometimes how similar, are the peoples and societies of China and the West. And, besides, these are entertaining stories and should be appreciated simply for their own sake.

DONALD F. LACH

FOR FURTHER READING

"Necrology of R. H. van Gulik (1910–1967)." *T'oung pao* 54 (1968): 116–24. Unsigned but probably by A. F. P. Hulsewe. At the end of the article appears a comprehensive but incomplete bibliography of Van Gulik's works, including the Judge Dee books.

Bishop, John L. "Some Limitations of Chinese Fiction." *Studies in Chinese Literature*, Harvard-Yenching Institute Studies, no. 21, pp. 237–45. Cambridge, Mass., 1966.

Hayden, George A. "The Judge Pao Plays of the Yüan Dynasty." Ph.D. dissertation, Stanford University, 1972.

Lin Yu-tang. *Lady Wu: A True Story*. London, 1937. A historical biography in which Judge Dee (here written "Di") figures.

Prousek, J. "Researches into the Beginnings of the Chinese Popular Novel." *Archiv Orientální* (Prague) 11 (1939): 91–132.

Shih Chung-wen. *The Golden Age of Chinese Drama: Yüan Tsachü*. Princeton 1976. Note especially pp. 100–112, on social justice in the courtroom stories.

Starrett, Vincent. "Some Chinese Detective Stories." In *Bookman's Holiday*, pp. 3–26. New York, 1942.

Van Gulik, Robert H. "Bibliography of Dr. R. H. van Gulik." Reproduced typescript. Boston [ca. 1970]. Compiled for the benefit of the Boston University Libraries—Mugar Memorial Library "Robert van Gulik Collection."

See also the postscripts to the various Judge Dee books, in which Van Gulik discusses the traditional Chinese system of justice, his sources for the Dee stories, and his working methods.

First Chapter: A CONNOISSEUR HAS A STRANGE EXPERIENCE IN
A CURIO SHOP; JUDGE DEE BEGINS HIS DUTIES AS MAGISTRATE
OF POO-YANG

> *A judge must be as a father and mother to the people,*
> *Cherishing the good and loyal, helping the sick and old.*
> *Though meting out stern punishment to every criminal,*
> *Prevention, not correction, should be his primary aim.*

IT is now six years since I withdrew from the prosperous tea
firm inherited from my father, and settled down to peaceful
retirement in our country villa outside the eastern city gate.
There I at last found time to devote myself entirely to my
favourite pastime, namely collecting material on the history of
crime and detection.

Since under our present glorious Ming Dynasty peace and
order prevail in the Empire and crimes and deeds of violence
are of rare occurrence, I soon found that it was the past I had
to turn to for data on mysterious misdeeds and their clever
solution by perspicacious magistrates. Engaged in this absorb-
ing study I had in the course of the years built up a remarkable
collection of authentic documents relating to famous criminal
cases, weapons actually employed in cruel murders, antique
burglar tools and numerous other relics pertaining to the
history of crime.

One of my most treasured items was a gavel, an oblong
piece of blackwood, many centuries ago actually used by
Judge Dee, our famous master-detective. On this gavel was
engraved the poem quoted here above. The records state that
Judge Dee always used this gavel when presiding at the
tribunal so as to be constantly reminded of his solemn duties
to the state and the people.

I quote the poem from memory, because I do not have that gavel any more. The horrifying experience I had this summer, about two months ago, made me abandon once and for all my criminological researches, and dispose of my entire collection of objects connected with gory misdeeds of the past. I have now transferred my interest to the collecting of celadon porcelain, and find this sedate hobby eminently suited to my fundamentally peace-loving disposition.

However, there is still one thing I must do before I can really settle down to a tranquil life. I must rid myself of all those haunting memories that today still come to disturb my sleep. To free myself of that recurring nightmare I must disclose the strange secrets that were revealed to me in so weird a manner, then and then only shall I be able to relegate to oblivion for ever the horrible experience that shocked me so deeply and brought me to the verge of insanity.

On this exceptionally fine autumn morning, sitting in my elegant garden pavilion and admiring the grace of my two favourite concubines as they tend the chrysanthemums with their slender hands—in these serene surroundings I at last dare to think back to what happened that fateful day.

It was late in the afternoon on the ninth day of the 8th moon—for ever that date shall remain engraved on my memory. It had been extremely hot at midday and later the weather became ever more sultry. I felt depressed and restless, and finally decided to go out in my palankeen. When my bearers asked me where to, on the spur of the moment I told them to take me to Liu's curio shop.

This shop that bears the lofty name of 'The Golden Dragon,' stands opposite the Temple of Confucius. Liu, the owner, is a greedy rascal, but he certainly knows his trade and often found me interesting curios relating to the history of crime and detection. I used to spend many a happy hour in his well-stocked shop.

When I had entered I only saw Liu's assistant. He told me that Liu was not feeling very well; he was upstairs, in the room where he keeps his more valuable items.

I found Liu there in a surly temper, complaining of a headache. He had closed the shutters in an attempt to keep out the stifling heat. In this semi-darkness the familiar room seemed strange and hostile to me, I thought of leaving then and there. But remembering the heat outside, I decided that I had better tarry awhile and have Liu show me a few things. Thus I sat down in the large arm-chair, vigorously fanning myself with my fan of crane-feathers.

Liu muttered something about not having anything special to show me. After having looked around aimlessly for a few moments, he took from a corner a black-lacquered mirror stand and placed it on the table before me.

When he had dusted it I saw that it was an ordinary cap-mirror. that is to say a mirror of polished silver mounted on top of a square box. Such a mirror is used by officials for adjusting their black gauze cap on their head. Judging by the tiny cracks that covered its lacquer frame, it seemed a fairly old specimen; but such are quite common and of slight value to the connoisseur.

Suddenly, however, my eye fell on a line of small characters inlaid in silver along the frame. Leaning forward I read:

'Property of the Dee official residence, Poo-yang'

With difficulty I suppressed an exclamation of astonished delight. For that must have been the cap-mirror of no one else than our famous Judge Dee! I recalled that according to the ancient historical records Judge Dee, while serving as magistrate of Poo-yang, a small district in Kiangsu Province, had unravelled with uncanny skill at least three mysterious crimes. Unfortunately, however, the details of those exploits have not been preserved. Since the surname Dee is not commonly met with, it was certain that this cap-mirror had indeed belonged to Judge Dee. All my lassitude had gone. Silently I blessed Liu's ignorance which had prevented him from identifying this priceless relic of one of the greatest detectives that ever lived in our Flowery Empire.

Assuming a laboriously casual air I leaned back in the chair and told Liu to bring me a cup of tea. As soon as he had gone downstairs I jumped up and, bending over the cap-mirror, examined it eagerly. Idly pulling out the drawer in the box under the mirror, I saw inside a folded judge's cap of black gauze!

I carefully unfolded the decaying silk. A cloud of fine dust descended from its seams. Apart from some moth holes the cap was still intact. I raised it reverently in my trembling hands, for this was the very cap the great Judge Dee had worn when presiding over the tribunal.

Only August Heaven knows what wanton whim made me lift this precious relic and place it on my own undeserving head. I looked in the mirror to see how it fitted me. Since age had dulled the polished surface it reflected only a dark shadow. Suddenly, however, this shadow assumed a definite shape. I saw a quite unfamiliar, haggard face staring at me with burning eyes.

That very moment a deafening thunderclap resounded in my ears. Everything went dark, I seemed to be falling down into a bottomless pit. I lost all notion of place and time.

I found myself floating through a mass of thick clouds. They gradually assumed human shape, I vaguely discerned a naked girl being brutally attacked by a man whose face I could not see. I wanted to rush to her aid but I could not move. I wanted to scream for help but no sound came from my lips. Then I was whirled through a succession of uncounted other hair-raising experiences, now a powerless spectator, then a tormented victim. When I was slowly sinking down in an evil-smelling pool of stagnant water, two comely girls came

A STRANGE EXPERIENCE IN A CURIO SHOP

to my rescue, they faintly resembled my two favourite concubines. But just when I was going to grasp their outstretched hands, a strong current bore me away, I was swirled round and round in a foaming vortex. I was in its centre, being slowly sucked down. When I came to I found myself confined in a dark, narrow space while a crushing weight was pressing me down with relentless force. I tried frantically to escape from under it, but all around my groping fingers met only a smooth iron wall. Just when I was suffocating the pressure was released and I greedily filled my lungs with fresh air. But when I tried to move I found to my horror that I was pinned spread-eagled to the floor. Thick ropes were attached to my wrists and ankles, their ends disappeared in a grey mist. I felt the ropes tightening, an excruciating pain pervaded all my limbs. A nameless terror constricted my heart. I knew that my body was slowly being torn asunder! I started to scream in agony. Then I woke up.

I was lying on the floor of Liu's room, drenched with cold perspiration. Liu was kneeling by my side calling out my name in a frightened voice. The old judge's cap had slipped from my head and was lying among the splinters of the broken mirror.

Assisted by Liu I rose and sank shivering into the arm-chair. Liu hurriedly brought a cup of tea to my lips. He said that just after he had gone down to fetch the teapot, there was a thunderclap followed by a torrential rain. He rushed upstairs to fasten the shutters, and found me prostrate on the floor.

I remained silent for a considerable time, slowly sipping the fragrant brew. Then I told Liu a rigmarole about my occasionally suffering from sudden fits, and had him call my palankeen. I was carried home through the pouring rain. Although the bearers had covered the palankeen with a piece of oil-cloth, I was drenched when I arrived.

I went straight to bed, feeling completely exhausted and

tormented by a splitting headache. Greatly alarmed, my First Lady had our physician called who found me delirious.

I was gravely ill for six weeks. My First Lady maintains that my final recovery was due entirely to her ardent prayers and daily burning incense in the Temple of the God of Medicine. But I ascribe it rather to the unremitting devotion of my two concubines who took turns sitting by my bedstead and administering the potions prescribed by the learned doctor.

When I was well enough to sit up, the doctor inquired what had happened in Liu's curio shop. Loath to recall my strange experience, I only said that I had suddenly felt dizzy. The doctor gave me a queer look but refrained from insisting. When taking his leave he observed casually that such attacks of malignant brain fever are often caused by handling old objects connected with violent death; for such things emanate an evil aura that may dangerously affect the mind of those who come in too close a contact with them.

When this shrewd physician had left I immediately called the house steward. I ordered him to pack my entire criminological collection in four large cases, to be forwarded to my First Lady's uncle Hwang. Although my First Lady never tires of singing his praises, this Uncle Hwang is in reality a mean, obnoxious fellow who delights in stirring up litigations. I indited a polite letter to him stating that I wished to make him a present of my entire criminological collection, as a slight mark of my deep respect for his wide knowledge of all matters connected with both civil and penal law. I should add that I have harboured a profound dislike for Uncle Hwang ever since by legalistic hair-splitting he swindled me out of a piece of valuable land. It is my fond hope that while studying my collection he also will some day come in too close contact with one of those macabre relics and be subjected to as shocking an experience as befell me in Liu's curio shop.

I shall now try to set forth in a connected manner the full

21

story of what I lived through when for a few brief moments I wore the cap of Judge Dee. I leave it to the indulgent reader to decide in how far this account of three ancient crimes represents actual happenings as revealed to me in this extraordinary manner, and in how far it is just a figment of my fever-tormented brain. I did not bother to check the facts with the historical records. For, as stated above, I have now completely abandoned my researches in the history of crime and detection. These inauspicious subjects hold no interest any more for me, happily engaged as I am in collecting the exquisite celadon ware of the Sung Dynasty.

*　*　*

Late in the evening of his first day in Poo-yang, his new post, Judge Dee was sitting in his private office behind the court room of the tribunal, engrossed in reading the district files. Two large bronze candles stood lighted on the desk loaded with piles of ledgers and documents. The flickering light played on the magistrate's green brocade robe and the glossy black silk of his cap. Occasionally he stroked his full black beard or caressed his long side-whiskers. But his eyes never strayed for long from the documents in front of him.

At a smaller desk opposite the judge Hoong Liang, his inseparable companion, was sifting the court files. He was a lean elderly man with a straggling white moustache and a thin goatee, dressed in a faded brown robe and wearing a small skull cap. He reflected that it would soon be midnight. From time to time he cast a furtive look at the tall, broad-shouldered figure behind the other desk. He himself had taken a long nap in the afternoon, but Judge Dee had not had one moment's rest that entire day. Although he knew the iron constitution of his master, Hoong was worried.

Formerly he had been a retainer of Judge Dee's father and used to carry the judge on his arms when he was still a child. Afterwards he had gone with him to the capital when the judge was completing his studies there, and he had also accompanied him when appointed in the provinces. Poo-yang was Judge Dee's third post as district magistrate. All those years Hoong had acted as his trusted friend and counsellor. Judge Dee was wont to discuss with him unreservedly all official and personal matters, and Hoong often gave him useful advice. In order to give Hoong official status, the judge had appointed him Sergeant of the tribunal, hence everybody always addressed him as 'Sergeant Hoong.'

Glancing through a bundle of documents Sergeant Hoong thought about the busy day Judge Dee had behind him. In the morning, when the judge and his suite consisting of his wives, children and servants had arrived in Poo-yang, the judge had gone immediately to the reception hall in the compound of the tribunal, while the rest of his suite went on to the magistrate's official residence in the northern part of the compound. There Judge Dee's First Lady, assisted by the house steward, had supervised the unloading of the luggage carts, and started to arrange their new quarters. Judge Dee had had no time to see the house. He had to take over the seals of the tribunal from Judge Feng, his predecessor. When that ceremony was over he had mustered the permanent personnel of the tribunal, from the senior scribe and the headman of the constables down to the keeper of the jail and the guards. At noon he had presided over a sumptuous repast in honour of the departing magistrate, and he had accompanied Judge Feng and his suite till outside the city gate, as prescribed by custom. Returned to the tribunal, Judge Dee had to receive the visits of the leading citizens of Poo-yang who came to bid him welcome to the district.

After a hurried evening meal taken in his private office Judge Dee had settled down there with the files of the tribunal, keeping the clerks busy hauling leather document boxes from the archives. After a couple of hours he had finally dismissed the clerks, but he himself did not seem to think of retiring.

At last, however, Judge Dee pushed away the ledger in front of him, and leaned back in his chair. Looking at Sergeant Hoong from under his bushy eyebrows he said with a smile:

'Well, Sergeant, what about a cup of hot tea?'

Sergeant Hoong rose quickly and brought the teapot from the side table. While he was pouring the tea Judge Dee said:

'Heaven has conferred its blessings on this district of Poo-yang. I see from the files that the land is fertile, there have been neither floods nor droughts, and the farmers prosper. Being situated on the Grand Canal that crosses our Empire from north to south Poo-yang derives much profit from the busy traffic. Both government and private ships always stay over in the excellent harbour outside the western city gate, there is a constant coming and going of travellers, so that the large merchant houses do a thriving business. The canal and the river that flows into it here abound in fish which provides a living for the poor, and there is a fairly large garrison stationed here, good custom for the small restaurants and shops. Thus the people of this district are prosperous and content, and taxes are paid on time.

'Finally, my predecessor, Judge Feng, evidently is a man of great zeal and ability, he has seen to it that all the records are brought up to date and the registers in perfect order.'

The Sergeant's face lit up as he said:

'This, Your Honour, is a most gratifying state of affairs. The last post Han-yüan was such a difficult one that I often worried about Your Honour's health!'*

Tugging at his thin goatee he continued:

'I have been going through the court records and found that crimes have been very rare here in Poo-yang. And those that occurred have been adequately dealt with. There is but one

* See "The Chinese Lake Murders".

24

case pending in the tribunal. It is a rather vulgar rape murder, which His Excellency Feng solved in a few days. When tomorrow Your Honour peruses the pertaining documents, you will see that only a few loose ends remain to be gathered.'

Judge Dee raised his eyebrows.

'Sometimes, Sergeant, those loose ends pose quite a problem! Tell me about that case!'

Shrugging his shoulders Sergeant Hoong said:

'This is really a very straightforward case. The daughter of a small shopkeeper, a butcher called Hsiao, was found raped and murdered in her room. It turned out that she had had a lover, a degenerate student called Wang. Butcher Hsiao filed an accusation against him. When Judge Feng had verified the evidence and heard the witnesses, it was proved that Wang was indeed the murderer, but he refused to confess. Judge Feng then put the question to Wang under torture, but the man lost consciousness before he could confess. Judge Feng had to leave the case at that point because of his impending departure.

'Since the murderer has been found and sufficient evidence collected against him to warrant questioning under torture, the case is practically finished.'

For a few moments Judge Dee remained silent, pensively stroking his beard. Then he said:

'I would like to hear the complete case, Sergeant.'

Sergeant Hoong's face fell.

'Midnight is approaching, Your Honour,' he said hesitantly, 'would it not be better if Your Honour retired now for a good night's rest? Tomorrow we shall have ample time for reviewing this case!'

Judge Dee shook his head.

'Even the bare outline you just gave me shows a curious inconsistency. After reading all those administrative documents, a criminal problem is just what I need to clear my brain! Have a cup of tea yourself, Sergeant, sit down comfortably and give me a summary of the facts!'

Sergeant Hoong knew the signs. Resignedly he returned to his desk and consulted a few papers. Then he began:

'Just ten days ago, on the seventeenth day of this month, a butcher called Hsiao Foo-han, who owns a small shop in Half Moon Street in the south-west corner of the city, came rushing in tears to the noon session of this tribunal. He was accompanied by three witnesses, namely Gao the warden of the southern quarter, Loong a tailor who lives opposite Hsiao's shop, and the master of the Butchers' Guild.

'Butcher Hsiao presented a written accusation against Wang Hsien-djoong, a Candidate of Literature; this Wang is a poor student who also lives near the butcher's shop. Hsiao claimed that Wang had strangled his only daughter Pure Jade in her bedroom and made off with a pair of golden hairpins. Butcher Hsiao mentioned that Candidate Wang had been having an illicit love affair with his daughter for six months already. The murder was not discovered until she failed to appear that morning for her usual household duties.'

'That Butcher Hsiao,' Judge Dee interrupted, 'must be either a complete fool or a greedy rogue! How could he permit his young daughter to conduct a love affair under his own roof, degrading his house to a brothel? No wonder that violence and murder took place there!'

Sergeant Hoong shook his head.

'No, Your Honour,' he said, 'Butcher Hsiao's explanation placed the crime in quite another light!'

Second Chapter: JUDGE DEE REVIEWS THE RAPE MURDER IN
HALF MOON STREET; HE STARTLES SERGEANT HOONG BY AN
UNEXPECTED STATEMENT

JUDGE DEE folded his hands in his wide sleeves.

'Proceed!' he said briskly.

'Until that very morning,' Sergeant Hoong continued,
'Butcher Hsiao had been completely ignorant of the fact that
Pure Jade had a lover. She slept in a garret that served as
laundry and sewing-room, and built over the godown that
stands somewhat apart from the shop. They have no servants,
all the housework there is done by the wife and the daughter.
Experiments made on the orders of Judge Feng showed that
even a loud voice in the girl's garret could not be heard either
in the butcher's bedroom, or by the neighbours.

'As to Candidate Wang, he is a member of a well-known
clan in the capital. But both his parents are dead and owing to
a family quarrel he is penniless. While preparing for the
second degree literary examination he has been eking out a
meagre living by teaching the children of the shopkeepers in
Half Moon Street. He rents a small attic over the shop of
Loong, an aged tailor, directly opposite Butcher Hsiao.'

'When did the love affair start?' Judge Dee asked.

'About half a year ago,' Sergeant Hoong answered, 'Candidate Wang fell in love with Pure Jade and the two arranged
secret meetings in the girl's room. Wang would go there
towards midnight, slip in through the window, and steal back
to his own quarters before dawn. Tailor Loong testified that
he had discovered Wang's secret after a few weeks and severely
reprimanded him, adding that he would inform Butcher
Hsiao about the disgraceful affair.'

The judge nodded. He said approvingly:

'That tailor was perfectly right!'

The Sergeant consulted a document roll before him. Then he said:

'Wang evidently is a cunning rascal. He fell on his knees and assured Tailor Loong that Pure Jade and he were deeply in love with each other. He swore to marry her as soon as he had passed his second degree. He would then be in a position to offer Butcher Hsiao a suitable wedding gift and to give his bride a proper home. Wang added that if his secret became known he would be barred from the literary examinations and that the affair would then end in disgrace for all concerned.

'Tailor Loong knew that Wang was a studious youngster who would certainly pass the examinations this autumn. Moreover he was secretly very proud that a scion of a noble family who would soon be an official had chosen the daughter of his neighbour as his bride-to-be. Finally he promised that he would not betray the secret, appeasing his own conscience by the consideration that after a few weeks the affair would be honourably concluded by Wang asking Pure Jade in marriage. However, in order to convince himself that Pure Jade was not a girl of loose morals, Tailor Loong from then on kept an eye on the butcher's shop; he testifies that Wang was the only man Pure Jade knew, and the only man who ever came near her room.'

Judge Dee sipped his tea. Then he said sourly:

'Be that as it may! Yet the fact remains that the conduct of these three people—Pure Jade, Candidate Wang and Tailor Loong is most reprehensible!'

'That point,' Sergeant Hoong observed, 'was duly brought out by Judge Feng's sharp denunciation of Tailor Loong for his connivance, and of Butcher Hsiao for his laxity in supervising his household.

'Now, when on the morning of the seventeenth Tailor

Loong learned about Pure Jade's murder, his affection for Wang changed into violent hatred. He rushed to Butcher Hsiao and told him all about Pure Jade's affair with Wang. I quote his actual words: "I, miserable wretch, condoned this sordid affair while all the time that dogshead Wang was using Pure Jade for his base lust. When she insisted that he marry her, he killed her and stole her golden hairpins in order to buy himself a wealthy wife!"

'Butcher Hsiao, distraught by rage and grief had Warden Gao and the master of his guild called. They held counsel together and all agreed that Wang was the murderer. The guildmaster drew up the written accusation and then they all went to the tribunal to charge Wang with this foul crime.'

'Where was Candidate Wang at that time?' Judge Dee asked. 'Had he fled from the city?'

'No,' the sergeant answered, 'he was caught immediately. When Judge Feng had completed hearing Butcher Hsiao, he sent out his constables to arrest Wang. They found him in his attic over the tailor's shop, fast asleep although it was well past noon. The constables dragged him to the tribunal. There Judge Feng confronted him with Butcher Hsiao's accusation.'

Judge Dee straightened himself. Leaning forward he placed his elbows on the desk and said eagerly:

'Now I am very interested to hear how Candidate Wang formulated his defence!'

Sergeant Hoong selected a few papers. After glancing them through he said:

'That rascal had an explanation for everything. His main point was——'

Judge Dee raised his hand.

'I prefer,' he said, 'to have it in Wang's own words. Read me the transcript!'

Sergeant Hoong looked astonished. He seemed about to make a remark but thought better of it. Hunched over the papers before him he began to read out in a monotonous voice the verbatim court record of Candidate Wang's statement.

'This ignorant student kneeling before Your Honour's dais is overcome with shame and mortification. He pleads guilty of the most reprehensible offence of having conducted a love affair with a maiden of unblemished reputation. It so happens that the attic where I sit every day reading the Classics faces the room of Pure Jade. It is on the corner of the blind alley on the other side of Half Moon Street. I often watched her as she was combing her hair in front of her window, and I resolved that she alone should be my future bride.

'It would have indeed been fortunate if I had confined myself to that resolution and waited till after my examination before taking any steps. Then I would have been in a position to approach a go-between with an appropriate wedding gift and thus have Pure Jade's father acquainted with my intentions in the customary and honourable way. One day, however, I chanced to meet Pure Jade alone in the alley. I could not refrain from engaging her in conversation. When she gave me to understand that my feelings were reciprocated I, who should have guided this innocent girl, fanned her own passion by my own: I arranged further meetings in the alley. Soon I persuaded her to allow me to visit her secretly in her room just once. Late on the appointed night I placed a ladder under her window and she let me in. Thus I enjoyed the pleasure which, if indulged in with an honourable maid, is forbidden by the Command of Heaven unless previously solemnified by the ceremony of marriage.

'And, just as a fire will burn higher when more fuel is added, my guilty passion exacted more frequent meetings. Since I feared that the ladder might be noticed by the night-watch or a late passer-by, I persuaded Pure Jade to let a long

JUDGE DEE DISCUSSES A CASE WITH SERGEANT HOONG

strip of white cloth dangle from her window, its other end being fastened to the leg of her bedstead. When I gave the strip a pull from below she would open her window and assist my ascent by hauling in the cloth. A casual observer would think this cloth a piece of laundry that people had forgotten to take inside for the night.'

Here Judge Dee interrupted the sergeant's reading by hitting his fist on the desk.

'The crafty rascal!' he exclaimed angrily. 'A fine thing indeed, a Candidate of Literature stooping to the tricks of thieves and burglars!'

'As I remarked before, Your Honour,' Sergeant Hoong said, 'that Wang is a base criminal! But I continue his statement:

'One day, however, Tailor Loong discovered my secret and he, honest man, threatened to tell Butcher Hsiao. But I, blind fool, disregarded this warning doubtless arranged by Merciful Heaven, and pleaded with him. Finally he consented to keep his silence.

'Thus the affair went on for nearly half a year. Then August Heaven on high could no longer countenance this violation of its Sacred Commands, and in one terrible blow it has smitten both innocent, poor Pure Jade and myself, miserable sinner. We had agreed that I should go to her again on the night of the sixteenth. That afternoon, however, my friend and fellow-student Yang Poo came to see me and told me that his father in the capital had sent him five silver pieces for his birthday. He invited me to join him in a small celebration at the Five Tastes Inn in the northern quarter of this city. During the meal I drank more wine than I could stand. When I left Yang Poo and walked out in the cool night air I realised that I was completely drunk. I intended to return home and lie down for an hour or so to sleep off the effects of intoxication before visiting Pure Jade, but I lost my way. Early this morning, just before dawn, I regained my senses and found myself lying in the midst of thorny brushwood among the ruins of an old mansion. I struggled up, my head was still heavy, I stumbled along without noticing much of my surroundings until somehow or other I reached the main street. I walked home and went straight up to my room. I lay down on my bed and fell asleep again straight away. It was only when Your Honour's constables came to fetch me that I learned about the terrible fate that had overtaken my poor bride-to-be.'

Sergeant Hoong stopped his reading and looked at the judge. With a sneer he said:

'Now comes the peroration of that sanctimonious hypocrite!'

'If Your Honour should decide that I must suffer the extreme penalty because of my unforgivable conduct towards this unfortunate girl or for having brought about indirectly her death, I shall welcome the verdict. It will deliver me from an intolerable existence which must for ever be clouded in darkness now that I have lost my beloved. But in order that her death be avenged, and for the sake of the honour of my family, I am compelled to deny most emphatically the crime of rape and murder of which I stand accused.'

The sergeant put the paper down. Tapping it with his forefinger he said:

'Wang's plan for escaping the just punishment for his foul crime is obvious. He emphasised his guilt in seducing the girl, but steadfastly denied that he murdered her. He is perfectly aware of the fact that the punishment for seducing an un-married girl, with her consent to the act so plainly established, is fifty blows with the bamboo, while the punishment for murder is an ignominious death on the execution ground!'

Sergeant Hoong looked expectantly at his master, but Judge Dee made no comment He slowly drank another cup of tea. Then he asked:

'What did Judge Feng say to Wang's statement?'

The sergeant consulted a document roll. After a while he said:

'During that session Judge Feng did not press Candidate Wang further. He immediately started on the routine investigation.'

'A wise procedure!' Judge Dee said approvingly. 'Can you find for me the report on his visit to the scene of the crime, and the findings of the coroner?'

Sergeant Hoong unrolled the document further.

'Yes, Your Honour, it is all set down here in detail. Judge Feng set out for Half Moon Street accompanied by his assistants. In the garret they found the naked body of a strongly-built and well-developed girl of about nineteen stretched out on the couch. Her face was distorted and her hair dishevelled. The mattress was awry and the pillow had fallen on the floor. A long strip of white cloth, one end tied to the leg of the bed, was lying crumpled on the floor. The chest wherein Pure Jade kept her scanty wardrobe was open. Against the wall opposite the bed there stood a large laundry tub, and in a corner a dilapidated small table with a cracked mirror. The only other furniture was a wooden footstool that lay overturned in front of the bed.'

'Was there no clue to the murderer's identity?' Judge Dee interrupted him.

'None, Your Honour,' Sergeant Hoong answered, 'a most diligent search failed to produce the slightest clue. The only discovery was a package of love poems addressed to Pure Jade which she had kept carefully wrapped-up in a drawer of the toilet table, although of course she could not read them. Those poems were signed by Candidate Wang.

'As to the autopsy, the coroner stated that death had ensued as a result of strangulation. The victim's throat showed two large bruises where the murderer's hands had choked her. He further listed numerous blue and swollen spots on her breast and arms, proving that the girl had fought back as well as she could. Finally, the coroner noted that certain signs proved that the girl had been raped before or during strangulation.'

The sergeant quickly glanced through the remaining part of the roll. Then he continued:

'During the ensuing days Judge Feng verified all the evidence brought forward in a most painstaking way. He sent——'

'You can skip the details,' Judge Dee interposed, 'I am convinced that Judge Feng performed that task in a thorough manner. Tell me the main points only. I would like to know, for instance, what Yang Poo had to say about the celebration in that inn.'

'Wang's friend Yang Poo,' the sergeant answered, 'confirmed his story in every detail, except that he did not think that Wang had been very drunk when he left him. Yang Poo used the words "slightly intoxicated." I may add that Wang could not identify the place where he allegedly awoke from his drunken sleep. Judge Feng did what he could, he had his constables take Wang to probable sites of ruined mansions all over the city and tried to make Wang identify one of those by mentioning some detail; but all in vain. Wang's body showed some deep scratches and his robe had some recent tears. Wang explained those as resulting from his stumbling among the thorny brushwood.

'Then Judge Feng devoted two days to a most thorough search of Wang's quarters and other likely places, without finding the stolen pair of golden hairpins. Butcher Hsiao made a sketch of them from memory. That drawing is attached to the record here.'

As Judge Dee held out his hand Sergeant Hoong detached a sheet of thin paper from the roll and placed it on the judge's desk.

'Good old handwork,' Judge Dee commented. 'Those buttons in the shape of a pair of flying swallows are delicately moulded.'

'According to Butcher Hsiao,' Sergeant Hoong said, 'these hairpins were an heirloom. His wife had always kept them locked away because they were supposed to bring bad luck to the wearer. A few months ago, however, Pure Jade had insistently begged to be allowed to wear them, and her mother had given them to her because she could not afford to buy any other trinket for her.'

The judge shook his head sadly. 'The poor wench!' he commented. After a while he asked:

'Now what was Judge Feng's final verdict?'

'Day before yesterday,' Sergeant Hoong said, 'Judge Feng recapitulated the evidence gathered. He began by stating that the missing hairpins had not been found. But he did not count this as a point in Wang's favour, since he would have had sufficient time for hiding them in some secure place. He conceded that Wang's defence was well formulated, but stated that it was only to be expected that a well-educated scholar would invent a very plausible story.

'The idea that the crime could be committed by a vagrant burglar he dismissed as most improbable. It is widely known that only poor shopkeepers live in Half Moon Street; and even if a thief would come there looking for loot he would certainly try to break into the butcher's shop or godown, and not choose a small garret under the roof. The testimony of all witnesses and also of Wang himself proved that the secret meetings were known only to the lovers and Tailor Loong.'

Looking up from the document roll Sergeant Hoong said with a faint smile:

'That Tailor Loong, Your Honour, is nearly seventy years and so enfeebled by age that he was immediately ruled out as a possible suspect.'

Judge Dee nodded. Then he asked:

'How did Judge Feng phrase his accusation? If possible I would like to hear it verbatim.'

Sergeant Hoong bent again over the roll. He read:

'When the accused again protested that he was innocent, His Excellency hit his fist on the table and shouted: "You dogshead, I, your magistrate, know the truth! After you had left the inn you went straight to the house of Pure Jade. The wine had given you the courage you coward needed, and you told her what you must have been planning to do for some time, namely that you had tired of her and wished to break off the relationship. A quarrel took place and in the end Pure Jade made for the door to call her parents. You tried to hold her back. The ensuing struggle roused your basest instincts, you possessed her against her will and then strangled her. Having perpetrated this foul deed you ransacked her clothes chest and made off with the golden hairpins so as to make it appear that the crime had been committed by a burglar. Now confess your guilt!" '

Having thus quoted from the record, Sergeant Hoong looked up and continued:

'When Candidate Wang persisted in his innocence, Judge Feng ordered the constables to give him fifty lashes with the heavy whip. After thirty lashes, however, Wang collapsed on the floor of the tribunal. After he had been revived by burning vinegar under his nose, he was so confused that Judge Feng gave up further questioning. That same evening the orders concerning Judge Feng's transfer arrived, so that he could not bring the case to its inevitable conclusion. However, he jotted down a brief note at the end of the record of that last session, stating his opinion.'

'Let me see that note, Sergeant!' Judge Dee said.

Sergeant Hoong unrolled the document to its very end, then brought it over to the judge.

Bringing the scroll nearer to his eyes Judge Dee read out:

'It is my considered opinion that the guilt of Candidate Wang Hsien-djoong has been established beyond all reasonable doubt. I recommend that after he has duly confessed, the death penalty in one of its more severe forms be proposed for this criminal. Signed Feng Yee, Magistrate of Poo-yang.'

Judge Dee slowly rolled the scroll up again. He took up a jade paper-weight and idly toyed with it for some time. Sergeant Hoong remained standing in front of the desk, looking at the judge expectantly.

Suddenly Judge Dee put the paper-weight down. He rose from his chair and stood there looking fixedly at his assistant.

'Judge Feng,' he said, 'is an able and conscientious magistrate. I ascribe his hasty verdict to the pressure of business engendered by his pending departure. If he had had time to study this case at leisure he would doubtless have arrived at quite a different conclusion.'

When he noticed the sergeant's perplexed look, Judge Dee smiled faintly. He quickly continued:

'I agree that Candidate Wang is a weak-kneed and wholly irresponsible youngster, who fully deserves a severe lesson. But he did not murder Pure Jade!'

Sergeant Hoong opened his mouth to speak. But the judge raised his hand.

'I won't say any more,' he said, 'until I have actually seen the persons involved, and examined the scene of the crime myself. Tomorrow I shall review the case in the tribunal, during the afternoon session. Then you will understand how I arrived at my conclusion.

'Well, what time is it now, Sergeant?'

'It is long past midnight, Your Honour.' Looking very doubtful the sergeant continued: 'I must confess that I can't see any flaw in the case against Wang. Tomorrow, when my brain is clearer, I shall reread the entire record!'

Slowly shaking his head he took one of the candles in order to light the way for the judge through the dark corridors leading to his own residence in the northern part of the compound.

But Judge Dee laid a hand on his arm.

'Don't bother, Sergeant!' he said. 'I don't think I should disturb my household so late in the night. They all had a strenuous day—and so had you! You may retire now to your own quarters. I shall rest on the couch here in my office. So: to bed and to sleep!'

Third Chapter: JUDGE DEE OPENS THE FIRST SESSION OF THE
TRIBUNAL; TAO GAN RELATES THE STORY OF A BUDDHIST
TEMPLE

THE following morning at dawn, when Sergeant Hoong
entered the private office with the breakfast tray he found
that the judge had already made his toilet.

Judge Dee ate two bowls of steaming rice gruel and some
salted vegetables and drank a cup of hot tea that the sergeant
poured out for him. When the early rays of the sun threw a
red light on the paper windows Sergeant Hoong blew out the
candles and assisted the judge in donning his long official robe
of heavy green brocade. Judge Dee noticed with satisfaction
that his servants had placed his cap-mirror on the side table.
He pulled out the drawer of the mirror stand and carefully
adjusted the black judge's cap with the wings of stiffened
gauze on his head.

In the meantime the constables had opened the massive,
copper-studded gates of the tribunal compound. Despite the
early hour a crowd of spectators was waiting in the street
outside. The rape-murder of the butcher's daughter had
caused great excitement in the quiet town of Poo-yang and
the citizens were eager to see the new magistrate conclude the
case.

As soon as the burly guard had sounded the large bronze
gong at the entrance, the spectators filed into the courtyard
and from there into the spacious court hall. All eyes were
riveted on the raised dais at the end of the hall and the high
bench covered with red brocade; for there the new magistrate
would presently appear.

The senior scribe arranged the judge's paraphernalia on the

bench. On the right the seal of the tribunal measuring two inches square, together with the seal pad. In the middle a double inkstone for rubbing red and black ink, with a separate writing brush for each colour. And on the left the blanks and forms used by the recording scribe.

Six constables stood facing each other in two rows of three in front of the bench. They carried whips, chains, hand-screws and the other awe-inspiring implements of their office. Their headman stood somewhat apart, nearer to the bench.

At last the screen behind the bench was drawn aside and Judge Dee appeared. He seated himself in the high arm-chair. Sergeant Hoong remained standing by his side.

Judge Dee surveyed for a moment the packed court hall, slowly stroking his beard. Then he knocked the gavel on the bench and announced:

'The morning session of the tribunal is open!'

To the disappointment of the spectators the judge did not reach for his red writing brush. That meant that he was not going to write out a blank for the warden of the jail to bring the accused before the bench.

Judge Dee ordered the senior scribe to hand him the records of a routine matter relating to the district administration, and disposed of that in a leisurely manner. Then he had the headman of the constables come forward and went over with him the pay-list of the personnel of the tribunal.

Looking sourly at the headman from under his thick eyebrows the judge rasped:

'There is one string of copper cash short! Explain where that money went to.'

The headman hemmed and hawed but could produce no plausible explanation of the difference.

'That sum will be deducted from your salary,' Judge Dee announced curtly.

He leaned back in the arm-chair. Sipping the tea that

Sergeant Hoong had offered him Judge Dee waited to see whether anyone in the audience wished to present a complaint. When none was forthcoming he raised his gavel and closed the session.

When Judge Dee had left the dais for his private office the crowd started to voice its disappointment.

'Get going!' shouted the constables. 'You people have seen what you came to see, hurry up now and don't keep us constables from our official duties!'

After the court hall had been cleared the headman spat on the floor and sadly shook his head. He said to some younger constables standing about there:

'You young ones had better look for another job! In this accursed tribunal of Poo-yang you will never make a decent living. Look, for the last three years we have been serving under His Excellency Feng, who asked an explanation for every missing silver piece. I thought that I had had my full share of service under a scrupulous magistrate! But now His Excellency Dee has succeeded him and he, may August Heaven preserve us, frowns on one string of copper cash! What a terrible state of affairs for us constables! Now tell me, why is it that easy-going and corrupt magistrates always shun Poo-yang?'

While the constables were muttering, Judge Dee was changing into a comfortable informal robe, assisted by a lean man, clad in a simple blue dress with a brown sash. He had a long, saturnine face, with a mole the size of a copper cash on his left cheek, from which sprouted three black hairs several inches long.

This was Tao Gan, one of Judge Dee's trusted lieutenants. Until a few years before he had earned a precarious living as a confidence man and he was therefore thoroughly familiar with loading dice, drawing up ambiguous contracts, forging seals and signatures, picking locks and all other tricks of city crooks.

Once Judge Dee had extricated him from a nasty situation, and since then Tao Gan had reformed. He served Judge Dee with unswerving loyalty. His alert mind and his talent for spotting unsavoury affairs had proved useful to the judge in solving more than one criminal case.

When Judge Dee had seated himself behind his desk two burly fellows entered and respectfully greeted him. Both were clad in long brown robes, girded with a black sash. They wore small, black pointed caps. These were Ma Joong and Chiao Tai, Judge Dee's other two lieutenants.

Ma Joong was well over six feet tall with 'shoulders like a bear.' His large, heavy-jowled face was clean-shaven except for a short moustache. Notwithstanding his great bulk, he moved with the swift grace that marks the experienced boxer. In his younger days he had served as bodyguard to a corrupt official. Once when his master extorted money from a widow, Ma Joong rose against him and almost killed him. Naturally he had to flee for his life so he joined the 'brothers of the green woods,' that is to say he became a highwayman. Once he attacked Judge Dee and his suite on the road outside the capital, but was so impressed by Judge Dee's personality that he gave up his profession then and there to become a devoted servant of the judge. Because of his great courage and remarkable strength, Judge Dee always employed him for arresting dangerous criminals and other risky undertakings.

Chiao Tai was a colleague of Ma Joong from his days in 'the green woods.' Though not as formidable a boxer as Ma Joong, he was an expert archer and skilful swordsman, and moreover possessed that dogged patience which is such an asset in the detection of crimes.

'Well, my braves,' Judge Dee said, 'I take it that you have had a look around in the city of Poo-yang and have an impression of the state of affairs.'

'Your Honour,' Ma Joong replied, 'His Excellency Feng

must have been a good magistrate. People here are prosperous and content. The inns serve tasty food at reasonable prices and the local wine is delicious. It seems that we shall have an easy time here!'

Chiao Tai assented happily, but Tao Gan had a doubtful look on his long face. He said nothing, but slowly let the long hairs of the mole on his cheek slip through his fingers. Judge Dee glanced at him.

'Are you of a different opinion, Tao Gan?' he enquired.

'As a matter of fact, Your Honour,' began Tao Gan, 'I chanced upon something that would seem to invite a thorough investigation.

'Making the rounds of the larger tea houses of this city, by force of habit I tried to find out about the sources of wealth of this district. I soon discovered that although there are about a dozen very wealthy merchants who handle the canal traffic, and four or five big landowners, their riches are a mere trifle when compared with the wealth of Spiritual Virtue, the abbot of the Temple of Boundless Mercy, in the northern suburb of the city. He is the head of that vast, newly-built temple compound and has about sixty baldpates under him. However, instead of fasting and praying those monks spend their time drinking wine, eating meat, and in general live off the fat of the land.'

'Personally,' Judge Dee interrupted, 'I will have no truck with the Buddhist crowd. I find myself completely satisfied with the wise teachings of our peerless Sage Confucius and his venerable disciples. I don't feel the need for meddling with the doctrines introduced by the black-robed foreigners from India. Our Imperial Court, however, in its august wisdom, has deemed that the Buddhist creed serves a purpose inasmuch as it ameliorates the morals of the common people and therefore has extended its gracious protection to the Buddhist clergy and their temples. If they flourish, then this is in

44

accordance with the Imperial Will and we must carefully refrain from criticism!'

Tao Gan, thus admonished, still seemed reluctant to leave the subject.

'When I say that the abbot is rich, Your Honour,' he continued after some hesitation, 'I mean to say that he must be as rich as the God of Wealth himself! They say that the monks' quarters are appointed as luxuriously as a Prince's palace. The sacrificial vessels on the altar in the main hall are all of pure, solid gold, and——'

'Spare me,' Judge Dee exclaimed, cutting his lieutenant short, 'all those details, which, moreover, are only based on hearsay. Come to your point!'

Tao Gan then said:

'Your Honour, I may be wrong, but I have a strong suspicion that the wealth of that temple is derived from a particularly sordid scheme.'

'Now,' Judge Dee remarked, 'your conversation begins to interest me. Proceed, but be brief!'

'It is widely known,' Tao Gan went on, 'that the main source of income of the Temple of Boundless Mercy is the large statue of the Goddess Kwan Yin which stands in the main hall. It is carved from sandalwood and must be well over a century old. Until some years ago it stood in a tumbledown hall surrounded by a neglected garden. The temple was inhabited by three monks who lived in a nearby shack. Only few people came to the temple to pray, and the incense fee they left was not enough to guarantee the three monks their daily bowl of watery rice. So every day they walked the streets with their alms-bowl in order to supplement their meagre income.

'Then, five years ago, a vagrant monk settled down in the temple. Although clad in rags, he was a tall, handsome man of imposing mien. He called himself "Spiritual Virtue." About a

45

year later the word spread that the sandalwood statue of the goddess had miraculous power and that childless couples who prayed at the temple always produced offspring. Spiritual Virtue, who by then had proclaimed himself abbot of the temple, always insisted that the women who desired a child must pass one night in pious meditation on a couch in the main hall directly in front of the statue.'

Tao Gan shot a quick look at his audience. Then he continued:

'In order to prevent malicious rumours the abbot himself pasted strips of paper over the door of the hall after the woman had entered, upon which he asked the husband to affix his seal. Moreover, the husband was required to pass the night there also, in the quarters of the monks. The following morning the husband was required to break the seal of the hall. So unfailing were the results obtained by repairing to this temple that its fame spread and soon childless couples from all over the district came to pray to the miraculous statue; rich presents and large sums of incense money were contributed by the grateful pilgrims after their wish had been realised.

'The abbot then rebuilt the main hall in magnificent style and added spacious quarters for the monks whose number soon swelled to over sixty. The garden was transformed into a beautiful park with goldfish ponds and artificial rocks. Last year the abbot added a number of elegant pavilions for the women who stayed in the temple overnight. He surrounded the entire compound with a high wall and built the resplendent three-storied gate that I admired just one hour ago.'

Here Tao Gan paused, waiting for Judge Dee's comment. The judge, however, remained silent. Then Tao Gan said:

'I don't know what Your Honour thinks about this. But if Your Honour's thoughts should happen to be similar to mine, then it is evident that this state of affairs cannot be allowed to continue!'

Judge Dee stroked his beard. He spoke thoughtfully:

'There are not a few phenomena in this world that elude the comprehension of common mortals. Far be it from me to deny immediately that this statue of the Goddess Kwan Yin possesses miraculous powers. Since, however, I have no urgent business for you, you might as well try to assemble more details about the Temple of Boundless Mercy. Report to me in due time.'

Then the judge leaned forward and selected a document roll from the pile on his desk.

'This,' he continued, 'is the complete record of the rape-murder in Half Moon Street, now pending in this tribunal. Last night I discussed this case with the sergeant here. I recommend that this morning all of you read through this record. I propose to hear this interesting case during the noon session of the tribunal. You will notice——'

Here the judge was interrupted by the entrance of an elderly man, the steward of his household. After three deep bows he said:

'Your Honour's First Lady has ordered me to enquire if, some time this morning, Your Honour could spare a few moments for inspecting the arrangements made in Your Honour's residence.'

Judge Dee smiled bleakly. He said to Sergeant Hoong:

'It is true that after our arrival here in Poo-yang I have not yet crossed the threshold of my own house! Small wonder that my ladies are somewhat dismayed.'

The judge rose. Putting his hands in his long sleeves he said to his lieutenants:

'During the noon session you will notice that there are weak points in the case against the accused Candidate Wang.'

Then he walked out into the corridor.

Fourth Chapter: A CANDIDATE OF LITERATURE IS HEARD IN
THE TRIBUNAL; JUDGE DEE GOES TO INVESTIGATE THE SCENE
OF A CRIME

JUDGE DEE had returned to his private office well before the
gong sounded for the noon session of the tribunal. He found
Sergeant Hoong and his three other lieutenants waiting for him.

The judge put on his official dress, placed the black cap on
his head and walked through the door-opening leading to the
dais in the court hall. He saw that the brief morning session
had apparently not discouraged the citizens of Poo-yang. The
court hall was packed with spectators, there was no standing
place left.

Having seated himself behind the bench, Judge Dee ordered
the headman of the constables to bring Butcher Hsiao before
him.

As the butcher approached the dais Judge Dee looked him
over. He decided that this was a simple, small shopkeeper,
honest but not too clever. When the butcher had knelt Judge
Dee addressed him:

'I, the magistrate, sympathise with you over the loss you
have suffered. My distinguished predecessor, Judge Feng, has
already admonished you about your laxity in supervising your
household. I shall not go into that matter again. There are,
however, several points in the evidence that I wish to verify.
Thus I must inform you that it may take some time before I
can close this case. Let me assure you, however, that justice
shall be done and that the murder of your daughter Pure Jade
will be avenged.'

Butcher Hsiao mumbled some words of respectful gratitude
and on a sign of the judge was led aside.

48

Judge Dee referred to the document in front of him. Then he said: 'The coroner will come forward!'

The judge gave him a quick look. The coroner seemed to be a shrewd young fellow. Judge Dee spoke:

'While your memory is still fresh I wish to check a few points of the autopsy. In the first place I desire your own general description of the physical features of the victim.'

'I respectfully inform Your Honour,' the coroner replied, 'that the girl was tall for her age, and sturdily built. I gather that she worked from morning till night in the household while also lending a hand in the shop. She had no physical defects and possessed the strong physique of a healthy, hard-working girl.'

'Did you,' Judge Dee asked, 'give due attention to her hands?'

'Certainly, Your Honour. His Excellency Feng was very particular about that because he hoped to find some shred of fabric or some other substance under her finger-nails that could serve as a clue to the murderer's dress. As a matter of fact she had the short nails of a working girl common to her class and no clue was discovered.'

Judge Dee nodded and continued:

'In your report you describe the blue marks left by the murderer's hands on the victim's throat. You also stated that these marks included the imprints of finger-nails. Describe those nail-marks in greater detail!'

The coroner thought for a few moments and then remarked:

'The nail prints showed the usual shape of a half moon. They had not penetrated deeply but the skin was broken in a few places.'

'This additional detail,' Judge Dee said, 'shall be entered into the records.'

He dismissed the coroner and ordered the accused Candidate Wang brought before him.

When the constables led Candidate Wang in front of the dais, Judge Dee gave him a sharp look. He saw a young man of medium height, clad in the long blue robe of a Candidate of Literature. He carried himself well, but had the narrow chest and hunched shoulders of a man who is a stranger to physical exercise. Evidently he passed most of his time among his books. He had a pleasant and intelligent face, with a broad forehead. But his mouth was weak. His left cheek showed a few ugly, badly-healed scratches.

When he was kneeling in front of the dais, Judge Dee thus harshly addressed him:

'You are the rascal Wang, the man who has besmirched the honour of the literati! Having had the privilege of studying the Classics and imbibing their lofty teachings, you chose to use your intelligence for the mean purpose of seducing an innocent, unlettered girl, an easy victim for your vile lusts. And if that were not enough in itself, you then raped and murdered her. There is not a single extenuating circumstance and the law shall be applied with full severity. I do not wish to hear your defence. I read it in the records of this case and consider it a disgusting document. I shall ask you some additional questions and you shall tell the complete truth.'

Judge Dee leaned forward in his chair and glanced through a paper. Then he said:

'In your statement you contend that on the morning of the seventeenth you woke up among the ruins of an old mansion. Give me an exact description of what you saw there!'

'Your Honour,' Wang answered in a faltering voice, 'to his great regret this candidate is in no position to obey your instruction. The sun had not yet risen. In the uncertain light that precedes dawn I only noticed a few piles of bricks that resembled a crumbled wall, surrounded by a thick growth of thorny bushes. These two features I remember distinctly. As I struggled to my feet, my head still heavy and my eyes blurred,

JUDGE DEE HEARS CANDIDATE WANG

I stumbled over the bricks. The thorns tore my robe and scratched my face and body. At that time my only thought was to leave the dismal place as quickly as possible. I vaguely remember walking at random through a number of small alleys. I kept my head down trying to clear my brain and worrying over Pure Jade who had been waiting for me in vain the night before——'

Judge Dee gave a sign to the headman of the constables, who immediately hit Candidate Wang in the mouth.

'Stop your lies,' the judge barked, 'and be careful to confine yourself to answering my questions!' He addressed the constables:

'Show me the scratches on this man's body!'

The headman gripped Wang by the collar of his robe and pulled him to his feet. Two constables roughly tore his robe down. Wang screamed with pain for his back was still raw from the whipping he had received three days earlier. Judge Dee saw several deep scratches on his breast, arms and shoulders, in addition to some bruises. He nodded to the headman. The constables forced Wang to his knees again without bothering to put the robe back over his shoulders. Then Judge Dee resumed the interrogation.

'You stated before that no one but the victim, yourself and Tailor Loong knew about your secret visits. This evidently is a loose statement. How can you be sure that some passer-by did not observe one of your escapades without your knowledge?'

'Before leaving the tailor's door, Your Honour,' Candidate Wang answered, 'I always carefully looked up and down the street, listening for footsteps. Sometimes the nightwatch approached and I had to wait until they had passed. Then I swiftly crossed the street and slipped into the dark alley next to Butcher Hsiao's shop. Once there I was safe, for even if someone were to pass through Half Moon Street, I could crouch in the shadows and remain unobserved. The only dangerous moment was when I climbed up, but then Pure Jade would be standing in the window to give warning if she saw someone approaching.'

'A Candidate of Literature, sneaking about in the night like a common thief!' Judge Dee said with a sneer. 'What an edifying spectacle! However, cudgel your brain and try to remember whether anything ever happened that gave you occasion to doubt.'

Candidate Wang remained in thought for some time. At last he said slowly:

'I recall, Your Honour, that about two weeks ago I had rather a bad fright. While I was watching from the tailor's door before crossing the street, I saw the nightwatch pass by, their leader sounding his wooden clapper. I waited till they had walked all through Half Moon Street. I could see them distinctly as they rounded the corner at the far end where the lighted lantern marks Doctor Fang's consulting-room.

'Yet, just as I was slipping into the blind alley opposite, I suddenly heard the clapper of the nightwatch again, and quite near too. I pressed myself against the wall and stood there in the shadows in a great fright. The sound of the clapper ceased and I expected the nightwatch to raise alarm, thinking that I was a thief. Nothing happened however. Everything remained dead quiet. Finally I decided that my imagination or the echo had played a trick on me. I left my hideout and tugged at the strip of cloth hanging from Pure Jade's window to inform her that I was there.'

Judge Dee turned his head and whispered to Sergeant Hoong, who was standing by his side:

'This is a new fact. Make a note of it!' Then, scowling at Candidate Wang, he said sourly:

'You are wasting the Court's time! How could the nightwatch have come back from that distance in so short a time?'

He turned to the senior scribe and ordered:

'Read out a summary of what the accused Wang has said at this session, so that he can verify it and affix his thumb-mark.'

The senior scribe read his notes aloud and Candidate Wang affirmed that they represented faithfully what he had said.

'Make him affix his thumb-mark!' Judge Dee ordered the constables.

The constables again pulled Wang to his feet roughly, pressed his thumb on the wet inkstone and told him to affix his mark on the paper that Judge Dee had pushed to the edge of the bench.

While Wang tremblingly obeyed, the judge noticed that he had the thin, cultivated hands of the scholar, along with the long nails affected by the literary class.

'Take the accused back to the jail!' Judge Dee shouted. Then he rose, and angrily shaking his long sleeves he left the dais. When he passed through the door leading to his private office, he heard the crowd of spectators start murmuring behind him.

'Clear the Court, clear the Court!' the headman of the constables shouted. 'This is no theatre where you can linger after the performance! Get a move on, do you expect the constables to serve you tea and cakes?'

When the last spectator had been pushed out of the hall, the headman moodily faced his subordinates.

'What a time we are heading for!' he exclaimed. 'A stupid judge who is also lazy—that is the kind of magistrate we devoutly pray for every day. But let August Heaven spare me service under a judge who is stupid and industrious at the same time! And a curmudgeon to boot. What a calamity!'

'Why did His Excellency not apply torture?' a young constable asked. 'That weak bookworm would have confessed at the first crack of the whip, to say nothing of crushing his hands and ankles in the screws. This case could have been over and done with!'

Another added:

'What is the use of these dilatory tactics? That fellow Wang is as poor as a rat in the gutter. There is no hope of getting a bribe out of him.'

'Sheer slowness of wit, that is what it is!' the headman said disgustedly. 'Wang's guilt is as clear as crystal and yet His Excellency wants to "verify points." Well, let us go to the kitchen and fill our rice bowls before those greedy guards eat everything.'

Meanwhile Judge Dee had changed into a simple brown robe, and had seated himself in the big arm-chair behind the desk in his private office. With a contented smile he sipped the tea that Chiao Tai had poured out for him.

Sergeant Hoong entered.

'Why are you looking so dejected, Sergeant?' the judge asked him.

Sergeant Hoong shook his head.

'I just mingled with the crowd outside the tribunal,' he said, 'and listened to their talk. If I may speak frankly, Your Honour, they are unfavourably impressed by this first hearing of the case. They can see no point in the interrogation. They opine that Your Honour failed to grasp the main issue, namely to make Wang confess his crime.'

'Sergeant,' Judge Dee said, 'if I did not know so well that your remarks are motivated only by your concern about my success as a magistrate, I would scold you severely. Our August Sovereign has appointed me to dispense justice, not to please the crowd!'

Judge Dee turned to Chiao Tai and said:

'Tell that Warden Gao to come here!'

When Chiao Tai had gone, Sergeant Hoong asked:

'Did Your Honour attach so much importance to Wang's

tale about the nightwatch because you think that those men are connected with this crime?'

Judge Dee shook his head.

'No,' he said, 'not for that reason. Even without having learned of the incident which Candidate Wang related today, my colleague Judge Feng closely questioned the nightwatch, as a matter of routine investigation of everyone who had been near the scene of the crime. Their headman was able to prove that neither he nor his two companions had had anything to do with it.'

Chiao Tai came back with Warden Gao, who bowed deeply before the magistrate.

Judge Dee looked sourly at him and said:

'So you are the warden in whose quarter this disgraceful affair took place. Don't you know that you are responsible for whatever irregularities occur there? Be more diligent about your duties! Make rounds day and night and don't waste the Government's time in inns and gambling dens!'

The warden hastily knelt down, knocking his head on the floor three times. Judge Dee continued:

'Now you shall lead us to Half Moon Street, so that we can have a look at the scene of the crime. I only wish to obtain a general impression. Apart from yourself I need only Chiao Tai and four constables. I shall go incognito, Sergeant Hoong will act as the leader of our party.'

Judge Dee put on a small black cap and they left the tribunal by the western side door, Chiao Tai and Warden Gao leading the way with the four constables bringing up the rear.

They first walked along the main street in a southern direction, till they came to the back wall of the Temple of the City God. There they turned west, and soon saw the green glazed tiles of the Temple of Confucius on their right. They crossed the bridge over the river that crosses the western section of the city from north to south. Here the pavement ended, they found themselves in the quarter of poor people. The warden turned left into a street lined on both sides with small shops and dilapidated houses, then entered a narrow, curved alley. This turned out to be Half Moon Street. Warden Gao showed them the shop of Butcher Hsiao.

As they stood in front of the shop, a crowd of onlookers gathered. Warden Gao shouted:

'These are officials of the tribunal investigating the scene of the crime on His Excellency's orders. Get a move on! Don't interfere with officials in the execution of their duty!'

Judge Dee noted that the shop stood on the corner of a very narrow side street and that its sidewall had no windows. The godown stood about ten feet behind it. The window of the garret where the girl had lived was visible a few feet above the top of the wall that connected the shop with the godown. On the opposite side of the alley rose the high, blind sidewall of the guild house on the other corner. Turning round and looking towards the street Judge Dee saw that Tailor Loong's shop was located exactly opposite the entrance of the alley. From the attic of the tailor shop one could see obliquely into the alley and obtain a view of the girl's window.

While Sergeant Hoong was asking Warden Gao some routine questions Judge Dee said to Chiao Tai:

'Try to climb up to that window!'

Chiao Tai smiled, tucked the slips of his robe in his belt and jumped up, grasping the top of the wall. He pulled himself up and found a hold for his right foot in a hole in the wall where a few bricks had dropped out. Then he raised himself slowly, pressing his body close to the wall, till he could put his hand on the window-sill. Pulling himself up again, he put his leg over the sill, and climbed inside.

Judge Dee nodded from below. Chiao Tai swung himself over the window-sill. He hung for a moment by his hands, then let himself drop down the five feet or so to the ground, where he landed with hardly a sound by using a boxer trick known as 'a butterfly descending on a flower.'

Warden Gao wanted to show them the victim's room, but Judge Dee shook his head to Sergeant Hoong, who said curtly:

'We have seen what we came to see. Let us return.'

A leisurely walk took them back to the tribunal.

After the warden had respectfully taken his leave, Judge Dee said to the sergeant:

'What I saw just now has confirmed my suspicions. Have Ma Joong called here!'

After a while Ma Joong entered, and bowed to the judge.

'Ma Joong,' Judge Dee said, 'I must charge you with a difficult and probably a dangerous job.'

Ma Joong's face lit up and he said eagerly:

'I am at your service, Your Honour!'

'I order you,' Judge Dee said, 'to disguise yourself as a low-class vagrant bully. You will frequent the haunts of the scum of this city and try to find a renegade Taoist or Buddhist mendicant monk or a ruffian who has taken on that guise. Your man is a tall, muscular fellow—but not the type of chivalrous highwayman you used to associate with when you were living in "the green woods." This is a degenerate brute whose faculties have been dulled by a life of violence and vile debauch. He has particularly strong hands with short, broken nails. I don't know what kind of robe he will be wearing when you find him, but probably it will be a ragged cowl. I am sure, however, that he, as all mendicant monks, will have with him the "wooden fish," that skull-shaped wooden hand gong those monks use for attracting the attention of the passers-by. The final proof of his identity is that he has, or till quite recently had in his possession a pair of solid gold hairpins of peculiar workmanship. This is a sketch of them, which you must memorise.'

'That is a fair enough description,' Ma Joong said. 'But who is this man and what crime did he commit?'

'Since I never met him,' Judge Dee said with a smile, 'I cannot tell you his name. But as to the crime he committed; he is the vile ruffian who raped and murdered the daughter of Butcher Hsiao!'

'That is a job I shall enjoy!' Ma Joong exclaimed excitedly and hurriedly took his leave.

Sergeant Hoong had been listening with growing astonishment to Judge Dee's instructions to Ma Joong. Now he exclaimed:

'Your Honour, this bewilders me completely!'

Judge Dee, however, just smiled and said:

'You have heard and seen what I heard and saw. Draw your own conclusions!'

IN the morning of that same day, when Tao Gan had left Judge Dee's private office, he changed into a quiet but distinguished-looking outer robe and put on a black gauze cap as is affected by gentlemen of leisure without official rank.

In this attire he walked through the northern city gate and strolled through the northern suburb. He found a small restaurant where he ordered a simple luncheon.

From the second floor where he sat by the window he could see through the lattice-work the curved roof of the Temple of Boundless Mercy.

As he paid his bill he said to the servant:

'What a magnificent temple that is! How pious the monks must be to receive such plentiful blessings from the Lord Buddha!'

The waiter grunted.

'Those baldheads may be pious,' he replied, 'but there is many an honest householder in this district who would gladly cut their throat!'

'Mind your language, my man!' Tao Gan said with feigned indignation. 'You are speaking to a devout believer in the Three Jewels.'

The waiter gave him a sullen look and went away without taking the tip that Tao Gan had left on the table. Tao Gan contentedly put the cash back into his sleeve and left the restaurant.

After a short walk he arrived at the three-storied gate of the temple. He ascended the stone steps and entered. Out of the corner of his eye he noticed three monks sitting in the gatekeeper's room. They scrutinised him carefully. Tao Gan walked slowly through the gate, then suddenly stopped short, felt in his sleeves, and looked to left and right as if undecided what to do.

One of the gatekeepers, an elderly monk, stepped up to him, and enquired politely:

'Can I be of any service to the gentleman?'

'This is very kind of you, Father,' Tao Gan said. 'I, a devout follower of the Path came here especially to offer this my humble votive gift to our Gracious Lady Kwan Yin. However, I find that unfortunately I left my small change at home. So I am unable to buy incense. I fear that I shall have to return and come back here some other day.'

As he spoke he took a beautiful bar of silver from his sleeve and let it weigh in the palm of his hand.

The monk, who cast an admiring eye on the silver bar, hastily said:

'Allow me, my Lord, to advance the incense money to you!'

So speaking he hurriedly went into the gatekeeper's room and reappeared with two strings of fifty copper cash each, which Tao Gan accepted with grave thanks.

Crossing the first courtyard, Tao Gan noticed that it was paved with polished stone slabs, while the reception rooms on both sides made a most elegant impression. Two palankeens were standing in front and there was much coming and going of monks and servants. Tao Gan passed two more courtyards, then saw the main hall of the temple directly in front of him.

This hall was on three sides surrounded by a marble terrace and overlooked a spacious courtyard paved with carved marble slabs. Tao Gan ascended the broad steps, crossed the terrace and stepped over the high threshold into the dimly-lit hall. The sandalwood statue of the goddess was over a fathom high. It was placed on a gilt pedestal and the light of two giant candles played on the golden incense burners and other sacrificial vessels on the altar.

Tao Gan bowed deeply three times and then, for the benefit of the group of monks standing about, made it appear as if with his right hand he dropped some cash in the large wooden offering box, while at the same time he let his left sleeve in which he had put the two strings of cash, swing against the outside of the box with a convincing thud.

He stood with folded hands for some time, bowed again three times and left the hall. He walked round it on the right side but found his passage barred by a closed gate. He stood debating whether or not to try to push this door open, when a monk came out, and asked:

'Does the gentleman wish to see His Reverence the Abbot?'

Tao Gan hastily excused himself and retraced his steps. He again passed the hall and then turned round the left corner. There he found a broad covered corridor which led to a flight of narrow steps that went down. At the bottom was a small gate with a notice reading:

ALL PERSONS EXCEPT THE TEMPLE PERSONNEL ARE RESPECT-
FULLY REQUESTED HERE TO ARREST THEIR STEPS

Ignoring this polite notice, Tao Gan swiftly pushed the door open, and found himself in a beautifully landscaped garden. A winding path led through flowering bushes and artificial rocks; in the distance the blue glaze of the tiled roofs and the red lacquered rafters of small pavilions shimmered through the green tree-tops.

Tao Gan assumed that this was the place where the ladies who visited the temple stayed overnight. He quickly slipped between two large bushes and, shedding his outer coat, put it on again inside out. Tao Gan had this coat specially made. Its lining consisted of rough hempcloth such as is worn by work-men and it showed several clumsy patches. He took off his gauze cap which proved collapsible, and stuffed it in his sleeve. He wound a strip of dirty cloth round his head and tucked his robe up so that his leggings showed. Finally he took a thin roll of blue cloth from his sleeve.

This contrivance was one of Tao Gan's many ingenious inventions. When unrolled, it proved to be a roughly sewn bag made of the blue cloth that people ordinarily use for wrapping up the bundles they carry. It had a square shape, but all kinds of queer folds and spare corners had been sewn in it. By fitting together, in various combinations, the dozen thin bamboo staves inside, Tao Gan could make this bag assume all kinds of shapes—from the square bundle containing laundry to the oblong package full of books. In his varied career this contraption had often proved extremely useful to him.

Tao Gan adjusted the bamboo staves inside in such a way that the bundle seemed to contain carpenter's tools. His transformation was completed in a few moments and soon he was walking down the pathway, his shoulders bent a little as if the bundle he was carrying under his arm was quite heavy.

The path led to an elegant small pavilion standing in the shadow of an old, gnarled pine tree. The red lacquered double door, studded with copper knobs, stood open and two novices were sweeping the floor.

Tao Gan stepped over the high threshold, and without a word went straight to a large couch that was standing against the back wall. He squatted down with a grunt, produced a piece of carpenter's string, and started measuring the couch.

One of the two young monks said:

'What, must the furniture be altered again?'

'Mind your own business!' Tao Gan said gruffly, 'do you grudge a poor carpenter a few copper cash?'

The two novices laughed and left the pavilion. As soon as he was alone Tao Gan stood up and looked round.

The room had no windows except for a round opening high

up on the back wall, which was so small that even a child would not be able to wriggle through. The couch on which he had pretended to start work was made of solid blackwood, intricately carved and inlaid with mother-of-pearl. Its coverlets and pillow were of heavy brocade. By its side stood a small table of carved rosewood, with a portable tea stove and a tea-set of fine porcelain. One of the side walls was entirely covered by a magnificent scroll picture on silk, showing an image of the goddess Kwan Yin painted in full colour. Against the wall opposite stood an elegant dressing-table of rosewood. On it was an incense burner and two large candles. The only other piece of furniture was a low footstool. Although the novices had just swept and aired the room, the fragrance of some thick incense still hung in the air.

'Now,' Tao Gan said to himself, 'we must locate the secret entrance.'

He first inspected the most likely place—the wall behind the scroll picture. He tapped it all over and tried to discover a groove or some other indication of a secret doorway, but all in vain. Then he inspected the other walls inch by inch. He pushed the couch away from the wall and scrutinised it closely. Climbing on the dressing-table, he felt all around the small window to see whether there was not a trick frame, that made it in fact larger than it seemed. But here also his efforts were fruitless.

This annoyed Tao Gan considerably, he prided himself on being an expert on secret contrivances.

'In old mansions,' he thought, 'one may find a trapdoor in the floor. These pavilions, however, were built only last year. I could imagine that the monks could have made secretly a hidden entrance in the wall, but they could never engage in such extensive work as digging tunnels underground without attracting attention from outside. Yet it is the only possibility left.'

So he rolled up the thick carpet that covered the floor space in front of the couch and went down on his hands and knees. He examined the stone flags one by one, prying in the grooves with his knife. However, all his labour was in vain.

Since he did not dare to stay in the pavilion too long, he had to give up. On the way out he hastily inspected the hinges of the heavy double door to see whether they concealed some trick. But they were perfectly normal. Tao Gan sighed and closed the double doors behind him, devoting a few moments to an inspection of the lock which was of the most solid kind.

He walked down the garden path, and three monks that met him only saw a grumpy old carpenter with his tool bag under his arm.

In the bushes near the entrance gate he changed back to his former attire and slipped out.

He strolled leisurely through the various courtyards and located the quarters of the monks, also the guest-rooms for the husbands of the ladies that came to visit the temple.

When he arrived at the main gate once more, he walked into the doorkeeper's room and found the same three monks that he had met when he entered.

'Accept my respectful thanks for the loan!' Tao Gan said politely to the eldest monk, without however making any attempt to take the strings of cash from his sleeve. Since it was awkward to let him stand there, the eldest monk invited him to sit down and asked him whether he would like a cup of tea.

Tao Gan accepted gravely. Soon the four of them were sitting round the square table, drinking the bitter tea that is served in Buddhist monasteries.

'You people,' Tao Gan said in a conversational tone, 'seem extremely averse to spending copper cash. I did not use those two strings of cash you lent me, because when I wanted to take off a few coppers to pay for the incense, it turned out that the string had no knot. How could I untie it?'

'This is a queer statement, stranger,' one of the younger monks said. 'Show me that string!'

Tao Gan took the string from his sleeve and handed it to the monk, who let it swiftly pass through his hands.

'Here,' he said triumphantly, 'if this is not a knot then I don't know what a knot is!'

Tao Gan took the string back without even looking at it, and said to the elder monk:

'This must be black magic! Do you want to bet me fifty cash that there is no knot in the string?'

'Done!' shouted the younger monk eagerly.

Tao Gan took up the string, made it whirl round and round in the air. Then he gave it back to the monk, and said:

'Now show me the knot!'

The three monks eagerly let the string pass through their hands, but search as they might among the cash, they could not discover a knot.

Tao Gan placidly put the string back in his sleeve. Throwing a single copper on the table, he said:

'I will give you a chance to get your money back. Spin this coin and I bet you fifty cash that the reverse comes up!'

'Taken!' the elder monk said and spun the coin. It came up with the reverse side.

'That squares the loan,' Tao Gan said. 'To compensate you for your loss, however, I am willing to sell you my bar of silver for fifty cash.'

So speaking he again produced the bar of silver and let it weigh in his palm.

By now the monks were completely confused. The elder one thought that Tao Gan was a bit queer in his head, but he was not going to let the bar of silver go by at one per cent of the price. Thus he produced another string of fifty cash and put it on the table.

普慈寺

TAO GAN PRACTISING HIS TRICKS IN A BUDDHIST TEMPLE

'You made a good deal,' Tao Gan observed, 'this is a nice bar, and moreover very easy to carry!'

He blew against the bar. It fluttered down on the table. It was, in fact, a very clever imitation made of tinfoil.

Tao Gan slipped the string of cash in his sleeve and took out another one. He showed the monks that the string was tied in a special knot. By pressing it between his fingertips it became a slipping knot which fitted exactly into the square hole of a copper cash. If one let the cash run through one's fingers the knot was invisible and moved along with the cash into which it was fastened. Finally Tao Gan turned over the coin that had been spun a few moments ago; it was the same on both sides.

The monks burst out laughing, for they now understood that Tao Gan was a professional swindler.

'The lesson you learned,' Tao Gan calmly remarked, 'was well worth a hundred and fifty copper cash. Now let me get down to business. I have heard people talk about the wealth that comes flowing into this temple, and I thought I would stroll round and have a look at things here.

'I hear that you have many distinguished visitors. Now it so happens that I am a good talker and a fine connoisseur of men. I thought that you people might employ me to locate prospective, shall we say, "clients" for you, and to persuade people who hesitate letting their wives stay here overnight.'

When the elder monk shook his head, Tao Gan hastily continued:

'You need not pay me much, you know. Say, for instance, only ten per cent of the incense money of those visitors whom I introduce to you.'

'My friend,' the elder monk said coldly, 'you are completely misinformed. I know that jealous people on occasion circulate nasty rumours about this temple, but that is just idle talk. I can well imagine that a crook like you thinks the worst of everything and everyone, but in this case you are completely wrong. All our blessings come from our Gracious Lady Kwan Yin, Amen.'

'No offence meant,' said Tao Gan cheerfully, 'people in my profession admittedly are a bit suspicious. Now I suppose that you take due precautions for safeguarding the honour of the lady visitors?'

'Of course,' the elder monk said. 'In the first place, our abbot, His Reverence Spiritual Virtue, is extremely cautious in admitting people. He first interviews newcomers in the reception room and if he has any doubt about their faith in the Lord Buddha, or about their financial, or let us rather say, their social background, he refuses to let them stay. When the lady has prayed with her husband in the main hall, the latter is expected to give a repast to the abbot and the elders. This is usually a bit expensive, but our kitchen is superb, though I say it in all humility.

'Finally the abbot conducts the couple to one of our guest pavilions in the back garden. You have not seen those, but you can take my word for it that they are appointed in the most elegant of tastes. There are six of them. Each has a life-size painted copy of the miraculous sandalwood statue which you saw in the main hall hanging on the wall. Thus the ladies can pass the night in meditation on the virtues of our Gracious Lady Kwan Yin, Amen! When the lady is inside, the husband locks the door and keeps the key. Moreover, our abbot always insists that a strip of paper be pasted over the door and that the husband impresses his seals thereon. These seals may not be broken by anyone other than the husband. The next morning it is he who unlocks the door. Do you see now that there is not the slightest reason for any dark suspicion?'

Tao Gan sadly shook his head and said:

'It is a great pity, but you are perfectly right! Now what happens if the prayer and the stay in the temple should fail to produce the desired result?'

'That,' the monk answered smugly, 'will happen only if the lady's mind is impure or if she does not genuinely believe in the Lord Buddha. Some ladies come back a second time, others we never see again.'

Pulling the long hairs on his cheek, Tao Gan asked:

'I suppose that when in due time a childless couple obtains the desired offspring, they don't forget the Temple of Boundless Mercy?'

'Indeed not,' the monk said with a grin, 'sometimes a special palankeen is needed to convey their presents here. And should on occasion this small courtesy be overlooked, our abbot usually sends a messenger to the lady concerned, just to remind her of her debt of gratitude to our temple.'

Tao Gan engaged the monks in some further desultory conversation without succeeding in eliciting more information from them.

After a while he took his leave and returned to the tribunal by a circuitous route.

TAO GAN found Judge Dee in his private office consulting with the senior scribe and the head of the archives about a disputed plot of land.

When the judge saw Tao Gan enter he dismissed the others and told him to call Sergeant Hoong.

Then Tao Gan gave a detailed report about his visit to the temple, omitting no detail except his little tricks with the faked silver bar and the strings of cash. When he had finished, Judge Dee said:

'Well, this settles our problem. Since you have found no secret entrance to the pavilion, we must accept the word of the monks. The statue of the goddess Kwan Yin has indeed miraculous powers, and will grant children to those devout women who earnestly pray to her.'

Both the sergeant and Tao Gan were greatly amazed at this pronouncement of the judge.

'The entire town,' Tao Gan said, 'is seething with rumours about the disgraceful things that go on in that temple! I beseech Your Honour to let me go there again, or else send Sergeant Hoong, to institute a more thorough investigation.'

Judge Dee, however, shook his head.

'For wealth and prosperity to incite envy,' he said, 'is unfortunately a common occurrence. The investigation of the Temple of Boundless Mercy is closed!'

Sergeant Hoong was going to make another attempt to persuade the judge, but being familiar with the indications given by Judge Dee's expression, he thought better of it.

'Moreover,' the judge added, 'if Ma Joong needs help in locating the murderer of Half Moon Street, Tao Gan must be ready to join him in the search.'

Tao Gan looked disappointed and would have said something, but just then the sound of the large gong resounded through the tribunal, and Judge Dee rose to don his official robes for the afternoon session.

The large crowd of spectators had gathered again in the court hall, for everyone expected that Judge Dee would now continue the hearing of the case against Candidate Wang that he had broken off that noon.

As soon as he had called the roll, Judge Dee glared at the crowd that filled the hall and spoke:

'Since the citizens of Poo-yang take such an interest in the proceedings of this tribunal, I avail myself of this opportunity to issue a general warning. It has come to my attention that some evil people in this district are disseminating malicious rumours regarding the Temple of Boundless Mercy. I, the magistrate, remind all of you of the fact that the Penal Code contains clear provisions against the spreading of libellous rumours and unfounded incriminations! Those who offend against the law shall be prosecuted according to the law.'

Then Judge Dee had the persons concerned in the dispute over the plot of land brought before him and devoted some time to deciding that issue. He did not call anyone concerned with the case of Half Moon Street.

As the session drew to its end, there was some commotion near the entrance of the court hall.

Judge Dee looked up from the document he was studying and saw an old lady who was trying to make her way through the crowd. The judge gave a sign to the headman, and he went with two constables to bring the lady before the dais.

The senior scribe bent over to Judge Dee's ear and whispered:

'Your Honour, that is a crazy old woman, who for months

on end has bothered His Excellency Feng with some imaginary complaint. I respectfully advise Your Honour to dismiss her.'

Judge Dee made no comment on this, but gave the woman a sharp look as she approached the dais. She seemed well past middle age and walked with difficulty, leaning on a long staff. Her robes were threadbare but clean and neatly patched. She had quite a distinguished face.

As she began to kneel, Judge Dee signalled to the constables.

'No aged and sick person shall kneel in my tribunal. Remain standing, Madam, and state your name and your complaint.'

The old lady bowed deeply and then spoke in an indistinct voice:

'This insignificant person is called Liang, *née* Ou-yang. I am the widow of Liang I-feng, in life a merchant in the city of Canton.'

Here her voice trailed off, thick tears flowed down her cheeks and her frail body shook with sobs.

Judge Dee had noticed that she spoke in Cantonese dialect, which was not easy for him to follow. Moreover she was evidently not in a condition to state her case. He addressed her:

'Madam, I can't keep you standing here so long. I shall hear you in my private office.' Turning to Sergeant Hoong who was standing behind his chair, Judge Dee said: 'Take this lady to the small reception room and have tea served to her there.'

When the old lady had been led away Judge Dee dealt with some routine matters and then closed the session.

Sergeant Hoong was waiting for the judge in his private office.

'Your Honour,' he said, 'the lady seems mentally deranged. When she had drunk a cup of tea, her mind was clear for a few moments. She gave me to understand that she and her family have been suffering some terrible wrong. Then she again started crying and her language became incoherent. I have

73

taken the liberty to send for an old maid of Your Honour's household to calm her down.'

'That was very wise, Sergeant,' the judge said. 'We shall wait till she is completely at ease and then see whether we can hear her. In most cases the wrongs such people speak of exist only in their deranged mind. Yet no one who appeals to this tribunal for justice shall be sent away before I have obtained a clear account of the case!'

Judge Dee rose from his chair and began pacing the floor, his hands behind him. Sergeant Hoong was just going to ask what was worrying him, when the judge stood still and said:

'Since we are alone now, I wish to make to you, my faithful friend and adviser, a final statement regarding the Temple of Boundless Mercy. Stand here, near to me, so that no one will hear.'

Speaking in a low voice, Judge Dee continued:

'You will understand that it serves no purpose to continue the investigation. In the first place, it is almost impossible to obtain definite proof. Tao Gan, in whose ability I place great confidence, failed to discover a secret entrance. And if the monks should, by some unknown means, perpetrate infamous acts, one need not hope that their victims will ever come forward to testify against them, and thus expose themselves and their husbands to ridicule and contempt and cast doubt on the legitimacy of their children. Besides, there is a still more cogent reason, which I shall tell you for your exclusive information, and in the strictest confidence.'

Speaking in a whisper, close to the sergeant's ear, Judge Dee continued:

'I have recently received disturbing news from the capital. It seems that the Buddhist Church, ever waxing in power, has now wormed its way into the Imperial Court. It started by a number of Court ladies being converted and now the black-robed crowd has even succeeded in obtaining the ear of our

74

August Sovereign. His Imperial Majesty has granted them consideration of their fallacious doctrines.

'The Chief Abbot of the White Horse Monastery in the capital has been appointed a member of the Grand Council, and he and his clique are meddling with the internal and external affairs of our Empire. Their spies and agents are everywhere. The loyal servants of the Throne are greatly worried.'

Judge Dee frowned and added in a still lower voice:

'This being so, you will understand what might happen if I were to open a case against the Temple of Boundless Mercy. We are not confronted with ordinary criminals, we are up against a powerful, national organisation. The Buddhist clique will immediately place itself behind the abbot and give him full support. They will start a campaign at Court, influence will be brought to bear in this province, and rich presents will be distributed in the right places. Even if I should produce irrefutable proof, long before I could complete such a case, I would find myself transferred to a distant post on the border. It is even possible that I might be sent to the capital in chains on a trumped-up charge.'

'Does this mean, Your Honour,' Sergeant Hoong said indignantly, 'that we are completely powerless?'

Judge Dee sadly nodded his head. After some reflection he said with a sigh:

'If only such a case could be initiated, solved, and the criminals convicted and executed—all on one and the same day! However, you know that our laws preclude such an arbitrary procedure. Even if I obtained a complete confession, the death sentence would have to be approved by the Metropolitan Court, and it takes weeks before my report would arrive there via the prefectural and provincial authorities. That would give the Buddhist clique ample time and opportunity to have the report suppressed, the case dismissed, and

75

myself removed from office in disgrace. Now I would gladly risk my career and even my life, if I could see the faintest chance of succeeding in removing this cancerous growth from our society. It may very well be, however, that such a chance will never come!'

'In the meantime, Sergeant, I charge you never to let one word of what has just transpired pass your lips and I forbid you ever to raise this question again. I am convinced that the abbot has his spies also among the personnel of this tribunal. Every word said about the Temple of Boundless Mercy is one word too much.

'Now go and see if the old lady can be questioned.'

When Sergeant Hoong returned with the old woman, Judge Dee made her sit down in a comfortable chair opposite his desk. Then he said kindly:

'I am exceedingly vexed, Madam, to see you in such distress. Now you told me that your husband's name is Liang, but you have not yet given me more details about the manner of his death or the wrong you suffered.'

With trembling hands the old lady fumbled in her sleeve and brought out a manuscript roll wrapped up in a piece of faded brocade. She presented this respectfully to the judge with two hands. She spoke in a faltering voice:

'May it please Your Honour to peruse these documents. Nowadays my old brain is so confused that I cannot think clearly for more than a few moments. I could never give you a consecutive account of the terrible wrong that myself and my family have suffered! Your Honour will find everything in those documents.'

Leaning back in her chair she started weeping again.

Judge Dee ordered Sergeant Hoong to give her a cup of strong tea and then unwrapped the package. It contained a thick roll of documents, yellowed by age and long use. Unrolling the first one, he saw that it was a long accusation, evidently written by an accomplished scholar, in beautiful style and elegant calligraphy.

Glancing through it, Judge Dee noted that it was a circumstantial account of a sanguinary feud between two wealthy merchant families of Canton, called respectively Liang and Lin. It had started when Lin had seduced Liang's wife. Thereafter Lin had relentlessly persecuted the Liang family, robbing them of all their possessions. When Judge Dee came to the end of the document and saw the date, he looked up in astonishment and said:

'Madam, this document is dated over twenty years ago!'

'Ruthless crimes,' the old lady answered in a soft voice, 'are not erased by the passage of time.'

The judge glanced through the other documents and saw that they all pertained to various later phases of the same case; the most recent paper was dated two years ago. At the end of every document, however, whether old or new, there always was the legend in vermilion ink, the magistrate's verdict reading 'Case dismissed because of insufficient evidence.'

'I observe,' Judge Dee said, 'that all this happened in the city of Canton. Why did you leave the old home of your family?'

'I came to Poo-yang,' the old lady said, 'because the main criminal, Lin Fan, happened to settle in this district.'

Judge Dee could not remember having heard this name. Rolling up the documents, he said kindly:

'I shall study these records with great care, Madam. As soon as I reach a conclusion, I shall ask you to come here again, for further consultation.'

The old lady slowly rose, and bowing deeply she said:

'For many years I have been waiting for a magistrate who would find a way to redress this terrible wrong. May August Heaven grant that the day has now come!'

Sergeant Hoong led her away. When he came back Judge Dee said to him:

77

'At first sight I would say that this is one of those vexing cases where a clever and well-educated rascal has enriched himself by ruining scores of other people, yet always escaping his just punishment. It is clear that sorrow and frustration have unhinged the mind of this old lady. The least I can do for her is to make a careful study of this case, although I doubt very much whether I shall be able to find a flaw in the defendant's arguments. I notice that the case has passed through the hands of at least one magistrate who is famous as an eminent jurist and who now sits on the Metropolitan Court.'

Then Judge Dee had Tao Gan called. When he saw the dejected face of his lieutenant he said with a smile:

'Cheer up, Tao Gan, I have now better work for you than to hang around the Buddhist crowd! Go to the place where that old Lady Liang lives. Gather all information you can get about her and her family. Then I want you to trace a wealthy man called Lin Fan, who must live somewhere in this city. You shall also report on him. It may help you to know that both persons are from Canton, and settled down here a few years ago.'

Judge Dee dismissed Sergeant Hoong and Tao Gan and had the senior scribe bring in some documents relating to the routine of the district administration.

Seventh Chapter: MA JOONG DISCOVERS A DESERTED TAOIST
SANCTUARY; A VIOLENT FIGHT TAKES PLACE IN THE TEMPLE
YARD

••

THAT afternoon after he had left Judge Dee's private office Ma
Joong had gone to his own quarters and altered his appearance
by means of a few simple changes.

He took off his cap, shook his hair loose, and bound it up
again with a dirty rag. He put on baggy trousers, strapping
their ends round his ankles with straw rope. Then he threw a
short, patched jacket over his shoulders and finally changed his
felt shoes for straw sandals.

In this disreputable attire he slipped out of the tribunal by
the side door and mingled with the crowd in the street. He
noticed with satisfaction that after one look at him people
hastily made way to let him pass. Street vendors instinctively
clutched their wares firmly under their arms when they saw
him approaching. Ma Joong scowled fiercely and for some
time rather amused himself.

It did not take him long to discover, however, that his task
was not as easy as he had thought. He had an execrable meal
in a street stall frequented by vagabonds, drank dregs of wine
in a den that smelled after the refuse it was built on, and heard
innumerable tales of woe and countless requests for the loan
of a few coppers. But all those people were but the comparatively innocent riff-raff that roams in the back streets of every
town—small pilferers and pick-pockets. He felt that he had
not yet come into touch with any of the local low-class
gangsters, who were well organised among themselves, and
knew exactly what was going on in the underworld.

It was only towards nightfall that Ma Joong obtained a faint clue. He was forcing another dram of terrible liquid down his throat in a street stall when he overheard part of the conversation of two beggars who were having their meal there. One asked about a good place to steal clothes. The other replied: 'The people at the Red Temple will know!'

Ma Joong knew that low-class criminals often gather round some dilapidated temple. However, since most temples have red lacquered pillars and gates, he was at a loss how to locate this particular one in a city where he had arrived only a few days before. He resolved to take a long chance. Walking to the market-place near the north gate of the city, he gripped a small ragamuffin by his neck and told him gruffly to take him to 'the Red Temple.' Without asking a single question, the ragged urchin took him through a maze of narrow, winding alleys to a dark square. There the boy wrenched himself loose and ran off as fast as he could.

Ma Joong saw the large red gate of a Taoist temple directly ahead, looming against the evening sky. On the right and left rose the forbidding walls of old mansions, all along their base a row of wooden shacks, their walls sagging at crazy angles. When the temple prospered, these had been the stalls of vendors catering to the crowd of the devout, but now they had been appropriated by the outlaws of the town.

The entire yard was strewn with filth and refuse. Its odour mingled with the nauseating stench of the cheap oil in which a ragged old man was frying cakes over an improvised charcoal fire. A smoking torch had been stuck in a crack in the wall and by its uncertain light Ma Joong discovered a group of men squatting in a circle, absorbed in a gambling game.

Ma Joong sauntered over to this group. A fat fellow with a naked torso and an enormous paunch was sitting on an overturned wine jar with his back against the wall. His long hair and his dishevelled beard were stiff with grease and dirt. He was following the game with heavy-lidded eyes, scratching

MA JOONG'S FIRST MEETING WITH SHENG PA

his belly with his left hand. His right arm, thick as a mast, rested on a knobbed stick. Three lean fellows were crouching round the dice board on the ground, while others squatted in the shadow farther away.

Ma Joong stood there for some time, following the rolling dice. No one seemed to pay the slightest attention to him. He was just debating with himself how he could strike up a conversation, when the huge fellow on the wine jar suddenly said, without looking up:

'I could use your jacket, brother!'

At once Ma Joong found himself the centre of attention. One gambler gathered up the dice, and rose from his crouching position. He was not as tall as Ma Joong, but his naked arms showed a certain wiry strength and the hilt of a dagger protruded from his girdle. Grinning he sidled up to Ma Joong's right side, fingering his dagger. The fat man left his wine jar, hitched up his trousers, spat with relish, and then, taking a firm hold on his knobstick, planted himself in front of Ma Joong.

With a leer he said:

'Welcome to the Temple of Transcendental Wisdom, brother! Am I far wróng when I take it that your devout spirit moved you to visit this holy place in order to present some votive gift? Let me assure you, brother, that that jacket of yours will be gratefully accepted!'

While speaking he prepared to strike.

In one glance Ma Joong took in the situation. The immediate danger was the ugly club in the fat man's right hand and the drawn dagger of the fellow on his right.

Just as the fat man was finishing his speech, Ma Joong's left arm shot out. Gripping the fat man's right shoulder, he pressed his thumb in the correct place temporarily laming the arm that held the club. The fat man swiftly closed his left hand round Ma Joong's left wrist, planning to pull him forward and hit Ma Joong in the groin with his knee. Practically at the same time, however, Ma Joong had raised his right arm with crooked elbow. He swung it back with all his might, crashing his elbow in the face of the man with the dagger, who fell down with a hoarse cry. Then, in one continuous motion, Ma Joong's right arm travelled forwards again, and hit the fat man a powerful blow on his unprotected diaphragm. The fat man let go his grip on Ma Joong's left wrist and doubled up on the ground gasping.

About to turn round to see whether the man with the dagger needed further attention, Ma Joong felt a crushing weight fall on his back. A muscular forearm closed round his throat from behind in a strangler's vice.

Ma Joong bent his powerful neck, pressing his chin in the other's forearm, at the same time groping behind his back. His left hand only tore a piece from his assailant's dress, but his right closed round a leg. He pulled it round with all his force, at the same time lurching forward to the right. Both men crashed to the ground, but Ma Joong was on top. His hip with his entire body weight behind it nearly broke his opponent's pelvis. The vice loosened. Ma Joong jumped up, just in time to dodge a dagger thrust from the lean fellow, who had scrambled up during these proceedings.

While he dodged, Ma Joong caught the wrist of the hand that wielded the dagger. Twisting the other's arm, he drew it over his shoulder. Then Ma Joong quickly ducked, and threw his opponent in a wide curve through the air. He crashed against the wall, and fell down on the empty wine jar, breaking it to pieces. He lay quite still.

Ma Joong picked up the dagger and threw it over the wall. Turning round he said to the shadowy figures in the background:

'I may seem a bit rough, brothers, but I have no patience with people who use daggers!'

He was answered by some non-committal grunts.

The fat man was still lying on the ground vomiting freely, groaning and cursing in between.

Ma Joong pulled him up by his beard, and threw him so that his back hit against the wall. The fat man landed there with a thud and sank into a squatting position, his eyes goggling at Ma Joong. He was still gasping for breath.

After quite some time, the fat man recovered slightly, and croaked in a hoarse voice:

'Now that, so to speak, the amenities have been complied with, would the honourable brother instruct us as to his name and profession?'

'My name,' Ma Joong replied casually, 'is Joong Bao and I am an honest street vendor, peddling my wares along the highways. Early this morning, when the sun was just rising, I met with a rich merchant. He took such a fancy to my wares that he bought the whole lot, paying me thirty silver pieces. Therefore I hurried here, to burn incense to the deities as a mark of my gratitude.'

The crowd guffawed and the prospective strangler asked whether Ma Joong had eaten his evening meal. When Ma Joong said no, the fat man shouted over to the oil cake vendor, and soon they were all gathered round the charcoal fire, eating oily cakes heavily seasoned with garlic.

It turned out that the fat man was called Sheng Pa. He proudly introduced himself as the chosen head of all the vagrant ruffians of the city and concurrently a counsellor of the Beggars' Guild. He and his men had settled down in the temple yard about two years ago. It used to be quite a prosperous place, but something untoward seemed to have happened there. The monks had left and the doors of the temple had been sealed up by the authorities. Sheng Pa said that it was a nice and quiet corner, yet not too far from the centre of the town.

Ma Joong confided to Sheng Pa that he found himself in a

somewhat awkward position. He had hidden the thirty silver pieces in a safe place but he was anxious to leave town as quickly as possible, since the merchant whom he had robbed might have reported to the tribunal. He did not relish the idea of walking through the street with a heavy bundle of silver in his sleeve. He would like to exchange it for some small trinket, that he could easily hide about his person. He did not mind losing on that deal.

Sheng Pa nodded gravely and said:

'That, brother, is a wise precaution. But silver is a mighty rare commodity. We usually deal exclusively in copper cash. Now, if one wishes to exchange silver for something of smaller bulk but of equal value, why, then there is nothing left but gold! And to tell you the truth, brother, in our crowd that auspicious yellow material appears but once in a life-time, if ever!'

Ma Joong agreed that gold was a rare treasure, but he added that it might just happen that a beggar would find a small golden trinket on the road, dropped down from the palankeen of some distinguished lady. 'News of such a lucky find,' he added, 'travels fast, and you as a counsellor of the Beggars' Guild would soon hear of it!'

Sheng Pa slowly scratched his belly and agreed that it was not impossible that some such thing might happen.

Ma Joong detected a marked lack of enthusiasm.

He fumbled in his sleeve and extracted a piece of silver. He weighed it on the palm of his hand and let the light of the torch play on it.

'When I hid my thirty silver pieces,' he said, 'I took one along for good luck. I wonder whether you would accept it as an advance payment on the commission due to you for acting as an intermediary for the proposed deal.'

Sheng Pa snatched the coin from Ma Joong's hand with amazing agility. With a broad smile he said:

'Brother, I shall see what I can do for you. Come back tomorrow night!'

Ma Joong thanked him, and took leave of his new friends with a few pleasant words.

Eighth Chapter: JUDGE DEE DECIDES HE WILL VISIT HIS COLLEAGUES; HE EXPLAINS THE RAPE MURDER IN HALF MOON STREET

WHEN he came back to the tribunal, Ma Joong quickly changed, then went to the main courtyard. He noticed that there was still a light in the judge's private office.

He found Judge Dee and Sergeant Hoong in conference.

When Judge Dee saw Ma Joong, he broke off the conversation and asked:

'Well, my friend, what is the news?'

Ma Joong reported briefly on his encounter with Sheng Pa and told the judge about the latter's promise.

Judge Dee was pleased.

'It would have been a piece of the most extraordinary good luck,' he observed, 'if you had found the criminal on the very first day. You have made an excellent start. News travels fast along certain channels in the underworld and I think you have now established contact with the right man. I have no doubt that in due time your friend Sheng Pa will give you a clue to the missing hairpins, and those will lead you to the murderer.

'Now, before you came, we were discussing the wisdom of my setting out tomorrow to pay courtesy visits to my colleagues in the neighbouring districts. Sooner or later I have to comply with the custom and the present seems an opportune time. I shall be absent from Poo-yang two or three days. In the meantime you will continue your efforts to apprehend the murderer of Half Moon Street. If you think it necessary, I shall order Chiao Tai to join in the search.'

Ma Joong thought it better if he went about it alone, since

two people enquiring after the same object might arouse suspicion. The judge agreed, and Ma Joong took his leave.

'It would be very opportune,' mused Sergeant Hoong, 'if Your Honour would be absent for a day or two, and the tribunal closed. Then there would be a valid reason for letting the case against Candidate Wang rest. The rumour is spreading that Your Honour is protecting Wang because he is a member of the literary class while his victim was but a poor shop-keeper's daughter.'

Judge Dee shrugged his shoulders and said:

'Be that as it may, I shall leave for Woo-yee tomorrow morning. The following day I shall proceed directly to Chin-hwa and return here on the third day. Since Ma Joong or Tao Gan may need instructions during my absence, you had better not accompany me, Sergeant; stay here and take charge of the seals of the tribunal. You will give the necessary instructions and see that suitable courtesy presents are prepared for my colleague Pan in Woo-yee, and Judge Lo, the magistrate of Chin-hwa. Have my travelling palankeen loaded with my luggage ready in the main courtyard early in the morning!'

Sergeant Hoong assured the judge that his orders would be executed without fail. Judge Dee leaned forward in his chair to read some documents that the senior scribe had placed on the desk for his inspection.

The sergeant seemed reluctant to go and remained standing in front of Judge Dee's desk.

After a while the judge looked up and asked:

'What is on your mind, Sergeant?'

'Your Honour, I have been thinking about that rape-murder, I have read and reread the records. But try as I may I cannot follow your reasoning. The hour is late but if before leaving tomorrow Your Honour would favour me with some further explanation, I will at least be able to sleep during the two nights that Your Honour will be away!'

Judge Dee smiled and placed a paper-weight on the document on his desk. Then he settled back into his arm-chair.

'Sergeant,' he said, 'order the servants to bring a pot of fresh tea and then sit down on the tabouret here. I shall explain to you what I think actually happened on the fateful night of the sixteenth.'

When he had drunk a cup of strong tea, Judge Dee began:

'As soon as I had heard from you the main facts of this case, I ruled out Candidate Wang as the man who raped Pure Jade. It is true that woman may sometimes raise in man strange and cruel thoughts; it is not without reason indeed that in his *Annals of Spring and Autumn* our Master Confucius on occasion refers to woman as "that fey creature"

'There are but two classes of people, however, who translate such dark thoughts into deeds. First, the low-class, utterly depraved habitual criminals. Second, rich lechers who through long years of debauch have become the slaves of their perverted instincts. Now I could possibly imagine that even a studious young man of sober habits like Candidate Wang, if he were in a frenzy of fear, would strangle a girl. But as to his raping her, what is more a girl with whom he had had intimate relations for more than six months, this seemed to me absolutely impossible. So I had to find the real criminal among the members of the two classes I referred to just now.

'I immediately discarded the possibility of a wealthy degenerate. Such persons frequent secret haunts where all vice and perversion can be indulged in if one is prepared to pay in gold. A wealthy man would probably not even be aware of the existence of a quarter of poor shopkeepers such as Half Moon Street. It is most unlikely that he would have had an opportunity to learn about Wang's visits, to say nothing of his ability to perform acrobatics at the end of a strip of cloth! Thus there remained the low-class, habitual criminal.'

Here the judge paused a moment. Then he continued in a bitter voice:

'Those despicable ruffians roam all through the town like hungry dogs. If in a dark alley they happen to meet a defenceless old man they knock him down and rob him of the few strings of copper cash he carries. If they see a woman walking alone they beat her unconscious and then rape her, tear the rings from her ears, and leave her lying in the gutter. Slinking about among the houses of the poor, if they see a door unlatched or a window left open, they creep inside and steal the only copper kettle, or a last set of patched robes.

'Is it not reasonable to assume that such a man when passing through Half Moon Street happened to discover Wang's secret visits to Pure Jade? Such a ruffian would immediately see the chance of having a woman who could not protest against his usurping her secret lover's place. However, Pure Jade defended herself. Probably she tried to shout or to reach the door in order to rouse her parents. Then he strangled her. Having committed this foul deed he calmly ransacked his victim's room for valuables, and made off with the only trinket she had.'

Judge Dee paused and drank another cup of tea.

Sergeant Hoong slowly nodded his head. Then he said:

'Your Honour has made it clear indeed that Candidate Wang did not commit this double crime. Yet I cannot see any definite evidence we could use in court.'

'If you want tangible proof,' Judge Dee answered, 'you shall have it! In the first place, you have heard the coroner's evidence. If Candidate Wang had strangled Pure Jade, his long fingernails would have left deep gashes in the girl's throat; the coroner only found shallow nailmarks, although the skin was broken here and there. This points to the short, uneven nails of a vagrant ruffian.

'Second, Pure Jade fought back with all her might when

she was being violated. Yet her worn-down fingernails could never have caused the deep, nasty scratches on Wang's chest and arms. Those scratches, by the way, were not caused by thorns, as Wang thinks; but that is a minor point to which I shall return in due time. As to the possibility of Wang having strangled Pure Jade, I may add in passing that having seen Wang's physique and having heard the coroner's description of the girl, I am convinced that if Wang had tried to strangle her he would soon have found himself being pushed out of the window! But that is neither here nor there.

'Third, when on the morning of the seventeenth the crime was discovered, the strip of cloth Wang used to climb up to the window was lying in a heap on the floor of the girl's room. If Wang had committed this crime, or if he had been in that room at all, how could he have left without the improvised rope? Wang is not an athlete, he required the girl's assistance to get up to the window. A muscular fellow with experience in housebreaking, however, would never bother to use that strip if forced to leave in a hurry. He would do exactly as you saw Chiao Tai do: swing himself down till he hung from the window-sill by his hands and then let himself drop.

'It is in this way that I obtained my picture of the criminal.'

Sergeant Hoong nodded with a contented smile.

'It is now perfectly clear to me,' he said, 'that Your Honour's reasoning is based on solid facts. When the criminal is caught, there is ample evidence to confront him with and to make him confess, if necessary by applying torture. Doubtless he is still in this city, he has no reason to get alarmed and flee to some distant place. It is known all over the town that Judge Feng was convinced of Candidate Wang's guilt, and that Your Honour concurred with his verdict.'

Caressing his whiskers Judge Dee nodded slowly and said:

'That ruffian will try to get rid of the golden hairpins and so he will betray himself. Ma Joong has established contact with the man who should know when the hairpins are offered for sale on the clandestine thieves' market. You know that a criminal will never dare to approach a goldsmith or a pawn-broker, for a description of stolen articles is circulated among those by the tribunal as a matter of routine. He must try his luck with his fellow criminals, and then the worthy Sheng Pa will soon hear about it. Thus, with reasonable luck, Ma Joong will get his man.'

Judge Dee took another sip of his tea, then took up his vermilion brush and bent over the document in front of him.

Sergeant Hoong rose. He pensively pulled at his moustache. After a while he spoke:

'There are still two points which Your Honour has not yet explained. How did Your Honour know that the criminal would be wearing the dress of a vagabond monk? And what could be the significance of the incident with the nightwatch?'

For a few moments Judge Dee remained silent. He concentrated on the document he was studying. He jotted down a remark in the margin, put down his brush and rolled up the document. Then he looked up at Sergeant Hoong from under his thick, black eyebrows and said:

'The queer incident about the nightwatch, related by Candidate Wang this morning, added the finishing touch to my mental picture of the criminal. You know that low-class criminals often take on the guise of a Taoist or Buddhist mendicant monk. It is excellent cover for their roaming through the city at all times of day and night. Therefore it was not the clapper of the nightwatch that Wang heard the second time, but——'

'The wooden hand-gong of the mendicant monk!' Sergeant Hoong exclaimed.

Ninth Chapter: TWO MONKS VISIT THE JUDGE WITH AN IMPORTANT MESSAGE; HE RECITES A BALLAD AT A DINNER WITH MAGISTRATE LO

THE next morning, as the judge was donning his travel robes, the senior scribe came in and announced that two monks from the Temple of Boundless Mercy had come to the tribunal with a message from the abbot.

Judge Dee changed into his formal robe and seated himself behind his desk. An elderly monk and a younger companion were shown in. As they knelt and touched their heads on the floor three times, the judge noticed that their yellow robes were of the finest damask, lined with purple silk. They carried rosaries of amber beads.

'His Reverence Spiritual Virtue, Abbot of the Temple of Boundless Mercy,' the elder monk chanted, 'has instructed us, ignorant monks, to transmit to Your Excellency his respectful greetings. His Reverence fully realises how heavy are the claims laid upon Your Excellency by official duties especially during these first days. Hence he does not dare to repair here himself for a longer visit. In due time, however, His Reverence shall give himself the privilege of appearing before Your Excellency to receive the benefit of your instruction. In the meantime, lest it be thought that His Reverence is lacking in respect for his magistrate, he begs you to accept a small courtesy gift, hoping that Your Excellency will measure it by the respectful feelings that inspired it rather than by its trifling value.'

Having thus spoken he gave a sign to the younger monk who rose and placed a small package wrapped in costly brocade on Judge Dee's desk.

Sergeant Hoong expected that the judge would refuse the present. To his utter amazement, however, Judge Dee only murmured the customary polite phrase of not being worth such great honour, and when the monk insisted he made no move to return the package. He rose from his chair, bowed gravely, and said:

'Please inform His Reverence that I am exceedingly sensitive to his thoughtfulness and transmit my thanks for the kind present, which I shall return at the proper time. Let His Reverence rest assured that although I am not a follower in the path of the Lord Sakyamuni, I am yet deeply interested in the Buddhist faith and that I eagerly anticipate the opportunity of being further instructed in its abstruse teachings by so eminent an authority as His Reverence Spiritual Virtue.'

'We shall respectfully obey Your Excellency's instructions. At the same time, His Reverence desired us to bring to Your Excellency's notice a matter that, though small in itself, yet was deemed of sufficient importance to be reported to this tribunal; all the more so since yesterday, during the afternoon session, Your Excellency was good enough to state so clearly that our poor temple enjoys your high protection in the same degree as every honest citizen of this district. Of late our temple has been visited by swindlers who have attempted to rob ignorant monks of the few strings of cash that rightfully are the temple's property and made numerous impertinent enquiries. His Reverence expressed the hope that Your Excellency would kindly issue the necessary instructions to curb the activities of these importunate rogues.'

Judge Dee bowed and the two monks took their leave.

The judge was greatly annoyed. He was aware that Tao Gan had been up to his old tricks again; also, that he had been traced back to the tribunal, which was worse. With a sigh Judge Dee ordered Sergeant Hoong to open the package.

Removing the elaborate wrappings, the sergeant saw three

shining bars of solid gold and an equal number of heavy silver.

Judge Dee had them wrapped again and put the package in his sleeve. It was the first time that Sergeant Hoong had seen the judge accept what was evidently a bribe and he was much distressed. Remembering Judge Dee's previous instruction, he did not dare to comment on the monks' visit and silently assisted the judge in changing back into his travelling costume.

Judge Dee slowly walked to the main courtyard in front of the large reception hall and saw that his official retinue was ready. His travel palankeen stood in front of the steps, with six constables in front and six behind; those in front carried placards mounted on long poles with the inscription 'The Magistrate of Poo-yang.' Six sturdy bearers stood ready by the shafts of the palankeen and twelve relays were carrying the judge's bundles of luggage.

Having found everything in order, Judge Dee ascended the palankeen, the bearers hoisted the shafts on their calloused shoulders. Slowly the procession moved across the courtyard and through the double gate.

As the cortège arrived in front of the tribunal, Chiao Tai, armed with bow and sword, guided his horse to the right of Judge Dee's palankeen, the headman of the constables, also on horseback, took up his position on the left.

Then the procession started out through the streets of Poo-yang. Two runners dashed in front beating their copper hand-gongs and shouting: 'Make way! Make way! His Excellency the Magistrate approaches!'

Judge Dee noticed that none of the usual cheers came from the crowd. As he looked through the lattice window of the palankeen, he saw many passers-by casting sullen looks at the procession. Settling back among the cushions with a sigh, the judge took Mrs Liang's documents from his sleeve and began to read them.

After they had left Poo-yang, the procession followed the

highroad which ran for hours on end through flat rice-fields. Suddenly Judge Dee let the roll drop into his lap. He looked out at the monotonous landscape with unseeing eyes. He attempted to survey all the consequences of the action he was contemplating, but could not arrive at a decision. Finally, the swinging movement of the bearers made him drowsy and the judge fell asleep. He awoke only as dusk was falling and the procession entered the city of Woo-yee.

Judge Pan, the magistrate of the district, received Judge Dee in the large reception hall of the tribunal and entertained him at a dinner attended by the leading lights of the local gentry. Magistrate Pan was several years Judge Dee's senior, but because of his failure of two literary examinations he had not been promoted.

Judge Dee found him an austere man of wide learning and independent spirit and soon realised that Pan had failed to pass the examinations because of his refusal to follow the literary fashion rather than because of lack of scholarship.

The meal was simple, the main attraction being the brilliant conversation of the host. Judge Dee learned much about the administrative affairs of the province. It was late when the party broke up, Judge Dee retiring to the guest quarters that had been prepared for him.

Early the next morning Judge Dee took his leave and proceeded with his suite to Chin-hwa.

The road led through a rolling country, gently waving bamboo groves blended with pine-covered hills. It was a fine autumn day and Judge Dee had the curtains of his palankeen rolled up so that he could enjoy the enchanting scenery. Yet the view could not make him forget the problems which preoccupied him. After a while weariness resulted from his pondering over the juridical technicalities of Mrs Liang's case, so he put the roll of documents back in his sleeve.

This case had barely left his troubled mind when he began

worrying whether Ma Joong would succeed in finding the murderer of Half Moon Street within a reasonable time. Now he regretted that he had not left Chiao Tai in Poo-yang to engage in a search for the murderer independently.

Harassed by doubts and misgivings Judge Dee was quite perturbed as the procession approached Chin-hwa. Then, to complete his misery, they missed the ferry over the river that flows by the town. That caused a delay of over an hour. It was well past dark when they finally entered the city.

Constables with lighted lanterns came out to meet them and assisted Judge Dee as he descended from his palankeen in front of the main reception hall.

Magistrate Lo greeted him ceremoniously and led Judge Dee to the spacious and very luxuriously appointed hall. Judge Dee thought to himself that Lo was exactly the opposite of Judge Pan. He was a short, fat, jovial young man; he had no side-whiskers but affected the thin, pointed moustache and the short beard that were fashionable in the capital at the time.

As they were exchanging the usual amenities Judge Dee heard faint sounds of music from the adjoining courtyard. Magistrate Lo apologised profusely and explained that he had invited a few friends to meet Judge Dee. When the hour had advanced far beyond the appointed time they assumed that Judge Dee had been detained at Woo-yee and begun dinner. Magistrate Lo proposed that the two of them eat in a side-room of the reception hall and have a quiet talk about official affairs of common interest.

Notwithstanding the polite speech, it was not difficult to see that a quiet talk was not Magistrate Lo's idea of a pleasant evening. Since Judge Dee himself was not in the mood for another serious discussion, he said:

'To tell you the truth I am a little tired, and, without intending to be frivolous, I still would prefer to join the dinner

97

that is already in progress and have an opportunity to make the acquaintance of your friends.'

Magistrate Lo seemed agreeably surprised and immediately conducted Judge Dee to the banquet hall in the second courtyard. There they found three gentlemen gathered round a festive dish, happily quaffing their wine cups.

They rose and bowed and Magistrate Lo introduced Judge Dee. The eldest guest, Lo Pin-wang was a well-known poet and a distant relative of the host. The second was a painter whose works were much in vogue in the capital and the third a Junior Graduate who was touring the provinces to broaden his mind. These three evidently were the magistrate's boon companions.

Judge Dee's entrance had a sobering effect on the company. After the usual polite compliments had been exchanged the conversation flagged. Judge Dee glanced about and ordered three rounds of wine drunk in succession.

The warm wine improved his own mood. He entoned an ancient ballad which earned the company's approval. Lo Pin-wang sang some of his own lyrics and after another round of wine Judge Dee recited some amatory verse. Magistrate Lo was delighted and clapped his hands. On this sign four exquisitely dressed singing girls appeared from behind the screen at the back of the hall where they had discreetly withdrawn when Magistrate Lo and his guest had entered. Two filled the wine cups, one played a silver flute, and the fourth executed a graceful dance, her long sleeves whirling in the air.

Magistrate Lo smiled happily and said to his friends:

'See, brothers, what a treacherous thing gossip is! Imagine that in the capital our Judge Dee here has the reputation of being something of a martinet. And now you can see for yourselves what a convivial fellow he really is!'

He then introduced the four girls by name. They proved to be as well-instructed as they were charming and Judge Dee was amazed at their skill in capping his verses and in improvising new words for well-known tunes.

Time passed quickly and the night was well advanced when the guests left in happy groups. It turned out that the two girls who had been pouring wine were the special partners of Lo Pin-wang and the painter, and they departed with their friends. The Junior Graduate had promised to take the musician and the dancer to a party in another mansion. So Judge Dee and Magistrate Lo found themselves alone at the banquet table.

The magistrate declared that Judge Dee was his bosom friend and in his mellow mood insisted that all empty formality be dispensed with and that they call each other elder and younger brother. The two left the table and strolled out on the terrace to enjoy the cool breeze and admire the full autumn moon. They sat down on small tabourets that stood by the carved marble balustrade. Here one obtained a beautiful view of the elegant landscape garden below.

After some animated discussion regarding the charms of the singing girls who had just left them, Judge Dee said:

'Although today was our first meeting, brother, I feel as if I had known you all my life! Allow me, therefore, to ask your advice about a very confidential matter.'

'I shall be delighted,' the other answered gravely, 'though my worthless advice will hardly be of use to a man of your riper wisdom.'

'To tell you the truth,' Judge Dee said in a low, confidential voice, 'I have a great love for wine and women. At the same time I like variety.'

'Excellent, excellent!' Magistrate Lo exclaimed, 'I completely agree with this profound statement! Even the choicest delicacies will pall on the palate if served every day!'

'Unfortunately,' Judge Dee continued, 'my present position precludes my frequenting the "pavilions of flowers and willows" in my own district in order occasionally to choose a tender blossom for enlivening my hours of leisure. You know how gossip will spread in a city. I would not like to impair the dignity of my office.'

'This fact,' the other sighed, 'together with the drudgery of the tribunal, is the one great inconvenience incidental to our high office!'

Judge Dee leaned forward and said in a low voice:

'Now suppose that I should chance to discover some rare blossom flowering here in your well-administered district. Would it be presuming too much on your friendship to assume that arrangements could be made for transferring those tender sprigs with due discretion to my own poor garden?'

Magistrate Lo immediately became enthusiastic. He left his seat and bowing deeply in front of Judge Dee, he said carefully:

'Rest assured, elder brother, that I am most flattered by this signal honour bestowed on my district! Condescend to stay a few days in my humble dwelling so that we may consider this weighty problem together from all angles in a leisurely way.'

'It so happens,' Judge Dee answered, 'that several important official affairs require my presence at Poo-yang tomorrow. However, the night is still young, and, should you deign to favour me with your help and advice, much could be accomplished between now and daybreak.'

Magistrate Lo clapped his hands excitedly, exclaiming:

'This ardour proves your romantic disposition! It shall be left to your gallantry to make a conquest in so short a time. Most of the girls have already formed attachments here, so it will not be easy to lure them away. However, you possess an imposing mien, although, if I may speak quite frankly, last spring those long side-whiskers definitively went out of fashion in the capital. So you must do your very best. I for my part shall see to it that the fairest of the fair present themselves here.'

Turning towards the hall, he shouted to the servants:

'Call the steward!'

Soon a middle-aged man with a crafty face appeared. He bowed deeply before Judge Dee and his master.

'I want you,' Magistrate Lo said, 'to go out at once with a palankeen and invite four or five damsels to accompany us while we sing odes to the autumn moon.'

The steward, who apparently was accustomed to such orders, bowed still deeper.

'Now instruct me,' Magistrate Lo said to the judge, 'as to your distinguished taste. What type do you generally prefer, beauty of form, passionate disposition, proficiency in the polite arts? Or does your taste mainly run to the delights of witty conversation? The hour is advanced, so most of the girls will be at home by now and there will be a wide choice. State your wish, elder brother, and my steward shall let himself be governed by your preference!'

'Younger brother,' Judge Dee said, 'there shall be no secrets between you and me! Allow me to state frankly that during my stay in the capital I have become tired of the company of those accomplished entertainers and their sophisticated manners. Now my tastes run, I am somewhat abashed to say, in rather a vulgar direction. Let me confess that I find myself attracted most by those flowers that blossom in quarters which people of our class ordinarily avoid.'

'Ha,' Magistrate Lo exclaimed, 'have not our philosophers stated that in final analysis the extreme positive merges with the extreme negative? You, elder brother, have reached that stage of sublime enlightenment that permits you to discover beauty where less-gifted persons can see only vulgarity. The elder brother commands, the younger brother obeys!'

Thereupon he beckoned the steward to come nearer and

whispered some words in his ear. The steward raised one of his eyebrows in astonishment. He bowed deeply again and disappeared.

Magistrate Lo led Judge Dee back to the hall, told the servants to bring in new dishes, and pledged Judge Dee a goblet of wine.

'Elder brother,' he said, 'I find your originality most stimulating. I am eagerly looking forward to a novel experience!'

After a comparatively short wait the crystal beads of the door-curtain tinkled and four girls entered. They were clad in garish robes and were too heavily made-up. Two were still quite young and not bad-looking despite their coarse make-up, but the faces of the other two, who were slightly older, clearly showed the ravages of their unfortunate profession.

Judge Dee, however, seemed very pleased. When he saw that the girls, ill at ease in such elegant surroundings, were hesitating, he left his seat and politely asked their names. The two younger ones were called Apricot and Blue Jade, the two others Peacock and Peony. Judge Dee conducted them to the table, but they remained standing there with down-cast eyes, at a loss as to what to say or do.

Judge Dee persuaded them to taste the various dishes, and Magistrate Lo showed them how to pour the wine. Soon the girls became more at ease and began to look around and admire their unaccustomed surroundings.

Of course, none of them could sing or dance and all were unlettered. But Magistrate Lo dipped his chopsticks in the gravy and amused the girls by drawing the written characters for their names on the table.

After the girls had each drunk a cup of wine and eaten a few choice morsels, Judge Dee whispered something in his friend's ear. Magistrate Lo nodded and had the steward called. He gave him some instructions and the steward soon returned

JUDGE DEE MEETS TWO GIRLS AT MAGISTRATE LO'S DINNER

with the message that the presence of Peacock and Peony was required at their house. Judge Dee gave them each a silver piece, and they took their leave.

Judge Dee now made Apricot and Blue Jade sit down on a tabouret on either side of him, taught them how to give a toast, at the same time engaging them in general conversation. Magistrate Lo amused himself hugely watching the judge's efforts as he drained one cup after the other.

Under Judge Dee's skilful questioning Apricot was now talking freely. It appeared that she and Blue Jade, who was her sister, were simple peasant girls from Hunan Province. Ten years before disastrous floods had brought the peasants to the verge of starvation, and their parents had sold them to a procurer from the capital. He first employed them as maids and when they had grown up he sold them to a relation in Chin-hwa. Judge Dee found that their rough profession had not yet affected their native honesty and he thought that with kindness and proper guidance they could be made into most agreeable companions.

As the hour of midnight approached Magistrate Lo at last reached the limit of his capacity. He had difficulty in keeping himself upright in his chair and his conversation became very confused. Seeing his condition, Judge Dee expressed his wish to retire.

Magistrate Lo left his chair assisted by two servants. He bade the judge a hazy good night. The steward he commanded:

'His Excellency Dee's orders are mine!'

When the jovial magistrate had been led away, Judge Dee beckoned to the steward to come over to him. In a low voice he said:

'I desire to purchase these two girls Apricot and Blue Jade. You will kindly arrange all details with the present owner, with great discretion. It shall in no way transpire that you are acting on my behalf!'

The steward nodded with a knowing smile.

Judge Dee took two gold bars from his sleeve and handed them to the steward.

'This gold should be more than sufficient for concluding the purchase. The remainder is to be used for conveying the two girls to my residence in Poo-yang.'

Then the judge added one silver bar and said:

'Please accept this small gift as your commission on this transaction.'

After repeated refusals, as prescribed by the rules of propriety, the steward accepted the silver. He assured the judge that everything would be arranged according to his orders, adding that his own wife would accompany the girls on their journey to Poo-yang. 'I shall now,' he concluded, 'give orders that these two girls be accommodated in Your Excellency's guest quarters.'

Judge Dee, however, remarked that he was tired and needed a good night's rest before he set out on his return journey next morning.

Apricot and Blue Jade took their leave, and Judge Dee was conducted to his quarters.

Tenth Chapter: TAO GAN CONSULTS WITH THE WARDEN ON
PAST AFFAIRS; HE HAS AN UNCOMFORTABLE TIME AMONG
THE DARK RUINS

••

IN the meantime Tao Gan had set out to learn more details
about Mrs Liang, according to Judge Dee's orders.

She did not live far from Half Moon Street, so Tao Gan first
went to pay a visit to Warden Gao. He timed his visit so that
he arrived there for the noon meal.

Tao Gan greeted the warden with the utmost cordiality.
Since Warden Gao thought it wise to be on good terms with
the lieutenants of the new magistrate, especially after the
scolding Judge Dee had just given him, he invited Tao Gan to
join him at a simple luncheon. The latter promptly accepted.

After Tao Gan had eaten heartily the warden brought out
his register and showed Tao Gan that Mrs Liang had arrived
in Poo-yang two years before, accompanied by her grandson
Liang Ko-fa.

Mrs Liang had registered her age as sixty-eight, and that of
her grandson as thirty. The warden remarked that Liang
Ko-fa had seemed much younger than that, he had thought
he rather looked like a youngster of twenty or thereabouts.
But he must, of course, have been at least thirty, because Mrs
Liang had said he had passed already his second literary
examination. He was a nice fellow who passed much of his
time loafing about the city. He had seemed to be interested
especially in the north-west quarter, and had often been seen
walking along the canal, near the watergate.

A few weeks after their arrival Mrs Liang had reported to
the warden that her grandson had been missing for two days
and that she feared that something untoward might have

happened to him. The warden had instituted the routine investigation but not a trace of Liang Ko-fa had been found.

Thereafter Mrs Liang had gone to the tribunal and filed an accusation with Judge Feng averring that Lin Fan, a wealthy Cantonese who had settled in Poo-yang, had abducted her grandson. At the same time she presented a number of older documents. From these it became clear that a feud of long standing existed between the houses Liang and Lin. Since Mrs Liang, however, could not produce a shred of proof that Lin Fan had had anything to do with the disappearance of her grandson, Judge Feng had dismissed the case.

Mrs Liang continued to stay in her little house, alone but for one elderly maid. Her advanced age together with brooding over her reverses had made the old lady a bit queer in the head. As to Liang Ko-fa's disappearance, the warden had no opinion. For all he knew he might have fallen into the canal and drowned.

Having learned these facts, Tao Gan thanked the warden cordially for his hospitality and went to have a look at Mrs Liang's house.

Tao Gan located it in a deserted, narrow back street not far from the southern watergate. It was one of a row of small, one-storied houses. He estimated that it could hardly contain more than about three rooms.

He knocked on the unadorned black front door. After a long wait he heard shuffling steps, and the peephole in the door opened. He saw the wrinkled face of a very old woman. She asked in a thin, querulous voice:

'What do you want?'

'Would Madame Liang be at home?' Tao Gan enquired politely.

The old woman gave him a suspicious look.

'She is ill and can't see anyone!' she croaked. And the peephole was slammed shut.

Tao Gan shrugged his shoulders. Turning round he surveyed the neighbourhood. It was very quiet, there was no one about, not even a beggar or a street vendor. Tao Gan wondered whether Judge Dee had been right in accepting straight off the good faith of Mrs Liang. She and her grandson might be clever actors, using a tale of woe to conceal some nefarious scheme perhaps in collusion with that Lin Fan. Such a deserted neighbourhood would provide excellent cover for a secret plot.

He noticed that the house directly opposite that of Mrs Liang was larger than the others, it was built of solid bricks and had a second story. The weather-beaten signboard announced that once it had been a silk shop. But all the windows were shuttered, it seemed uninhabited.

'No luck here!' Tao Gan muttered. 'I had better go and see whether I can learn more about Lin Fan and his household!'

He set out on the long walk to the north-west quarter.

He had found Lin Fan's address in the register at the tribunal, but he met with unexpected difficulties in locating the house. The Lin mansion was situated in one of the oldest parts of the city. Many years ago the local gentry used to live there, but later they had moved to the more fashionable east quarter. A rabbit warren of narrow, winding alleys had sprung up around the once stately residences.

After many a wrong turn Tao Gan finally found the house, a large mansion with an imposing gate. It had solid double doors, lacquered red and heavily studded with copperwork. The high walls on either side were in excellent state of repair. Two large stone lions flanked the gate. The place had a grim and forbidding appearance.

Tao Gan thought of walking along the outer wall in order to locate the kitchen entrance and at the same time get an impression of the size of the Lin Compound. But he saw that that would be impossible. On the right he found his progress blocked by the wall of the adjoining mansion while on the left there was a heap of ruins.

He retraced his steps round the corner till he came to a small vegetable shop. He bought an ounce of pickles and as he was paying he casually enquired about business.

The greengrocer wiped his hands on his apron and said:

'This is not a place to make large profits. But I can't complain. I and my family are strong and healthy so that we can work from morning till night. Thus we have our daily bowl of gruel, a few vegetables from the shop and once a week a piece of pork. What more can a man desire of life?'

'Seeing that your shop is so near that large mansion round the corner,' Tao Gan remarked, 'one would have thought that you had quite a good customer there.'

The greengrocer shrugged his shoulders.

'It is just my bad luck that of the two large mansions in this vicinity, one has been empty for years, while the other is inhabited by a bunch of foreigners. They came from Canton and can hardly understand their own language! Mr Lin has a plot of land in the north-western suburb, along the canal, and every week the farmer brings in a cartload of their own vegetables. They don't spend a single copper cash in my shop!'

'Well,' remarked the lieutenant, 'I have lived in Canton for some time and I know that the Cantonese are quite a sociable breed. I suppose that Mr Lin's servants occasionally drop in here for some conversation?'

'Don't know a single one of them!' the greengrocer answered disgustedly. 'They go their own way and seem to think that they are better people than us northerners. But what is all this to you?'

'To tell you the truth,' Tao Gan answered, 'I am a skilled mounter of pictures and I was wondering whether in such a large mansion, quite far from the street of the mounters, they would not have some scroll pictures to be repaired.'

'No chance, brother,' the greengrocer said, 'pedlars and itinerant workmen never get their foot over that threshold.'

Tao Gan, however, was not easily discouraged. When he was round the corner he took his small trick bag from his sleeve and adjusted the bamboo staves inside so that it seemed to contain the jars of paste and the brushes of the mounter. Then he walked up the steps to the gate and gave a resounding knock on the door. After a while a small peephole opened and a sullen face looked at him through the grating.

In his younger days Tao Gan had roamed all over the Empire and he spoke a number of local dialects. Thus he addressed the doorkeeper in quite creditable Cantonese, saying:

'I am a skilled mounter of pictures who learned my trade in Canton. Is there nothing for me to repair here?'

The doorkeeper's face lit up as soon as he heard his native dialect. He opened the heavy double door.

'I shall have to enquire about that, my friend! But since you speak a decent language and lived in our magnificent City of the Five Rams, you can come in for a while and sit down in my room.'

Tao Gan saw a well-kept front courtyard surrounded by a row of low buildings. While he was waiting in the gate-keeper's room, he was struck by the deep silence that reigned in this mansion. There was no shouting of servants or the sounds of people moving about.

When the gatekeeper returned, he looked more sullen than ever. In his footsteps followed a squat, broad-shouldered fellow, clad in the black damask favoured by the Cantonese. The man had an ugly, broad face, with a thin, irregular moustache. His air of authority seemed to indicate that he was the steward of the mansion.

'What do you mean, you rascal,' he barked at Tao Gan, 'by barging in here? If we want a mounter we can call one. Get out of here!'

Tao Gan could do nothing but mumble an apology and take his leave. The heavy doors closed behind him with a thud.

Slowly walking away, Tao Gan reflected that it was not much use to make another try in broad daylight. As it was a crisp autumn day, he resolved to walk out to the north-western suburb and have a look at the Lin farm.

He left the city by the north gate. After half an hour's walk he found himself at the canal. Cantonese are rather rare in Poo-yang. He located the farm of Mr. Lin without much difficulty by asking some peasants.

It proved to be quite a large plot of fertile land, stretching for over half a mile along the canal. In the middle stood a neatly-plastered farmhouse with two large godowns at the back. A path led to the waterside where he saw a small wharf with a junk moored to its side. Three people were busy loading the junk with bales wrapped in straw matting. Except for them, the place seemed deserted.

Having convinced himself that there was nothing in this peaceful rural scene to arouse suspicion, Tao Gan walked back and entered the city again by the north gate. He found a small inn and ordered a frugal meal of rice and one bowl of meat soup, persuading the waiter to let him have a small dish of fresh onions gratis. His walk had given him an excellent appetite. He picked up the last grains of rice carefully and drained the soup bowl till the last drop. Then he put his head on the table using his folded arms as a pillow and soon was snoring.

When he woke up, it was dark. Tao Gan thanked the waiter profusely and then walked out, leaving such a small tip that the indignant waiter had half a mind to call him back.

Tao Gan walked straight to the Lin mansion. Fortunately a brilliant autumn moon was in the sky and he encountered little trouble finding his way. The vegetable shop had closed for the night and the neighbourhood was utterly deserted.

Tao Gan made for the ruins on the left of the gate. Carefully picking his way through thick undergrowth and fallen bricks, he succeeded in finding the old gate to the second courtyard. He climbed over the heap of rubbish that obstructed the door opening and saw that part of the wall of the courtyard was still standing. Tao Gan thought that if he could climb on top he might be in a position to look over the outer wall of the Lin mansion.

After a few futile attempts he succeeded in securing a foot-hold among the fallen bricks and hoisted himself to the top of the wall. He stretched out on his belly and found that from this precarious perch he had an excellent view of the compound. It consisted of three courtyards, each surrounded by rows of imposing buildings and connected by ornamental gateways. The entire compound, however, seemed dead. There was nobody to be seen and aside from the gatekeeper's lodge, there were only two windows in the back courtyard that showed a light. This seemed very curious to Tao Gan, since such a large compound usually presents a busy picture so early in the evening.

Tao Gan remained lying atop of the wall for over an hour, but nothing stirred in the compound below. Once he thought he saw something move stealthily in the shadows in the front courtyard, but he suspected that his eyes had tricked him, for he could not detect the slightest sound.

Finally he decided to leave his observation post. As he let himself down, a loose brick slipped from under his foot. He fell into the undergrowth, upsetting a pile of bricks that toppled with a crash. Tao Gan cursed heartily, for he had bruised his knee and badly torn his robe. He scrambled up and started to find his way back. However, as bad luck would have it, a cloud obscured the moon just at that moment and it was pitch dark.

Tao Gan realised that a wrong step might mean a broken

arm or leg. So he just squatted down where he was and waited for the moon to reappear.

He had not been waiting long when he suddenly had the feeling that he was no longer alone. During his past hazardous life he had developed an instinct for danger and now he was certain that somewhere among the ruins someone was looking at him. Tao Gan remained motionless, straining his ears. But he heard nothing except an occasional rustling in the undergrowth which could have been caused by some small animal.

Yet, when the moon had come out again, he took the precaution of not moving for some time, carefully scrutinising his surroundings. He could not, however, discover anything out of the ordinary.

He rose slowly to a crouching position and with difficulty succeeded in finding his way out of the ruined mansion, moving with the greatest care and keeping in the shadows as much as possible.

Tao Gan heaved a sigh of relief when he was back in the alley. Walking past the vegetable shop he quickened his pace, for that silent, deserted neighbourhood frightened him badly.

Suddenly he found to his dismay that he had taken a wrong turn. He was now in a narrow alley that was wholly unfamiliar to him.

As he looked round to orientate himself, he saw two masked figures detach themselves from the shadows behind. They came towards him. Tao Gan ran as fast as he could. He rounded a number of corners, hoping to outrun his pursuers or to find a larger thoroughfare where his attackers would not dare to follow him.

Unfortunately, far from reaching the main street, he found himself in a narrow blind alley. When he turned round his pursuers were already entering it. He was trapped.

'Hold it, fellows!' Tao Gan shouted, 'there is nothing that can't be settled by friendly consultation!'

The two masked men paid no attention to his words. As they closed in on him, one aimed a vicious blow at his head.

In a crisis Tao Gan generally depended more on his tongue than on his fists. His training in boxing was limited to a few friendly bouts with Ma Joong and Chiao Tai. He was, however, by no means a coward, as more than one ruffian, deceived by Tao Gan's placid mien, had occasion to remember.

Tao Gan ducked the blow and slipping past his first attacker, tried to trip up the other. But he lost his foothold and when he attempted to regain his balance, the man gripped his arms from behind. Seeing the evil glint in the eyes of his attackers, Tao Gan realised that there was more at stake than his money. These two men were out for his life.

He shouted for help as loudly as he could. The man behind him turned him round, pinning his arms to his back in a vice-like grip, while the other pulled a knife. Tao Gan knew in a flash that this was probably the last job he would do for Judge Dee.

He kicked backwards with all his might and tried to free his arms, but all in vain.

Just at that moment a third ruffian of huge build and with dishevelled hair came rushing into the alley.

Eleventh Chapter: A NEWCOMER UNEXPECTEDLY MIXES
HIMSELF IN THE FIGHT; THE LIEUTENANTS OF JUDGE DEE
TAKE COUNSEL TOGETHER

SUDDENLY Tao Gan felt his arms free. The man behind him
slid past the newcomer and ran towards the entrance of
the alley. The third man aimed a ferocious blow at the head
of the ruffian with the knife, but he ducked and the blow
went wild. Then that fellow also ran, the newcomer on his
heels.

Tao Gan heaved a deep sigh, wiped the perspiration from
his forehead and straightened his robes. Then the tall man
came back and said in a surly voice:

'So you have been at your old tricks again!'

'I always value your company, Ma Joong,' Tao Gan said,
'but I have seldom valued it as much as a few moments ago!
Now what are you doing here in that queer attire?'

Ma Joong answered gruffly:

'I was on my way home from an interview with my friend
Sheng Pa at the Taoist temple. I lost my way in this accursed
maze of streets. Passing this alley I heard someone bleating for
help. So I ran in here to offer the help that seemed so urgently
required. If I had known that it was only you, I would
certainly have waited a bit till you had had the thrashing you
fully deserve for always trying to cheat people!'

'If you had waited a bit,' Tao Gan exclaimed indignantly,
'you would have waited just a bit too long!' Stooping, he
picked up the knife that had been dropped by his second
attacker and handed it to Ma Joong.

Ma Joong, letting the weapon weigh on his palm, scrutinised
the long, evil-looking knife as it shone in the moonlight.

'Brother,' he said admiringly, 'this would have cut through your belly like a scythe through grass! I regret all the more that I could not catch those bastards. They must be quite familiar with this accursed neighbourhood. They slipped away in a dark side street and had disappeared completely before I knew what was happening. Why did you choose such a dismal place for picking a quarrel with people?'

'I was not picking a quarrel,' Tao Gan answered sourly. 'I was investigating the mansion of that Cantonese dogshead Lin Fan, on His Excellency's orders. As I was walking back, I was suddenly attacked by those two cut-throats.'

Ma Joong looked at the knife in his hand again.

'My friend, henceforth you had better leave the investigation of dangerous people to me and Chiao Tai. Evidently you were discovered while you were spying on that mansion and Mr Lin conceived a dislike for you. Let me tell you that it was he who sent those two fellows after you, to get you out of the way. This happens to be a peculiar style of knife that is always carried by ruffians of Canton.'

'Now that you say that,' Tao Gan exclaimed, 'I remember that one of those dogsheads seemed familiar to me! They had covered up the lower part of their face with scarves, but the build and carriage of one of them reminded me of that surly steward in the Lin mansion.'

'That being so,' Ma Joong said, 'those people are engaged in some nefarious scheme, else they would not take it so badly when someone tried to find out what they were doing. Come along now, let us return home!'

They walked again through the maze of winding alleys and, having finally located the main street, they strolled back to the tribunal.

They found Sergeant Hoong sitting all by himself in the deserted office of the senior scribe, poring over a chess board.

The sergeant made them sit down for a cup of tea while Tao

Gan told all about his expedition to the Lin mansion and Ma Joong's timely intervention.

'I still regret,' he concluded, 'that His Excellency has ordered discontinuation of the investigation of the Temple of Boundless Mercy. I had rather deal with those addle-pated baldheads than with these Cantonese ruffians. And at the temple I made at least a bit of money!'

Sergeant Hoong observed:

'If His Excellency wishes to initiate a case on the basis of Mrs Liang's accusation, it will have to be done with the utmost dispatch.'

'Why the hurry?' asked Tao Gan.

'If you were not so upset by tonight's adventures,' the sergeant answered, 'you would doubtless have realised this point yourself. You saw that Mr Lin's house, although it is a large, well-kept mansion, is practically deserted. This can only mean one thing, namely that he and his people are about to leave this town. The womenfolk and most of the servants must have been sent ahead already. The distribution of the lighted windows shows that aside from the gatekeeper, only Lin Fan himself and a couple of his trusted assistants remain. I would not be surprised if that junk you saw near Lin's farm is all ready to set sail for the south.'

Tao Gan crashed his fist on the table, exclaiming:

'Of course you are right, Sergeant! That explains everything! Well, His Excellency will have to take a decision in the very near future, so that we can serve notice on my friend Lin Fan that a case is pending against him and that he will have to stay where he is. And would not I like it to serve that notice on that bastard! I must confess, however, that I have not the faintest idea what his secretive behaviour has to do with old Mrs Liang.'

'His Excellency,' the sergeant explained, 'has taken the documents presented by Mrs Liang away with him on his journey. I have not yet seen them, but from chance remarks of the judge I understand that there is no direct proof of any kind against Mr Lin. Well, in the meantime His Excellency will certainly have evolved some clever plan.'

'Shall I go again to the Lin mansion tomorrow?' enquired Tao Gan.

'I think,' Sergeant Hoong replied, 'that for the time being you had better leave Lin Fan and his mansion alone. Wait till His Excellency has heard your report!'

Tao Gan agreed and asked Ma Joong what had happened at the Temple of Transcendental Wisdom.

'Tonight,' Ma Joong said, 'I received good news. The worthy Sheng Pa asked me whether I would eventually be interested in a nice golden hairpin. At first I pretended to be none too eager, and said that hairpins went in pairs and that I would prefer a golden bracelet or some such thing which I could wear under my sleeve. Sheng Pa insisted that a hairpin could easily be made into an armband and finally I let myself be persuaded. Tomorrow night Sheng Pa shall arrange my meeting the party concerned.

'Now where one of the hairpins is we shall certainly find the other, and if tomorrow night I shall not be able to meet the murderer himself, then it will at least be someone who knows who he is and where I can find him.'

Sergeant Hoong looked pleased.

'You did not do badly, Ma Joong! What happened further?'

'I did not leave there right away,' Ma Joong answered, 'but stayed on for a friendly round of gambling and let them win about fifty cash. I observed that Sheng Pa and his friends practise a few tricks, familiar to me through the kind lessons of our friend Tao Gan here! Since I wanted to create a cordial atmosphere I pretended not to notice anything.

'Thereafter we engaged in a desultory conversation and they told me all kinds of horrifying tales about that Temple of

Transcendental Wisdom. You must know that I happened to ask Sheng Pa why he and his men lived in those miserable shacks in front, while by secretly forcing a side door of the temple they could find a comfortable shelter against wind and rain within, using the cells vacated by the monks.'

'I had been wondering about that too!' Tao Gan observed.

'Well,' Ma Joong continued, 'Sheng Pa told me that they would certainly have done so, were it not for the fact that the temple is haunted. Late at night they often hear groans and the clanking of chains behind those sealed doors. One of the men once saw a window open and a devil with green hair and red eyes scowled at him. Now you can believe me when I say that Sheng Pa and his gang are tough customers, but they don't like getting involved with ghosts and goblins!'

'What a gruesome tale!' Tao Gan said. 'Why did the monks leave the temple? It is usually not so easy to make that lazy crowd leave a place once they are settled comfortably. Do you think they were chased out by devils or malignant foxes?'

'I don't know about that,' Ma Joong said, 'I only know that the monks just left there and went Heaven knows where.'

Thereupon the sergeant told a hair-raising story about a man who married a nice young girl. She later turned out to be a fox-spirit and bit through her husband's throat.

When he had finished, Ma Joong observed:

'All this talk about ghosts gives me a strong desire for something better to drink than tea!'

'Well,' Tao Gan said, 'that reminds me! Near Lin Fan's mansion I bought some pickled nuts and salted vegetables, in order to get into conversation with the greengrocer. I dare say that those would go well with a cup of wine!'

'Now this is a Heaven-sent opportunity,' Ma Joong declared, 'to get rid of that money you filched in the Temple of Boundless Mercy! You know that money stolen in a temple brings bad luck if you dare to keep it!'

For once Tao Gan made no objections. He sent a sleepy servant out to buy three pints of good local wine. When it had been warmed on the tea stove they had many a round and did not retire till after the hour of midnight.

Early the next morning the three friends met again in the chancery of the tribunal.

Sergeant Hoong went to inspect the jail. Tao Gan disappeared into the archives to search for documents relating to Lin Fan and his activities in Poo-yang.

Ma Joong walked over to the quarters of the guards, and when he saw that the constables were loafing there, while the guards and the runners were gambling, he ordered them all to assemble in the main courtyard. To their great dismay he put them for two hours through a stiff military drill.

Then he had luncheon with Sergeant Hoong and Tao Gan, and returned to his own quarters for a good afternoon nap. He expected to have quite a strenuous evening.

WHEN night had fallen, Ma Joong once more donned his
disguise. Sergeant Hoong had authorised the comptroller to
issue him thirty silver pieces from the coffers of the tribunal.
Having wrapped these in a piece of cloth, Ma Joong put the
package in his sleeve. Then he set out again for the Temple of
Transcendental Wisdom.

He found Sheng Pa in his usual place, sitting with his back
against the wall, scratching his naked torso. He seemed completely absorbed in the gambling.

But when he saw Ma Joong he greeted him cordially and
bade him sit down by his side. When Ma Joong had squatted
he spoke:

'I thought, brother, that by now you would have invested
the copper cash you won from me the other night in buying
yourself a nice jacket. What will you do when winter comes
and you find yourself unprotected?'

Sheng Pa gave him a reproachful look.

'Brother,' he said, 'your language is offensive to me. Did I
not tell you that I am a counsellor of the Beggars' Guild? Far
be it from me ever to obtain a piece of clothing through a
mercenary procedure so odious to me as buying. However,
let us get to the business on hand.'

Bringing his head close to Ma Joong's ear, he continued in a
hoarse whisper:

'Everything has been arranged! Tonight you will be able to
leave the city. The fellow who wants to sell a golden hairpin
for thirty silver pieces is a vagrant Taoist mendicant monk.

He will be waiting for you tonight in Wang Loo's tea house, behind the Drum Tower. You will easily recognise him, he said he will be sitting all by himself at a table in a corner. There will be two empty cups under the spout of the teapot in front of him. You are supposed to identify yourself by commenting on those tea cups. The rest is up to you.'

Ma Joong thanked him profusely and promised that when he revisited Poo-yang, he would come to pay his respects without fail. Then he took a hurried leave.

He strode briskly to the Temple of the War God. He saw the Drum Tower silhouetted against the evening sky. A street urchin guided him to a small but busy shopping centre directly behind the tower. He glanced down the bustling street and found Wang Loo's signboard without difficulty.

He pulled aside the dirty door curtain. A dozen or so people were crowded around rickety tea tables. Most of them were clad in rags and a nauseating smell enveloped the place. He spotted a monk sitting alone at a table in the corner farthest from the door.

As he approached him Ma Joong was assailed by doubt. The waiting man was indeed clad in a ragged Taoist cowl. His head was covered by a greasy, black Taoist cap, and a wooden hand-gong hung from his girdle. But far from being tall and muscular, this man was short and fat. Even though he looked sufficiently disreputable with his dirty, sagging face, he definitely was not the type of violent rogue Judge Dee had described. Yet there could hardly be a mistake about this being his man.

Ma Joong sidled up to the table and said casually:

'Brother, since there are two empty tea cups I wonder whether I could sit down with you and moisten my parched throat!'

'Ha,' grunted the fat man, 'here you are, my disciple! Sit

down and have a cup of tea. Have you brought the holy book with you?'

Before sitting down Ma Joong stretched out his left arm and let the other feel the package in his sleeve. The stranger's nimble fingers quickly identified the shape of silver pieces. He nodded and poured Ma Joong a cup of tea.

After they had taken a few sips, the fat man said:

'Now I shall show you the passage where the doctrine of the Supreme Void is most lucidly explained.'

As he spoke he produced a dirty volume from his bosom. Ma Joong took the thick, dog-eared book and noted the title was *Secret Tradition of the Jade Emperor*, a famous Taoist classic.

Ma Joong leafed through the book but failed to see anything out of the ordinary.

'I want you to read,' the monk said with a sly smile, 'the tenth chapter.'

Ma Joong found the place and raised the book nearer to his eyes as if to see better. A long golden hairpin had been inserted in the heart of the book, alongside the spine. The head of the pin consisted of the figure of a flying swallow exactly like the sketch that the judge had shown him. Ma Joong noticed the superb workmanship of the pin.

He hastily closed the book and put it in his sleeve.

'This book,' he said, 'will doubtless prove most illuminating! Let me now return the treatise you so kindly lent me the other day.'

As he spoke Ma Joong produced the package of money and handed it to the fat man, who hurriedly put it in the bosom of his cloak.

'I must leave now,' Ma Joong said, 'but tomorrow night we shall meet here again to continue our discussion.'

The fat man mumbled some polite words and Ma Joong rose and left the tea house.

Looking up and down the street Ma Joong saw that a curious crowd had gathered round an itinerant fortune-teller. He joined them but took a position that allowed him to keep an eye on the door of Wang Loo's tea house. After a short while the little fat monk emerged from the door and walked briskly down the narrow street. Ma Joong followed him at a distance, avoiding the circles of light cast by the oil lamps of the street vendors.

His quarry strode along as rapidly as he could with his short legs, heading in the direction of the northern gate. Suddenly he turned into a narrow side alley. Ma Joong looked around the corner. No one else was about. The little man had halted in front of a small house and was about to knock on the door. Ma Joong ran noiselessly up behind him.

Clapping his hand on the fat man's shoulder, he jerked him round and gripped him by the throat, growling:

'One sound and you are done for!'

Then he dragged him farther into the alley until he found a dark corner, where he pinned the monk against the wall.

The fat man trembled all over and whined:

'I shall give you back the silver! Please don't kill me!'

Ma Joong took the package from him and put it back in his sleeve. Then he shook the stranger roughly.

'Tell me where you got that hairpin!' he demanded.

The other began in a faltering voice:

'I found it in the gutter. Some lady must have——'

Ma Joong gripped his throat again and cracked his head against the wall. It struck the stone with a dull thud. He hissed:

'Tell the truth, you dogshead, and save your wretched life!'

'Let me talk,' the other implored as he gasped for air.

Ma Joong released his throat and stood threateningly over him.

'I am,' the fat monk whined, 'one of a small gang of six vagabonds, masquerading as Taoist mendicant monks. We

124

live in a deserted guard house in the East City at the foot of the wall. Our leader is a rough fellow called Hwang San.

'Last week, when we were taking our afternoon nap, I happened to open my eyes and saw Hwang San take a pair of golden hairpins from the seam of his robe to examine them. I closed my eyes again and pretended to be asleep. For some time I had been planning to leave the gang, they are much too violent for my taste. It seemed to me that this was the opportunity for obtaining the needed funds. So two days ago when Hwang San came home dead drunk, I waited till he was snoring. Then I felt the seam of his robe until I found one hairpin. He stirred and I did not dare to look for the other one but fled instead.'

Ma Joong was inwardly exceedingly pleased with this information. However, he did not relax his furious scowl.

'Lead me to that man!' he barked.

The fat man started to tremble again all over and whimpered:

'Please don't deliver me to that man! He will beat me to death!'

'The only man you need be afraid of is me!' Ma Joong said gruffly. 'At the first sign of treachery I shall drag you to a quiet corner and cut your filthy throat. Get going!'

The fat man led him back to the main street. After a short walk they reached a maze of small alleys and finally arrived in a dark and deserted area along the city wall. Ma Joong could vaguely distinguish a tumbledown hut which was built against the wall.

'Here it is,' the fat man blubbered and turned to run away. But Ma Joong gripped him by the collar of his robe and dragged him along until they stood in front of the hut. Ma Joong kicked against the door and shouted:

'Hwang San, I have brought a golden hairpin for you!'

Sounds of stumbling were heard inside, a light went on and

presently a huge, bony fellow emerged. He was as tall as Ma Joong but lacked the latter's weight.

Lifting up the oil lamp, he surveyed his visitors with small, mean eyes. Then he cursed roundly and growled at Ma Joong:

'So that wretched rat stole my hairpin. Now what do you have to do with that?'

'I want to buy the pair of them. When this bastard produced only one, I knew he was holding out on me. I gently persuaded him to tell me where I could find the other one.'

The other guffawed. He had uneven, yellow teeth.

'We shall do business, brother!' he said. 'But first let me kick in the ribs of this fat sneak thief—just to show him how to behave towards his betters!'

He put down the oil lamp as a preliminary to action. The fat man suddenly kicked the lamp over with surprising deftness. Ma Joong let go of his collar and the terrified thug ran away as fast as an arrow from the bow.

Hwang San swore and wanted to run after him. Ma Joong caught him by the arm saying quickly:

'Let the wretch go! You can settle with him later. I have urgent business with you.'

'Well,' Hwang San growled, 'if you have cash with you we might make a deal. I have had bad luck all my life and somehow I have a feeling that those accursed hairpins will land me in trouble if I don't sell them quickly. You have seen one of them; the other is exactly the same. What will you give?'

Ma Joong looked around warily. The moon had come out and he noticed that the place seemed completely deserted.

'Where are the other fellows?' he enquired. 'I don't like to do business in front of witnesses!'

'Don't worry,' Hwang San reassured him, 'they are all away making the rounds in the shopping centres.'

'In that case,' Ma Joong said coldly, 'you can keep your hairpin, you wretched murderer!'

MA JOONG'S FIGHT UNDER THE CITY WALL

Hwang San swiftly sprang back.

'Who are you, you bastard?' he shouted angrily.

'I am the lieutenant of His Excellency Judge Dee,' Ma Joong answered, 'and I am going to take you to the tribunal as the murderer of Pure Jade. Now will you come along or shall I have to beat you to a pulp first?'

'I have never heard of the wench,' Hwang San barked, 'but I know your dirty kind of constable and the corrupt judges for whom you act as running dog! Once you get me in the tribunal you will pin some unsolved crime on me and then torture me till I confess. I'll take my chance with you!'

As he spoke the last words he aimed a vicious blow at Ma Joong's middle.

Ma Joong parried and swung at Hwang San's head. The latter, however, caught the blow in the approved way and followed up with a quick thrust at Ma Joong's heart.

Blow was exchanged for blow wihout either of them being able to score a real hit.

Ma Joong realised that he had found his equal in this art. Hwang San was lean but his bones were unusually thick so that their body weight would be about the same. As to Hwang San's boxing, this was of such superior quality that Ma Joong placed him in the eighth, or next-highest grade. Ma Joong himself was of the ninth grade, but this advantage was neutralised by the fact that Hwang San was thoroughly familiar with the ground and repeatedly forced Ma Joong to make a stand on an uneven or slippery patch.

After a strenuous fight, Ma Joong lashed out and succeeded in crushing Hwang San's left eye with an elbow blow. Hwang San countered with a kick on Ma Joong's thigh, which greatly impeded his footwork.

Then suddenly Hwang San aimed a kick at Ma Joong's groin. Ma Joong leaped back and caught his opponent's foot in his right hand. He was going to press Hwang San's knee down with his left hand, keeping his leg stretched to prevent him from drawing near, and kick his opponent's other leg out from under him. But he slipped and missed. Hwang San immediately bent his knee and dealt Ma Joong a fearful blow on the side of the neck.

This blow is counted among the nine fatal strokes of boxing. If Ma Joong had not happened to have his head turned so that his jaw caught half of the blow, he would have been finished then and there. As it was, he let go of Hwang San's foot and staggered backwards. The effects of the disrupted blood circulation blurred his eyes. At that moment he was completely at the mercy of his opponent.

A great boxer of antiquity, however, once stated: 'A fight between two people of equal strength, weight and technique, is decided by the spirit.' Although Hwang San had mastered all the physical aspects of the art, he had a low, brutish mind. Since Ma Joong was defenceless, Hwang San could have chosen any one of the nine, clean death blows, but his base instinct prompted him to aim a nasty kick at Ma Joong's groin.

To repeat the same blow twice is one of the basic mistakes in boxing. Ma Joong's blood circulation was so badly disturbed that he was unable to execute any complicated move; he did the only thing he could in the circumstances: he clasped Hwang San's lower leg in both arms and twisted it round with all his strength. Hwang San emitted a hoarse cry as his knee joint was dislocated. At the same time Ma Joong drove his body forward, fell down together with Hwang San, and sank on his middle with his knees. Then Ma Joong felt his strength give out. He rolled over and over till he was well out of the reach of Hwang San's flailing arms. Lying on his back, Ma Joong concentrated on those secret breathing exercises that restore the normal circulation of the blood.

When he felt that his head was clear and his nervous system restored to normal, Ma Joong scrambled up and went over to Hwang San. His opponent was making frantic attempts to get up. Ma Joong placed an accurate kick on Hwang's jaw, his head crashed backwards and struck the ground. Then from around his middle Ma Joong unwound the long, thin chain used for binding criminals and secured Hwang San's hands behind his back. Drawing them as high up to the shoulders as they would go, Ma Joong slipped one end of the chain in a running noose round Hwang San's neck. If he made the slightest attempt at freeing his hands the thin chain would cut into his throat.

Ma Joong squatted down by his side.

'You nearly got me, you rascal!' he said. 'Now spare His Excellency and me unnecessary trouble and confess your crime!'

'If my accursed bad luck had not again caught up with me,' Hwang San gasped, 'you would have been dead now, you dog of a constable! As to my confessing to any crime, leave that to your corrupt master.'

'Have it your own way!' Ma Joong said coldly.

He walked into the nearest alley and pounded on the door of a house till a sleepy man opened it. Ma Joong identified himself and ordered the man to fetch the warden of the quarter, with instructions to come immediately with four men and a couple of bamboo poles.

Then he went back to stand guard over his prisoner who let out a stream of the foulest curses.

When the warden and his men arrived they made a stretcher of the poles for carrying Hwang San. Ma Joong threw an old robe over him that he had found in the hut and they went back to the tribunal.

Hwang San was handed over to the warden of the jail. Ma Joong ordered a bone-setter called to put Hwang's knee right.

Sergeant Hoong and Tao Gan were sitting up waiting for Ma Joong in the chancery. They were very happy when they heard the news of the criminal's capture.

The sergeant said with a broad grin:

'This indeed calls for a snack and a few rounds!'

The three headed for the main street and entered an all-night restaurant.

Thirteenth Chapter: JUDGE DEE SOLVES THE RAPE-MURDER
OF HALF MOON STREET; A CANDIDATE OF LITERATURE MOANS
OVER HIS CRUEL FATE

JUDGE DEE returned to Poo-yang late in the afternoon of the
next day.

After a hasty meal in his private office, during which Sergeant
Hoong related the latest developments briefly, the judge had
Ma Joong and Tao Gan called in to present their reports.

'Well, my brave,' Judge Dee said to Ma Joong, 'I hear that
you found our man. Tell me the entire story!'

Ma Joong related his adventures of the two preceding
nights and concluded:

'That man Hwang San corresponds in every detail to the
description Your Honour gave me. Furthermore, these two
hairpins are exactly identical with the sketch in the files here.'

Judge Dee nodded contentedly.

'If I am not greatly mistaken we shall be able to close this
case tomorrow. You will see to it, Sergeant, that all persons
connected with the rape-murder of Half Moon Street are
present at the morning session of the tribunal.

'Now, Tao Gan, let us hear what you have discovered about
Mrs Liang and Mr Lin Fan.'

Tao Gan gave a detailed account of his investigation, including the attempt on his life and Ma Joong's well-timed
intervention.

Judge Dee expressed approval of Tao Gan's decision not to
continue the investigation of the Lin mansion pending his
return.

'Tomorrow,' Judge Dee announced, 'all of us shall have a
conference here regarding the case of Liang *versus* Lin. I shall

then tell you what conclusions I arrived at by studying the records and explain the action I propose to take.'

Then the judge dismissed his lieutenants and had the senior scribe bring in the official correspondence that had accumulated during his absence.

The news of the capture of the criminal of Half Moon Street had spread like wildfire through Poo-yang. Early the next morning a large crowd assembled in the tribunal long before the appointed hour.

When Judge Dee was seated behind the bench, he took up his vermilion brush and filled out a slip for the warden of the jail. Two constables dragged in Hwang San and pushed him to his knees in front of the dais. He groaned with pain as he bent his knee, but the headman shouted:

'Shut up and listen to His Excellency!'

'What is your name,' Judge Dee enquired, 'and for what crime are you brought before this tribunal?'

'My name——' Hwang San began. The headman of the constables hit him on the head with his club and barked:

'You dog, speak reverently in front of your magistrate!'

'This insignificant person,' Hwang San said in a surly voice, 'is called Hwang, personal name San. I am an honest mendicant monk who has resigned from all worldly affairs. Last night I was suddenly assaulted by one of the runners of this tribunal and dragged to jail for some unknown reason.'

'You dogshead!' Judge Dee shouted, 'what about your murdering Pure Jade?'

'I don't know whether the wench was called Pure Jade or Impure Jade,' Hwang San said in a surly tone. 'But let me tell you that you won't pin the death of that harlot in Mother Pao's place on me! She hanged herself and I was not there at the time. That can be proved by several witnesses.'

'Spare me your sordid stories,' Judge Dee said sourly. 'I, the magistrate, tell you that on the night of the sixteenth you foully murdered Pure Jade, the only daughter of Butcher Hsiao Foo-han!'

'Your Honour,' Hwang San replied, 'I don't keep a calendar and I have not the faintest idea of what I did or did not do on that particular date. And the names you mention mean nothing to me.'

Judge Dee sat back in his chair. He pensively stroked his beard. Hwang San answered his conception of the rape-murderer in every detail and the hairpins had been found in his possession. Yet Hwang San's denial had the unmistakable ring of truth. Suddenly a thought struck the judge. He leaned forward in his chair and said:

'Look up at your magistrate and listen carefully while I refresh your memory. In the south-west corner of this city, over the river, there is a street of small shopkeepers. It is named Half Moon Street. On the corner of that street and a narrow alley is a butcher's shop. The butcher's daughter lived in a garret over the godown at the back of the shop. Now did not you effect entry into the girl's room by means of a strip of cloth that was hanging outside the window? And did not you rape and strangle her, making off with her golden hairpins?'

Judge Dee saw a flash of understanding in the one shifty eye that Hwang San was still able to open. The judge knew that this was after all his man.

'Confess your crime!' Judge Dee shouted at him, 'or shall I put the question to you under torture?'

Hwang San muttered something and then said in a loud, clear voice:

'You can accuse me of any crime you like, you dog-official. But you will wait long before I confess to a crime I did not commit!'

'Give that wretch fifty lashes with the heavy whip!' Judge Dee ordered.

The constables tore off Hwang San's robe, baring his muscular torso. The heavy thong swished through the air and slashed across the accused's back. Soon Hwang San's back was a mass of torn flesh and his blood stained the flagstones. However, he did not scream, emitting only deep groans. After the fiftieth blow he fell unconscious and his face struck the stone floor.

The headman revived him by burning vinegar under his nose and then offered him a cup of strong tea which Hwang San disdainfully refused.

'This,' Judge Dee remarked, 'is but the beginning. If you don't confess, I shall subject you to real torture. Your body is strong and we have the whole day before us.'

'If I confess,' Hwang San said hoarsely, 'you will chop my head off. If I don't confess I shall die under torture. I prefer the latter! I am willing to stand a little pain for the pleasure of getting you, dog-official, into trouble!'

At that the headman smashed Hwang San on the mouth with the butt of the whip. He was going to strike him again when the judge raised his hand. Hwang San spat some of his teeth on to the floor and uttered a horrible curse.

'Let me have a close look at this insolent dog,' Judge Dee said.

The constables jerked Hwang San to his feet and Judge Dee looked into his one, cruel eye. The other eye was a mass of swollen flesh as a result of the blow he had received in the fight with Ma Joong.

Judge Dee thought to himself that this was the type of degenerate, habitual criminal that would probably stand by his word and die under torture rather than confess. In his mind he rapidly reviewed what Ma Joong had told him about last night's encounter and his conversation with Hwang San.

'Let the criminal kneel down again!' the judge commanded. Then he took up the golden hairpins that lay on his desk. He threw them over the edge. They clattered to the floor, in front of Hwang San. He looked sullenly at the shining gold.

Judge Dee ordered the headman to bring Butcher Hsiao before him.

As the butcher knelt at Hwang San's side, Judge Dee said:

'I know that an evil destiny is connected with these hair needles. I have not, however, heard your full account of them.'

'Your Honour,' Butcher Hsiao began, 'in the old days, when my family still was fairly well off, my grandmother bought these pins in a pawnshop. By that unfortunate act she drew a fearful curse on our house. For a terrible destiny is connected with these things, caused by who knows what gruesome crime in the past. A few days after she got them two robbers broke into her room, killed my grandmother and stole the hairpins. They were caught while trying to sell the pins and they were beheaded on the execution ground. Had but my father then destroyed these harbingers of evil! He, however, was a virtuous man, blessed be his memory, and he let his feelings of filial piety prevail over his judgement.

'The next year my mother fell ill, complaining of a mysterious headache, and after a long illness she died. My father lost the little money he had and died shortly afterwards. I wanted to sell the hairpins, but my wife, the stupid person, insisted that they should be kept in reserve for a day of great need. And instead of keeping the evil things locked safely away, she let our only daughter wear them. And see what terrible fate befell the poor girl!'

Hwang San had listened intently to the tale which was told in simple language familiar to him.

'Accursed be Heaven and Hell!' he burst out, 'it would have to be me to steal those hairpins!'

A murmur arose from the crowd of spectators.

'Silence!' shouted Judge Dee.

He dismissed the butcher and addressed Hwang San in a conversational tone.

'No one can ever escape the decree of destiny. It does not matter whether you confess or not, Hwang San. The hand of Heaven is against you and you will never escape—here or in the Nether World!'

'What do I care after all, let us get this over and done with,' Hwang San replied. Then, addressing the headman he said: 'Let me have a cup of that filthy tea, you bastard!'

The headman was highly indignant, but at a peremptory sign of the judge he gave Hwang San a cup of tea.

Hwang San gulped it down, spat on the floor and said:

'I don't care whether you believe it or not, but if there was ever a man who has been persecuted by bad luck his whole life, it is me. A fine strong fellow like me should have ended his days at least as the head of a great robber gang. But what happened? I am one of the best boxers in the Empire, I had a master who knew all the tricks. But as bad luck would have it he had a nice-looking daughter, I liked her but she did not like me. I don't stand for nonsense from a woman, so I raped the foolish wench and had to flee for my life.

'Then I met a merchant on the road. He looked for all the world like the god of wealth in person. I just hit him once, just to make him amenable. Of course, the feeble wretch had to die then and there! And what did I find in his girdle? Nothing but a bunch of worthless receipts. And so it was always.'

Hwang San wiped off some of the blood that had oozed from the corners of his mouth and continued:

'A week or so ago I sauntered through the smaller streets in the south-west quarter, looking for some late passer-by to intimidate into giving me some alms. Suddenly I saw a fellow slip across the street and disappear into a narrow alley. I thought it was a thief and followed him to share the loot. But by the time I had entered that alley the fellow was nowhere to be seen and everything was dark and quiet.

'A few days later—and if you say it was the sixteenth then it was the sixteenth—I found myself in that neighbourhood again. I thought I might as well have another look into that alley. It was completely deserted but I saw a long strip of good cloth hanging outside an upper window. I thought that that was a piece of laundry that people had forgotten to take in for the night. So I walked over to take it along, to have at least something for my trouble.

'Standing close to the wall, I gave it a gentle tug to make it come down. Suddenly the window above opened, I heard a soft woman's voice, and noticed that the strip was slowly being hauled in. I knew at once that the wench had a tryst with a secret lover and thought that that was my chance to steal whatever I would like; for she would never dare to raise the alarm. Thus I took hold of the strip and pulled myself up on the window-sill. I was standing in the room while the woman was still busy hauling in the strip.'

Hwang San leered and went on:

'She turned out to be a young comely wench, which was not hard to see since she was, so to speak, all undressed for the part. Now I am not a man to let a chance like that go by, so I clapped my hand over her mouth, and whispered: "Keep your mouth shut! Close your eyes and just imagine that I am the fellow you were expecting." That girl, however, fought like a tigress and it took me some time to subdue her. Even after I had finished with her she would not keep quiet. She made a run for the door and started shouting. I strangled her then and there.

'I hauled in the strip of cloth to keep that paramour of hers away and then rummaged through her possessions to look for money. With my bad luck I should have known better. I did not find one single copper cash, only those accursed hairpins.

138

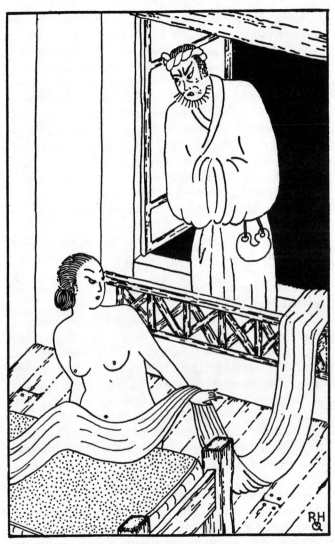

AN UNEXPECTED VISITOR SURPRISES PURE JADE

'Now let me put my thumb-mark on that scrap of paper your scribbler is working on. I don't want to hear the story read out again! For the girl's name you can put in anything you like. Let me go back to the jail. My back hurts.'

'The law,' Judge Dee said coldly, 'says that the criminal shall hear his confession before he affixes his thumb-mark.'

He ordered the senior scribe to read aloud Hwang San's confession as he had noted it down. When Hwang San had sullenly agreed that it was correct, the paper was placed before him and he affixed his thumb-mark to it.

The judge said in a solemn voice:

'Hwang San, I pronounce you guilty of the double crime of rape and murder. There are no extenuating circumstances and this was even a particularly brutal murder. It is my duty, therefore, to warn you that the higher authorities will probably condemn you to the extreme penalty in one of its more severe forms.'

He gave a sign to the constables and Hwang San was led back to his cell.

Judge Dee had Butcher Hsiao brought before him once more.

'A few days ago,' said the magistrate, 'I promised you that in due time I would bring the murderer of your daughter to justice. Now you have heard his confession. Terrible indeed is the curse that August Heaven chose to lay on those golden hairpins. Your poor daughter was raped and murdered by a low ruffian who did not even know her name and cared less.

'You can leave the hairpins here. I shall have them weighed by a goldsmith and the tribunal shall pay you their value in silver.

'Since this despicable criminal has no property, no blood money can be paid to you. However, you shall presently hear my arrangements for the compensation of your loss.'

Butcher Hsiao began to thank the judge profusely, but the

magistrate stopped him and told him to stand back. Then he ordered the headman to bring Candidate Wang before him.

The judge examined the latter closely and noticed that his recent exoneration of the double crime of rape and murder had done nothing to lighten his grief. On the contrary, the confession of Hwang San had shocked him deeply, tears were streaming down his cheeks.

'Candidate Wang,' Judge Dee said gravely, 'I could have you punished severely for seducing the daughter of Butcher Hsiao. You have, however, already received thirty lashes and since I believe you when you say that you were deeply in love with the victim, I take it that the memory of this tragedy will be a heavier punishment than this tribunal could ever impose.

'Yet this murder must be redressed and the family of the victim compensated. I therefore rule that you shall marry Pure Jade posthumously as your First Wife. The tribunal shall advance to you a suitable brides-gift and the ceremony shall be conducted in the proper way, Pure Jade's soul-tablet taking the place of the bride. When you have passed your examination, you shall repay your debt to the tribunal in monthly instalments. At the same time you shall pay a sum to Butcher Hsiao every month, to be fixed by me on the basis of your official salary, till a total of five hundred silver pieces is reached.

'When in due course you shall have paid off those two debts, you shall be allowed to marry a second wife. But never shall she or any other secondary wife be allowed to usurp the place of Pure Jade, who shall be considered as your First Wife till the end of your days. Butcher Hsiao is an honest man, you shall honour and serve him and his wife as a dutiful son-in-law. They, on their part, shall forgive you and stand by you as your own parents would have done if they were still alive. Now go and devote yourself to your studies!'

Candidate Wang repeatedly knocked his head on the floor, sobbing freely. Butcher Hsiao knelt by his side and thanked

Judge Dee for his wise arrangements for restoring the honour of his family.

As they rose, Sergeant Hoong bent over to the judge and whispered something in his ear. Judge Dee smiled thinly and said:

'Candidate Wang, before you go one minor point remains to be cleared up. Your statement about the way you spent the night from the sixteenth to the seventeenth is true in every detail save for one mistake which you made in good faith.

'During my first reading of the records it seemed already impossible to me that a thorny bush could have produced such deep gashes on your body. When in the uncertain light of dawn you saw piles of bricks and some undergrowth, you quite naturally took it that you had landed among the ruins of an old mansion. In fact, however, you had come to a plot where a new house was being built. The masons had left piles of bricks lying around for the outer walls and preparations had been made for erecting the plaster inner walls in the usual way, that is by constructing rows of thin bamboo stakes, as a frame for the plaster. You must have fallen on their sharp points, which would cause exactly that type of gashes. If you feel so inclined you may search for such a plot in the vicinity of the Five Tastes Inn, I don't doubt that you will then find the place where you passed that fateful night. Now you may go.'

Then Judge Dee rose and left the dais with his lieutenants.

As he passed through the screen that opened on his private office, a murmur of admiration rose from the crowd of spectators.

Fourteenth Chapter: JUDGE DEE RELATES THE HISTORY OF AN
ANCIENT FEUD; HE OUTLINES HIS PLANS FOR TRAPPING THE
MURDERER

JUDGE DEE spent the rest of the morning writing for the
higher authorities a detailed report on the murder in Half
Moon Street, proposing the extreme penalty for the criminal.
Since all capital sentences had to be endorsed by the Throne it
would take several weeks before Hwang San could be executed.

During the noon session the judge dealt with a few routine
problems of the district administration. Thereafter he had his
noon meal in his own residence.

Back in his private office he had Sergeant Hoong, Tao
Gan, Ma Joong and Chiao Tai called in. When they had
respectfully greeted the judge he addressed them:

'Today I shall tell the four of you the entire story of the case
Liang *versus* Lin. Have fresh tea brought in and be seated
comfortably! It is a long story.'

All sat down in front of Judge Dee's desk. While they were
sipping their tea, the judge unrolled the documents that Mrs
Liang had given him. Having sorted those papers out he
placed them under paper-weights and leaned back in his chair.

'You will hear,' he began, 'a long story of foul murders and
ruthless violence, and you will often wonder how August
Heaven could ever allow such cruel injustice! I for one have
seldom read a more stirring record.'

Judge Dee fell silent, slowly stroking his beard. His lieutenants looked at him expectantly.

Then the judge sat straight in his chair.

'For the sake of convenience,' he said briskly, 'I shall divide
the complicated material into two parts. The first comprises

143

the origin and development of the feud in Canton, the second covers happenings here in Poo-yang, after the arrival of Lin Fan and Mrs Liang.

'Strictly speaking I am not competent to review the events of the first phase. Those cases have been dismissed by the local tribunal of Canton and by the Provincial Court of Kwangtung Province, I cannot review their verdicts. However, although this first phase of the feud does not directly concern us we cannot afford to ignore it because it supplies the background of the developments here in Poo-yang.

'I shall begin, therefore, by summing up the first part, omitting all judicial technicalities, names and other details not germane to the subject.

'About fifty years ago there lived in Canton a wealthy merchant named Liang. In the same street lived another rich merchant, by the name of Lin. He was his closest friend. Both were honest and industrious men of great business ability. Their houses flourished and their ships sailed the seas as far as the Gulf of Persia. Liang had one son, Liang Hoong, and one daughter whom he gave in marriage to Lin Fan, the only son of his friend Lin. Shortly afterwards old Mr Lin died. On his deathbed he solemnly enjoined his son, Lin Fan, for ever to foster the ties of friendship that existed between the houses Lin and Liang.

'In the ensuing years, however, it became evident that though Liang Hoong was the very image of his father, Lin Fan was a wicked and cruel man of mean, greedy character. While Liang Hoong, after his old father had retired from business, continued the sound trade policy of the firm, Lin Fan engaged in various dubious deals in the hope of gaining quick and unjust profits. The result was that, while the house of Liang continued to flourish, Lin Fan gradually lost the greater part of the vast capital inherited from his father. Liang Hoong did what he could to help Lin Fan, always giving him

LIANG HOONG MURDERED BY ROBBERS

good advice, defending him against other merchants who accused him of not standing by his contracts, and on more than one occasion he even lent Lin Fan considerable sums of money. This generosity, however, evoked only scorn and spite on the part of Lin Fan.

'Liang Hoong's wife bore him two sons and a daughter, while Lin Fan remained childless. Envy changed Lin Fan's scorn of Liang Hoong into a deep hatred. Lin Fan came to consider the house of Liang as the source and origin of all his reverses and misfortunes and the more Liang Hoong helped him, the greater Lin Fan's hatred became.

'Affairs came to a crisis when Lin Fan once happened to see Liang Hoong's wife and at once conceived a violent passion for her. At the same time a risky business deal of Lin Fan's miscarried and he found himself heavily in debt. Since he knew that Mrs Liang was a virtuous woman who would never dream of deceiving her husband, Lin Fan evolved a vile scheme to appropriate by force both Liang Hoong's wife and his riches in one and the same blow.

'Lin Fan's shady deals had brought him into contact with the Cantonese underworld. Thus when he heard that Liang Hoong was going to travel to a neighbouring town to collect a vast sum of gold, partly for himself, but for the greater part on behalf of three other large Cantonese trade concerns, he hired brigands who intercepted Liang Hoong outside the city on his return. They killed him and stole the gold.'

Judge Dee looked gravely at his lieutenants. Then he went on quickly:

'On the day that this nefarious plan was carried out, Lin Fan went to the Liang mansion and stated that he had to see Mrs Liang on an urgent and private matter. When she received him, Lin Fan told her that her husband had been attacked on the road and the gold stolen. He said that Liang Hoong had been wounded, but that there was no fear for his life. His servants had temporarily put him up in a deserted temple in the northern suburb and from there Liang Hoong had sent for him, Lin Fan, for a secret consultation.

'It was Liang Hoong's wish that his mishap be kept a deep secret until his wife and his father, by liquidating part of their assets, could realise enough money to cover the loss of the gold that he had collected for the three firms. Disclosure of the loss would affect his and their credit. He also desired Mrs Liang to accompany Lin Fan to the temple immediately, so that they could have a consultation together and decide what assets could be liquidated at short notice. Mrs Liang believed the story, which was so typical of the prudent character of her husband, and set out with Lin Fan, having left the house secretly, by a back door.

'As soon as they arrived at the deserted temple, Lin Fan told Mrs Liang openly that his story was only partly true. He informed her that her husband had been killed by the robbers, but that he, Lin Fan, loved her and would look after her. Mrs Liang was outraged beyond words and wanted to flee to denounce Lin Fan. He, however, held her back and that night possessed her against her will. Early the next morning Mrs Liang pierced her finger with a needle and wrote an apology to her father-in-law in blood on her handkerchief. Then she hanged herself with her girdle from a roof-beam.

'Lin Fan searched her body. He found the handkerchief with the last message and this gave him an idea for covering up his crime. The message read:

'Since Lin Fan has lured me to this lonely place and violated me, having brought disgrace on your house, your slave, now an unchaste widow, feels that death is the only atonement for her crime.

'Lin Fan tore off the right edge of the handkerchief, which contained the first line of the message and burned the strip.

The rest of the message, starting "Having brought disgrace, etc.," he put back in the dead woman's sleeve.

'Then Lin Fan returned to the Liang mansion where he found old Mr and Mrs Liang grieving over the murder of Liang Hoong and the loss of the money. A passer-by had discovered Liang Hoong's body and reported the crime. Feigning to share the sorrow of Liang Hoong's old parents, Lin Fan enquired after the widow. And when they told him that she was missing, after much pretended hesitation Lin Fan said that he felt it his duty to inform them that he knew that Mrs Liang had a lover, whom she used to meet secretly in a deserted temple. He suggested that Mrs Liang might be found in her trysting place. Old Mr Liang hurried to the temple and discovered the body of his daughter-in-law hanging from the roof-beam. Having read her last message he thought that she had killed herself in a sudden attack of remorse when she heard that her husband had been killed. Unable to bear all this grief, that evening old Mr Liang killed himself by taking poison.'

Judge Dee paused and motioned to Sergeant Hoong to pour the tea. The judge took a few sips and remarked: 'From here old Mrs Liang who now lives here in Poo-yang becomes the central figure of this case.' Then he continued:

'Old Mr Liang's wife was an intelligent and very energetic woman, who always had taken an active part in the affairs of her husband's family. Knowing the virtuous character of her late daughter-in-law, she suspected foul play. She issued all necessary orders for the liquidation of the Liang assets to make good the loss of the three firms. At the same time she dispatched the trusted house steward to the deserted temple for an investigation. Now when Mrs Liang wrote her message she had spread out the handkerchief on her pillow, and part of the blood had stained the cover. From these faint traces the first sentence of the message could be reconstructed. When the steward reported this to old Mrs Liang, she knew that Lin Fan had not only raped Liang Hoong's wife but also arranged his murder; for it was he who told her of Liang Hoong's death before the body had been discovered.

'Mrs Liang then accused Lin Fan of this double crime before the tribunal of Canton. At that time, however, Lin Fan's foul deed had supplied him with a large amount of gold. He bribed a local official and had witnesses deliver false testimony, including one depraved young man who presented himself as the lover of the late Mrs Liang. The case was dismissed.'

Ma Joong opened his mouth to ask a question. But Judge Dee raised his hand, and went on:

'At about the same time Lin Fan's wife, the sister of Liang Hoong, disappeared and could nowhere be found. Lin Fan pretended to be greatly distressed, but it was generally surmised that he had secretly killed her and concealed her dead body. He hated every member of the Liang family, including the wife that had born him no children.

'Such are the facts set forth in the first document of Mrs Liang. It is dated twenty years ago.

'Now I come to the further development of this feud. The Liang family had now been reduced to the old lady, her two grandsons, and one granddaughter. Although their capital had shrunk to about one-tenth through compensating the three firms, the good name of the house of Liang was unimpaired and its various branches continued to prosper. Under the capable direction of old Mrs Liang, the main firm rapidly recovered its losses and the family started to flourish once more.

'In the meantime Lin Fan, always trying to increase his ill-gotten gains, had organised a large smuggling ring. The local authorities became suspicious of his activities. Lin Fan knew that smuggling was not a crime that could be dealt with by the local authorities and that he might be indicted before the Provincial Court, where his influence was nil. Thus he decided on another evil scheme, calculated to divert the attention of the authorities, and at the same time wreck the house of Liang.

'He bribed the harbourmasters and secretly had several cases of contraband placed among the cargo of two junks of the Liang firm. Then he hired a man to denounce old Mrs Liang. The damning evidence was duly found and all the property of the Liang firm and its branches was confiscated by the Government. Mrs Liang again accused Lin Fan, but the case was dismissed, first by the local, thereafter by the Provincial Court.

'Mrs Liang realised that Lin Fan would not rest until her entire family had been exterminated. So she took refuge on a farm outside the city, the property of one of her own cousins. This farm was located on the site of a demolished fortress. One of the old stone redoubts was still standing, the farmer was using it as a granary. Mrs Liang thought that this redoubt would provide an adequate shelter if Lin Fan hired brigands to attack them, so she had it prepared for an emergency.

'A few months later Lin Fan indeed sent a band of outlaws to destroy the farm and kill its inhabitants. Mrs Liang, her three grandchildren, the old steward, and six trusted servants barricaded themselves inside the stone redoubt, where they had stored food and water. The ruffians tried to ram the gate but the solid iron doors withstood their onslaught. Then they assembled dry wood and threw lighted faggots through the cross-barred windows.'

Here Judge Dee paused a moment. Ma Joong clenched his big fists on his knees. Sergeant Hoong angrily pulled at his thin moustache.

'Those inside were nearly suffocating,' Judge Dee continued, 'and they had to make a sortie. Mrs Liang's younger grandson, her granddaughter, the old steward and six servants were hacked to pieces by the brigands. During the general confusion, however, Mrs Liang herself succeeded in escaping together with her elder grandson, Liang Ko-fa.

'The leader of the ruffians reported to Lin Fan that all had been killed and Lin Fan thought that now the entire house of Liang had been exterminated. This ninefold murder excited great indignation in Canton and some merchants who were acquainted with the feud between the two families realised that it was again Lin Fan who was responsible for this atrocious crime.

'By then, however, Lin Fan had become one of the richest merchants of the city and nobody dared to oppose him. He, moreover, professed to be greatly distressed about the affair and offered a substantial reward for information about the whereabouts of the brigands. Their leader made a secret understanding with Lin Fan, sacrificing four of his men, who were arrested, pronounced guilty, and beheaded with great pomp and circumstance.

'Mrs Liang and her grandson Liang Ko-fa had found shelter with a distant relative in Canton and for some time remained in hiding, living under an assumed name. She succeeded in collecting evidence against Lin Fan. On a certain day, five years ago, she emerged from her hiding-place and accused Lin Fan of the ninefold murder.

'This crime had become so famous that the local magistrate hesitated to protect Lin Fan; popular opinion was turning against him. It cost Lin Fan large sums to have this accusation finally dismissed. He thought that it would be wise to disappear for a few years, especially since a new provincial governor had been appointed who was famous for his integrity. Thus he placed his affairs in the hands of a trusted steward, put a few of his servants and concubines on three of his large river junks, and secretly left the city.

'It took Mrs Liang three years to discover where Lin Fan

had gone. As soon as Mrs Liang learned that Lin Fan had settled down here in Poo-yang, she decided to follow him and seek a means of revenge. Her grandson, Liang Ko-fa, accompanied her. For is it not written that a son shall not live under the same sky with his father's murderer? Two years ago grandmother and grandson arrived in this city.'

Here Judge Dee paused for a while and drank another cup of tea. Then he went on:

'We now come to the second part of this case. That is covered by Mrs Liang's accusation filed with this tribunal, two years ago. In this document,' he said, tapping the scroll in front of him, 'Mrs Liang accuses Lin Fan of having abducted her grandson, Liang Ko-fa. She says that immediately after their arrival, Liang Ko-fa started to make enquiries about Lin Fan's activities here in Poo-yang and that he told her that he had found evidence, sufficient for opening a case against him.

'Unfortunately at that time he gave his grandmother no further particulars about his discoveries. Mrs Liang maintains that Lin Fan caught him while making enquiries in the vicinity of the Lin mansion. For justifying this accusation, however, she had to fall back on the old feud between the two families. She is in no position to adduce any proof that Lin Fan is in any way concerned with Liang Ko-fa's disappearance. This being so, one cannot blame my predecessor, Judge Feng, for having dismissed this case.

'Now I shall outline to you what course of action I intend to take. During the long hours spent in my palankeen while travelling to Woo-yee and Chin-hwa, I have given considerable thought to this problem. I arrived at a theory about Lin Fan's criminal activities here in Poo-yang and this theory has been borne out by some facts reported by Tao Gan.

'In the first place I asked myself why Lin Fan chose this small district of Poo-yang as a hide-out. A man of his wealth and influence would ordinarily prefer a large city or even the capital, where he could live unnoticed and still enjoy ease and comfort.

'Remembering Lin Fan's association with the smuggling trade, and keeping in mind his extremely greedy nature, I arrived at the conclusion that his choice was determined by the fact that this city is situated most favourably for the smuggling of salt!'

A flash of understanding passed over Tao Gan's face. He nodded pensively as the judge went on:

'Salt has since the time of our glorious Han dynasty been a monopoly of the Imperial government. Poo-yang is situated on the canal, and not far from the salt pans along the coast. I think, therefore, that Lin Fan settled down in Poo-yang to enrich himself further by smuggling salt. It is quite in accordance with his mean, greedy character that he preferred a lonely but profitable exile to a comfortable but expensive life in the capital.

'Tao Gan's report confirmed my suspicions. Lin Fan chose that old mansion, in a deserted neighbourhood and within convenient distance of the watergate, because its location was suitable for the secret transport of the salt. The plot of land he bought outside the city wall is also part of this scheme. It takes quite some time to walk there from the Lin mansion, since one has to make the detour through the northern city gate. But if you look at a map of the town, you will see that the distance by water is very short. It is true that the heavy grating of the watergate prevents boats from passing through there, but smaller bales could easily be transferred through the grating from one boat to another. The canal supplies Lin Fan with the means for transporting the salt by junk anywhere he likes.

'Now it is most unfortunate that at present Lin Fan has apparently suspended his smuggling activities and is preparing to return to his native city. I doubt whether we still can collect evidence against him. He will have destroyed all traces of his illegal trade.'

Sergeant Hoong here interrupted:

'It is evident, Your Honour, that Liang Ko-fa had found proof of the smuggling and intended to attack Lin Fan from that angle. Couldn't we institute another thorough search for Liang Ko-fa? Perhaps Lin Fan keeps him imprisoned somewhere!'

Judge Dee shook his head.

'I fear,' he said gravely, 'that Liang-Ko-fa is no longer among the living. Lin Fan is completely ruthless, as Tao Gan has reason to know. The other day Lin Fan thought that Tao Gan was an agent of Mrs Liang and only a lucky coincidence prevented his being assassinated on the spot. No, I fear that Lin Fan has killed Liang Ko-fa.'

'That leaves little hope for catching Lin Fan,' said the sergeant. 'It will be practically impossible to collect evidence of that murder, now that two years have gone by.'

'That,' Judge Dee replied, 'is unfortunately true. I have, therefore, decided on the following course of action.

'As long as Lin Fan thought that Mrs Liang was his only adversary, he knew exactly what counter measures to take against her plans and he did not make a single mistake. But I'll give him to understand that from now on he'll have to reckon with me. My intention is to frighten him, to harry and press him so much that he will resort to some desperate step which will give us an opening for attacking him.

'Now listen carefully to my instructions.

'In the first place, this afternoon the sergeant will bring my name card to Mr Lin and announce that tomorrow I shall pay him a quite informal visit. On that occasion I shall let it transpire that I suspect him of some crime and make it plain that he cannot leave the city.

'Second, Tao Gan shall find out who owns the plot of land

next to the Lin mansion. Tao Gan will then inform the owner that the tribunal orders that those ruins are to be cleared away because they serve as a shelter for vagabonds. Half of the cost shall be borne by the district administration. You will contract the workmen, Tao Gan, and have them start tomorrow morning under your supervision, assisted by two constables.

'Third, Sergeant Hoong, after his visit to the Lin mansion, will go directly to the garrison headquarters and hand the commander my written instructions to the effect that the military guards of the four city gates are to hold for questioning, on some pretext or other, every Cantonese that enters or leaves the city. Further, a few soldiers shall be on guard duty at the watergate, both day and night.'

Rubbing his hands Judge Dee concluded contentedly:

'That should give Lin Fan ample food for thought! Has any of you other suggestions?'

Chiao Tai said with a smile:

'We might also do something about that farm of his! What about my going tomorrow to the plot of government land outside the city wall, opposite Lin Fan's farm? I could set up an army tent there and stay for a day or two, doing some fishing in the canal. There I can keep a close watch on the watergate and on the farm, and do that so conspicuously that the people on the farm won't fail to notice it. They will doubtless report my spying activities to Lin Fan, and that should add to his worries!'

'Excellent!' the judge exclaimed. Turning to Tao Gan, who sat there pensively pulling the long hairs on his cheek, he continued:

'Have you got any proposal, Tao Gan?'

'Lin Fan is a dangerous man,' Tao Gan remarked. 'When he finds that pressure is being brought to bear on him, he may well plan to kill Mrs Liang. With his accuser dead, the case against him would collapse. I propose that we have her guarded. When I went to her house, I noticed that the silk shop opposite is deserted. Your Honour might consider posting Ma Joong and one or two constables there to see that nothing untoward happens to the old lady.'

Judge Dee thought this over for a while, then he replied:

'Well, until now Lin Fan has made no attempt at harming Mrs Liang here in Poo-yang. But we'd better take no chances. Ma Joong, you shall go there today.

'Now, as a final measure, I shall address a circular to all military guard posts along the canal north and south of this city, with the request to halt and search for contraband every junk bearing the marks of the Lin firm.'

Sergeant Hoong smiled and said:

'Well, in a few days Lin Fan will feel like "an ant in the middle of a hot frying pan," as our proverb goes!'

Judge Dee nodded.

'When Lin Fan,' he said, 'has come to know all these measures he will feel trapped. Here he is far from Canton, the city where he wields his power, and he has sent away most of his henchmen. Moreover, he does not know that I have not a shred of evidence against him. He will ask himself whether Mrs Liang has given me some facts that he does not know or whether I have discovered evidence about his smuggling, or perhaps received additional information against him from my colleague in Canton.

'I hope that these doubts will worry him so much that he acts rashly and gives us a hold on him. I admit that it is a small chance. But it is the only one we have!'

THE next day, after the noon session of the tribunal, Judge Dee changed into an informal blue robe and put on a small black cap. Then he proceeded to the Lin mansion in his palankeen accompanied by only two constables.

As they arrived in front of the large gate, Judge Dee lifted the curtain of his palankeen and saw a dozen or so workmen clearing the ruins on the left. Tao Gan was supervising their work, sitting on a pile of bricks in full view of the peephole in the gate, looking exceedingly pleased.

As soon as a constable had knocked, the double gate of the Lin mansion swung open and Judge Dee's palankeen was carried into the main courtyard. The judge descended and saw a tall, spare man of imposing mien waiting for him at the foot of the steps that led to the reception hall.

Except for a squat, broad-shouldered man whom Judge Dee took to be the steward, no other servants were in evidence.

The tall man bowed deeply and spoke in a low, toneless voice:

'This person is the merchant Lin, named Fan. Your Excellency deign to enter my poor hovel.'

They ascended the steps and entered a spacious hall, simply but elegantly furnished. They sat down on chairs of carved ebony, and the steward served tea and Cantonese sweetmeats.

The usual amenities were exchanged. Lin Fan spoke the northern language fluently, but with a marked Cantonese accent. While they were talking, Judge Dee unobtrusively surveyed his host.

Lin Fan seemed about fifty years old. He had a long, lean face with a sparse moustache and a grey goatee. Judge Dee was particularly struck by Lin Fan's eyes; they had a queer, fixed stare and seemed to move with his head. The judge reflected that if it were not for those eyes, one would find it difficult to believe that this dignified, polite gentleman was responsible for at least a dozen foul murders.

Lin Fan wore a dark robe of severe simplicity; a black damask jacket as is favoured by the Cantonese, and on his head an informal cap of black gauze.

'My visit,' Judge Dee began, 'is entirely unofficial. I wished to have a very informal consultation with you about a certain matter.'

Lin Fan bowed deeply and said in his low, monotonous voice:

'This person is an ignorant small merchant, but such as I am I place myself unreservedly at Your Excellency's disposal.'

'A few days ago,' Judge Dee continued, 'an old Cantonese lady called Liang presented herself in the tribunal and told a long, incoherent story about all kinds of crimes she said you had committed against her. I could not quite follow what it was all about. One of my assistants later informed me that the lady is mentally deranged. She left a collection of documents which I have not bothered to read, since they will contain only the vagaries of her poor distracted mind.

'Unfortunately the law does not permit me to dismiss the case without at least the formality of one hearing. Thus I decided to pay you this friendly visit, to consult with you in an informal manner about how to dispose of this case, giving the old lady some kind of satisfaction and mutually saving much waste of time.

'You will understand that this is, on my part, quite an

irregular procedure, but it is so evident that the old lady is mentally deranged, while you are a man of such unquestioned probity, that in this case I felt justified in taking this step.'

Lin Fan left his seat, and bowed deeply in front of the judge to express his thanks. When he was seated again, he slowly shook his head and said:

'This is a sad, sad story. My late father was the best friend of Mrs Liang's late husband. I myself have for many years sedulously endeavoured to continue and strengthen the traditional bonds of friendship between our two houses, although sometimes that was a most distressing task indeed.

'I must inform Your Excellency that while my affairs prospered, those of the Liang family steadily declined. This was due partly to a series of reverses and calamities that could not have been prevented and partly to the fact that Liang Hoong, the son of my father's friend, lacked sound business sense. Time and again I lent them a helping hand, but apparently Heaven had turned against the house of Liang. Liang Hoong was killed by robbers and the old lady took over the direction of their firm. Unfortunately she made grave errors in judgement and lost heavily. Then, hard pressed by her creditors, she let herself be enticed to join a gang of smugglers. They were found out and all the property of the family was confiscated.

'Then the old lady went to live up country. There their farm was burned by a band of brigands who killed two of her grandchildren and several servants. Although I had had to break off our relations after the smuggling case, this outrage done to a family which had been so close to my own was more than I could bear. I put up a generous reward and had the satisfaction of bringing the murderers to justice.

'In the meantime, however, all these misfortunes had affected Mrs Liang's mind and she conceived the idea that it was I who had been the cause of everything.'

'What a preposterous notion!' Judge Dee interrupted. 'You were her best friend!'

Lin Fan nodded slowly and sighed:

'Yes! Your Excellency will understand that this affair has caused me great distress. The old lady has been persecuting me, calumniating me and has tried by all possible means to turn people against me.

'I can tell Your Honour in confidence that Mrs Liang's machinations were the main reason why I resolved to leave Canton for a few years. Your Excellency will understand my position. On the one hand I could not bring myself to invoke the protection of the law against all those false accusations of this lady who, after all, is the head of a house to which I have been related by marriage. On the other hand, if I left the accusations unanswered, my credit in the City of Canton would be affected. I thought I would find rest here in Pooyang, but she followed me and accused me of abducting her grandson. His Excellency Feng dismissed the case forthwith. I suppose that now Mrs Liang has brought this same accusation before you?'

Judge Dee did not immediately answer this question but had a few sips of tea while tasting the sweets that Lin Fan's steward offered him. Then he said:

'It is most unfortunate that I cannot just dismiss this vexing case. Much though I dislike to cause you this trouble, in due time I will have to summon you to the tribunal, to hear your defence, purely as a matter of form, of course. I am confident that I shall then be able to dismiss the case.'

Lin Fan nodded. His curious still eyes fixedly regarded Judge Dee.

'When does Your Excellency propose to hear this case?'

Judge Dee caressed his side-whiskers for a while and then answered:

'That, I fear, is very difficult to say. There are a number of other matters pending and my predecessor left some arrears in administrative affairs. Moreover, in order to keep up appearances, my senior clerk will have to make a study of Mrs Liang's documents, and make an abstract for me. No, I would not like to commit myself to a definite date. But rest assured that I shall expedite everything as much as possible!'

'This person would deeply appreciate that,' Lin Fan said, 'for the fact is that several important matters demand my presence in Canton. I had been planning to set out tomorrow, leaving my steward in charge here. It is my impending departure that gives this humble abode such a deserted appearance and is the reason for the poor service, for which I profoundly apologise. Most of my servants left here one week ago.'

'I repeat,' Judge Dee said, 'that I shall do my utmost to have this matter settled in the very near future. Although I must confess that I greatly regret that you must leave us. This district feels honoured by the presence of such an eminent man from our famous emporium in the south. We can offer you so little of the luxury and refinement you are accustomed to in the city of Canton! I rather wondered what made so prominent a man choose Poo-yang as a place for temporary retirement.'

'That,' Lin Fan answered, 'is easily explained. My late father was an unusually active man. He used to travel up and down the canal in our junks for personal inspection tours of the various branches of our firm.

'On passing Poo-yang he conceived a great love for its charming scenery and decided to build a villa here after his retirement. Alas, Heaven took him away while he was still in the full force of his years, before he could execute his plan. I thought it was my filial duty to see to it that the house of Lin possessed a mansion in Poo-yang.'

'A most commendable act of filial piety!' Judge Dee remarked.

'Perhaps,' Lin Fan continued, 'I might decide later to make this mansion into a memorial hall, dedicated to my late father. The house is old, but well built and I have added such improvements as my limited means permitted. Will Your Excellency give me the honour of leading you round in this humble abode?'

Judge Dee agreed and his host led the magistrate across a second courtyard to a ceremonial hall, even larger than the first.

The judge saw that the floor was covered by a thick carpet that must have been woven especially for this hall. The pillars and beams were covered with intricate carving, inlaid with mother-of-pearl. The furniture was of fragrant sandalwood and the windows were not covered with paper or silk, but consisted of thin segments of shell, which filled the hall with a soft, diffuse light.

The other rooms showed the same elegant luxury.

When they came to the back courtyard, Lin Fan smiled thinly, and said:

'Since all the womenfolk have left already, I can even show you the family quarters.'

Judge Dee politely refused, but Lin Fan insisted that he should see everything and took him through all the rooms. Judge Dee understood that Lin Fan wanted to show him that there was nothing in his house that he needed to hide.

When they had returned to the hall, Judge Dee drank another cup of tea and engaged his host in a general conversation.

It transpired that Lin Fan's firm acted as banker for some highly-placed persons in the capital, and that the house of Lin had branches in most of the important cities of the Empire.

Finally Judge Dee took his leave. Lin Fan ceremoniously conducted him to his palankeen.

While he was ascending, Judge Dee turned round and again assured Lin Fan that he would do everything in his power to have Mrs Liang's case disposed of as soon as possible.

Once returned to the tribunal, Judge Dee went to his private office. Standing by his desk, he casually looked through the documents that the scribe had placed there during his absence. He found it difficult, however, to take his thoughts off his visit to Lin Fan. The judge realised that he was up against a most dangerous adversary, who commanded vast resources. Somehow he doubted whether Lin Fan would fall into the trap he was setting for him.

While the judge was reflecting on this problem, his house steward entered. Judge Dee looked up.

'What brings you here to the chancery?' he enquired. 'I trust that in my household everything is in order?'

The steward looked uncomfortable and apparently did not know how to begin.

'Well, my man,' the judge said impatiently, 'speak up!'

The steward then said:

'A few moments ago, Your Honour, two closed palankeens arrived in the third courtyard. The first carried an elderly woman, who informed me that she was bringing two young ladies, on Your Honour's orders. She did not vouchsafe any further explanation. Now the First Lady is resting, I did not dare to disturb her. I consulted with the Second and the Third Lady, but they said that no instructions had been left with them. So I made bold to come here, to report to Your Honour.'

Judge Dee seemed pleased with this news and said:

'The two young ladies shall be accommodated in the fourth courtyard. One maidservant shall be assigned to each of them. You will transmit my thanks to the woman who brought them, and then dismiss her. Later this afternoon I myself shall see to the rest.'

The steward looked relieved, bowed deeply and took his leave.

Judge Dee spent the afternoon with the senior scribe and the head of the archives, to work out a complicated civil suit relating to the division of an inheritance. It was quite late when he returned to his family quarters.

The judge went straight to the rooms of his First Lady. He found her checking the household accounts with the steward.

She rose hurriedly when she saw the judge enter. He dismissed the steward and seating himself at the square table, he bade his wife to sit down again.

The judge enquired whether his children made good progress with their tutor and his wife answered him politely; but she kept her eyes down, and the judge knew that she was dismayed.

After a while Judge Dee said:

'You doubtless have heard that two young women have arrived here this afternoon.'

'I have thought it my duty,' his wife said in a detached voice, 'to go to the fourth courtyard myself in order to ascertain that they are provided with everything they need. I have assigned to them the maids Aster and Chrysanthemum. As my lord will know, the latter is an accomplished cook.'

Judge Dee nodded his assent. After a while his wife continued:

'After I visited the fourth courtyard I have been wondering whether my lord would perhaps not have been better advised if you had previously acquainted me with your intention of enlarging our household and deigned to entrust to this person the proper selection.'

Judge Dee raised his eyebrows.

'I am distressed,' he said, 'that you do not approve of my choice.'

'I would never,' his First Lady said coldly, 'presume to disapprove of your preference. It is the harmonious atmosphere of your house that I am thinking of. I could not fail to notice that those new arrivals are somewhat different from the other ladies of your household and I fear that this disparity in education and taste will not be conducive to the maintenance of the pleasant relations that heretofore have prevailed in your mansion.'

The judge rose and said curtly:

'In that case your duty is perfectly clear. You will see to it that this disparity, the existence of which I acknowledge, is corrected within the shortest possible space of time. You will personally instruct those two young ladies. Have them taught embroidery and the other lady-like arts, including some elementary writing. I repeat that I quite see your point and I have decided, therefore, that for the time being they shall associate only with you. I shall keep myself informed of their progress!'

The First Lady also had risen when the judge made to leave, and now she said:

'It is this person's duty to draw your attention to the fact that our present income is barely sufficient to cover the expenses of your household in its present enlarged form.'

The judge took a bar of silver from his sleeve and placed it on the table.

'This silver,' he said, 'will be utilised for purchasing material for their dresses and for other expenses deriving from this addition to my household.'

His wife bowed deeply and Judge Dee left the room. Heaving a deep sigh he realised that the difficulties had only begun.

He walked through the winding corridors to the fourth

courtyard and there found Apricot and Blue Jade admiring their new surroundings.

They knelt before the judge and thanked him for his favour. Judge Dee bade them rise.

Apricot respectfully presented a sealed envelope to him, holding it with both hands. Judge Dee opened it and found the receipt of the house to which the two girls had belonged, together with a polite note of the steward of Magistrate Lo.

The judge put the note in his sleeve; the receipt he handed back to Apricot and told her to keep it carefully, in case their former owner pretended any future claim on them. Then he said:

'My First Lady will personally look after your well-being, and tell you all there is to know about the routine of this household. She will buy material for your new dresses. Until those are ready, you will confine yourselves to this courtyard for ten days or so.'

After a few kind words he went back to his private office and told the servants to prepare his couch for the night there.

It was a long time before sleep would come.

The judge was full of doubts and asked himself anxiously whether he was not taking on too much. Lin Fan was a man of great wealth and influence, a dangerous and ruthless opponent. The judge also felt deeply the estrangement that had sprung up between himself and his First Lady. Thus far his harmonious family life had always been a haven of peace to fall back upon when he was troubled by the burden of his official duties or worried about a difficult criminal case.

Harried by these worries, the judge did not fall asleep until the second nightwatch had been sounded.

Sixteenth Chapter: A WEALTHY MERCHANT DRINKS TEA IN THE RECEPTION HALL; JUDGE DEE SETS OUT IN A FORTUNE-TELLER'S DISGUISE

THE next two days brought no new developments in the case Liang *versus* Lin.

Judge Dee's lieutenants came in to report regularly, but Lin Fan made no move whatsoever. He seemed to pass his days confined in his library.

Tao Gan had told the workmen who were clearing away the ruins to leave the old wall of the second courtyard standing. They had hacked out an easy ascent and levelled its top. Tao Gan had now a comfortable observation post and he sat there sunning himself, overlooking the Lin mansion and scowling at the steward whenever he came out in the courtyard.

Chiao Tai reported that the Lin farm was inhabited by three men who were either busy looking after the vegetables or working on the large junk that was still moored to the landing. Chiao Tai had caught two beautiful carp in the canal which he presented to Judge Dee's kitchen.

Ma Joong had found a fairly large attic over the silk shop opposite Mrs Liang's house and there amused himself by teaching boxing and wrestling to a promising young constable. He reported that Mrs Liang had not once gone out, he had only seen the old hag leave the house to buy vegetables. He had noticed no suspect characters lingering about there.

On the third day the military guards of the southern gate arrested an incoming Cantonese, on the suspicion of being connected with a burglary in the southern suburb. He carried a bulky letter addressed to Lin Fan.

Judge Dee read it carefully but could find nothing suspicious. It was a detailed account sent by one of the representatives of the Lin firm in another city regarding the conclusion of a business transaction. Judge Dee was amazed at the sums of money involved. This deal alone seemed to have realised several thousand silver pieces.

The letter was copied out and the messenger set free. That afternoon Tao Gan reported that the man had presented himself at the Lin mansion.

On the evening of the fourth day Chiao Tai intercepted Lin Fan's steward on the bank of the canal. He must have swum down the river and then dived under the grating of the water-gate, without the soldiers on guard noticing him.

Chiao Tai assumed the role of a highway robber. He knocked the steward down and relieved him of a letter addressed to a high official in the capital. Judge Dee found that this letter suggested in veiled terms that the magistrate of Poo-yang be transferred to another post without delay. Significantly a draft authorising the payment of five hundred gold bars was enclosed.

The next morning a servant of the Lin mansion brought a letter to the judge in which Lin Fan reported that his steward had been attacked and robbed by a highwayman. Judge Dee had a poster put up offering a reward of fifty silver pieces for information regarding this dastardly assault. He kept the stolen letter in his file for future use.

This was the first good news, but it seemed to be the last. One week passed by without any new developments.

Sergeant Hoong noticed that the judge was worried. He had lost his usual equanimity entirely and was often in an irritable temper.

The judge had developed an extraordinary interest in military affairs and would study circular reports from the other magistrates in the province for hours. He kept careful

JUDGE DEE ENTERTAINS LIN FAN AT TEA

notes about an armed uprising in the south-west corner of the province where zealots of a new religious sect had joined a band of brigands. Since it was most unlikely that this disorder would reach Poo-yang, Sergeant Hoong was at a loss to understand why Judge Dee was so interested in this affair.

The judge even went so far as cultivating the friendship of the garrison commander of Poo-yang who, apart from his military ability, was a rather dull man. Judge Dee engaged him in long conversations about the distribution of the military forces in the province.

The judge did not vouchsafe any explanation to the sergeant. The latter felt hurt about the judge not taking him into his confidence and was all the more unhappy because he was aware of the troubles in Judge Dee's household.

Judge Dee occasionally spent the night in the courtyard of his Second or Third Lady, but mostly he slept on the couch in his private office.

Once or twice he had paid a morning visit to the fourth courtyard and had a cup of tea with Apricot and Blue Jade. After having talked to them for a while, he had returned to the tribunal.

Two weeks after Judge Dee's visit to Lin Fan, the latter's steward came to the tribunal with his master's calling card and enquired whether Lin Fan might come to see the judge that afternoon. Sergeant Hoong informed the steward that the judge would feel much honoured.

That afternoon Lin Fan arrived in a closed palankeen. Judge Dee received him most cordially. He had him sit down by his side in the large reception hall of the tribunal and insisted that he partake of some fruit and cakes.

Lin Fan's impassive face was as inscrutable as ever while in his monotonous voice he pronounced the usual polite enquiries.

Then Lin Fan asked whether anything had been discovered

that might be a clue to the ruffian who had attacked his servant. 'My steward,' Lin Fan continued, 'was on his way to my farm to transmit a message. He had left the city by the northern gate and as he was walking along the river outside the watergate, this ruffian knocked him down, robbed him and then threw him in the water. Fortunately my man could crawl on to land, else he would have drowned.'

'Ha, that rascal!' Judge Dee exclaimed angrily. 'First he assaults a man and then he tries to drown him! I shall raise the reward to one hundred silver pieces.'

Lin Fan gravely thanked the judge. Staring at Judge Dee with his still eyes he asked:

'Has Your Excellency found time yet to make some preparations for the hearing of my case?'

Judge Dee sadly shook his head and answered:

'My senior scribe is working on those documents every day! Some points, however, will have to be checked with Mrs Liang, and, as you know, she has only very few moments that her brain is entirely clear. I trust, however, that everything will be in order soon. The matter has my constant attention.'

Lin Fan bowed deeply.

'These two things,' he continued, 'are but small matters. I would not have intruded upon your valuable time were it not that I find myself confronted with a problem that only Your Excellency can solve for me.'

'Feel free to speak frankly,' Judge Dee said, 'and consider me completely at your service!'

Lin Fan smiled his bleak smile. He stroked his chin and said:

'Your Excellency, being in constant touch with the highest authorities in the land, is naturally completely conversant with the internal and external affairs of our Empire. It will probably never have occurred to you how ignorant we merchants are of those problems. Yet a knowledge thereof would often save us thousands of silver pieces.

'Now I learn from my representative in the city of Canton that a rival firm has secured the informal advice of an official, who has deigned to act as their honorary counsellor. I feel that my own small firm should follow their example. Unfortunately, a poor merchant like this person has no connections at all in the official world. Therefore I would greatly appreciate if Your Excellency would grant me the favour of suggesting a name to me.'

Judge Dee bowed and said earnestly:

'I feel immensely honoured that you condescend to ask my worthless opinion, and regret all the more that since I am but an insignificant magistrate of a small district, I could not think of one friend or acquaintance with enough experience and knowledge to act as honorary adviser to such a great firm as the house of Lin.'

Lin Fan sipped his tea.

'I understand that my rival offers ten per cent of his income to this honorary counsellor,' he said quietly, 'as a slight mark of appreciation of the thought he gives to their problems. This percentage does, of course, not mean much to a high official, but even so I would compute it at five thousand silver pieces monthly, which should help in the household expenses.'

Judge Dee stroked his beard. He observed:

'I hope you will understand how deeply it grieves me that I cannot help you in this matter. If I did not esteem you so highly, I could, of course, give you an introduction to some of my colleagues. In my opinion, however, the best is hardly good enough for the house of Lin!'

Lin Fan rose.

'I offer Your Excellency my apologies for having broached this subject so abruptly. I only wish to stress that the sum I mentioned off-hand is but a rough computation; it might as well turn out to be double that amount. Well, perhaps some further reflection might bring a name to Your Excellency's memory.'

Judge Dee also rose and said:

'I regret this exceedingly, but I could never find in my limited circle of friends a man who has the necessary high qualifications.'

Lin Fan once more bowed deeply and took his leave. Judge Dee personally conducted him to his palankeen.

Sergeant Hoong noticed that after this visit Judge Dee was in high spirits. He told the sergeant about his conversation with Lin Fan and remarked:

'The rat knows it is caught and starts gnawing at the trap!'

The next day, however, the judge relapsed into his dejected mood. Even the enthusiastic reports of Tao Gan as to how he annoyed the Lin steward failed to bring a smile to Judge Dee's lips.

Another week passed.

After the noon session of the tribunal, Judge Dee sat alone in his private office, listlessly looking through some official papers.

He heard the vague murmur of voices in the corridor outside. Two clerks were standing there engaged in desultory talk. Suddenly Judge Dee caught the word 'uprising.'

He jumped up from his chair and tiptoed to the paper window. He heard one of the clerks saying:

'—thus there is no fear of this uprising spreading further. I just heard, however, that the governor of our province, as a precaution, wishes to concentrate a substantial military force near Chin-hwa, as a show for the population.'

Judge Dee eagerly glued his ear to the paper. He heard the other clerk say:

'That explains it! My friend the corporal told me that, as an emergency measure, the garrisons of all districts in this neighbourhood have received orders to leave for Chin-hwa tonight.

Well, if that is true, the official communication should be under way to this tribunal, and——'

Judge Dee did not listen further. He hurriedly unlocked the iron chest in which he kept confidential documents and took out a large bundle along with some papers.

When Sergeant Hoong came in he was amazed at the change that had come over the judge. All his apathy had left him and he said in a crisp voice:

'Sergeant, I shall have to leave the tribunal at once on a most important secret investigation! Listen carefully to my instructions. I shall have no time to repeat them and to give you an explanation. Execute my orders to the letter. Tomorrow you will understand what this is all about.'

The judge handed Sergeant Hoong four envelopes.

'Here are four of my calling cards, addressed to four leading citizens of this district, all of unquestioned probity and greatly esteemed by the local people. I have selected these names after much reflection, taking into account also the location of their houses.

'They are Bao the retired General of the Left Wing, Wan the retired judge of the Provincial Court, Ling the master of the Guild of Goldsmiths, and Wen the master of the Guild of Carpenters. Tonight you will go to see them on my behalf. Inform them that tomorrow morning, one hour before dawn, I will need them as witnesses in a case of the greatest importance. They are not to say a word about this to anyone. I expect them to be ready in the courtyard of their respective houses, with their palankeens and a suitable retinue.

'Then you will secretly recall Ma Joong, Chiao Tai and Tao Gan from their posts. Replace them by constables. Tell my lieutenants to stand by in the main courtyard of this tribunal tomorrow morning two hours before dawn. Ma Joong and Chiao Tai on horseback and in full battle array, armed with sword and bow!

'The four of you will quietly rouse the entire personnel of the tribunal including all clerks, constables and runners. My official palankeen will be standing ready in the main courtyard. The personnel will take their appointed places around it, the constables with their clubs, chains and whips. All this should be done as quietly as possible. The lanterns should not be lighted. You will see that my official robe and cap are placed in my palankeen. The personnel of the jail shall guard the tribunal.

'Now I must leave. I shall see you tomorrow morning, two hours before dawn!'

Before the sergeant could say a word, the judge had taken his bundle and left the office.

Judge Dee hurried to his own mansion and went directly to the fourth courtyard. There he found Apricot and Blue Jade embroidering a robe.

He talked earnestly with them for about half an hour. Then he opened his bundle. It contained, among other things, a fortune-teller's outfit, complete with the high black cap and the placard that advertised his trade, bearing in large letters the inscription:

MASTER PENG

FAMOUS ALL OVER THE EMPIRE. HE FORETELLS
THE FUTURE ACCURATELY ON THE BASIS
OF THE SECRET TRADITION
OF THE YELLOW EMPEROR

Apricot and Blue Jade helped the judge change into this disguise. After he had placed the rolled-up placard in his sleeve, the judge looked intently at the girls, and said slowly to Apricot:

'I place my full trust in you and your sister!'

The two girls bowed deeply.

Judge Dee left by a small back-door. He had expressly

chosen this fourth courtyard as quarters for Apricot and Blue Jade, because besides being somewhat apart from the rest of his mansion, it had this back-door that opened on the park behind the tribunal by which he could leave the compound unnoticed.

As soon as he was in the main street, Judge Dee unrolled his placard and mingled with the crowd.

He spent the rest of the afternoon walking about at random in the back streets of the town, drinking innumerable cups of tea in small inns and street stalls. If someone approached him to have his fortune told, the judge excused himself on the ground that he was on his way to an appointment with an important client.

When night had fallen, he ate a simple meal in a modest restaurant not far from the northern gate. He reflected that he had the whole evening before him. While he was paying the waiter, it occurred to him that he might as well go and have a look at the Temple of Transcendental Wisdom; Ma Joong's lively description of Sheng Pa and his ghost stories had aroused Judge Dee's curiosity. The waiter told him that the temple was not far from there.

By frequently asking the way, Judge Dee finally found the alley that led to the temple. He carefully picked his way through the darkness, guided by a light he saw ahead.

Once arrived in the temple yard, he saw the scene that had become familiar to him through Ma Joong's account.

Sheng Pa was seated in his usual place against the wall. His henchmen were gathered round him, watching the rolling dice.

They gave Judge Dee a suspicious look, until they saw his placard.

Sheng Pa spat contemptuously. He said sourly:

'Go away quickly, my friend, and make haste! It saddens me sufficiently to look back upon my past, let alone that I should enjoy looking at my future. Bore yourself into the wall like a unicorn, fly up in the sky like a dragon, but by all means disappear. In my humble opinion you constitute a dismal sight!'

'Could I by any chance find here,' Judge Dee asked politely, 'a man called Sheng Pa?'

Sheng Pa leaped to his feet with amazing agility. Two of his followers approached Judge Dee threateningly. Sheng Pa said gruffly:

'I have never heard of anybody of that name. What do you mean by asking us, you bastard?'

'Well,' Judge Dee replied meekly, 'there is no reason to get excited! I happened to meet a colleague of mine, who when he saw that I was walking in this direction handed me two strings of copper cash. He said that his friend of the Beggars' Guild had entrusted him with those to be transmitted to a man called Sheng Pa, to be found in the yard of this temple. But since he is not here, I think I had better forget the entire episode!'

And the judge turned round to go.

'Hey, you crooked dogshead!' Sheng Pa exclaimed angrily. 'Know that I am Sheng Pa himself. Don't you dare to steal the money that belongs rightfully to the counsellor of the Beggars' Guild!'

Judge Dee hastily produced two strings of cash and Sheng Pa grabbed them from his hands. Immediately he started counting them.

When he had found everything in order, he said:

'Brother, I apologise for my rudeness! It was very kind of you to execute this errand. But let me tell you that we have had queer visitors here of late. One was quite a likeable ruffian, whom I thought I was helping out of a nasty spot. And now the word is being passed around that far from being an honest man, he belongs to the tribunal. What is the Empire coming to if one cannot trust his friends any more? He was a nice fellow to play dice with too!

'Well, since you did me this favour, sit down and rest yourself a while. You know the future, so I don't suppose there is any money for us in a game of dice with you.'

Judge Dee squatted down and joined the general conversation. He had made a profound study of the ways of the underworld, and using their slang freely, he told a few stories that earned general approval.

Then the judge started upon a gruesome ghost story.

Sheng Pa raised his hand and interrupted him saying sternly:

'Brother, hold your tongue! The unholy crowd are our neighbours. I shall not allow their being commented upon unfavourably in my presence!'

When Judge Dee expressed his surprise at this statement, Sheng Pa told him the story of the deserted temple at their back, without adding anything to what the judge already knew. Judge Dee said:

'Well, I for one would never say anything to their detriment, in a way ghosts and goblins are my business relations. As a fortune-teller I often have to consult them and they have brought me in quite a bit of money. For my part, I always try to do them little favours, like placing oil cakes in deserted corners that they frequent. They are very fond of those.'

Sheng Pa slapped his hand on his knee and exclaimed:

'So that is where those oil cakes I missed yesterday night went to! Well, well, one learns every day!'

Judge Dee saw one of Sheng Pa's henchmen chuckle, but he pretended not to notice anything and continued:

'Would you mind if I had a closer look at that temple?'

'Since you know how to handle ghosts and goblins,' Sheng Pa said, 'by all means go! You might tell them that I and my friends are decent persons whose well-earned night-rest ought not to be disturbed by ghostly phenomena!'

Judge Dee borrowed a torch and ascended the high flight of steps that led to the front gate of the temple.

The doors were of heavy wood, locked by an iron crossbar. The judge raised his torch and noticed that a strip of paper had been pasted over the padlock. The inscription read: 'The tribunal of Poo-yang' and the seal was that of his predecessor, Judge Feng. The date was two years before.

Judge Dee walked round the terrace till he found a smaller side door, also barred and locked. The upper panel, however, consisted of an open grating.

The judge extinguished his torch against the wall and, standing on his toes, he looked into the pitch-dark interior of the temple.

He stood very still, straining his ears.

Far away back in the temple he seemed to hear faint sounds of shuffling footsteps, but they could also have been caused by bats flying about. After a while everything was silent again. The judge did not quite know whether or not his ears had deceived him.

He waited patiently.

Then he heard faint sounds of knocking, which, however, ceased abruptly.

Although the judge stood and listened for a long time, everything remained silent as the grave.

Judge Dee shook his head and reflected that this temple certainly would have to be investigated. There might be a natural explanation for the shuffling sounds, but he thought that the knocks seemed very uncanny.

When he returned to the yard below, Sheng Pa asked him:

'Well, you were quite some time. Did you see anything?'

'Nothing to speak of,' Judge Dee replied, 'just two blue devils rolling dice with fresh human heads.'

'August Heaven!' Sheng Pa exclaimed, 'what a crowd! But unfortunately one can't choose one's neighbours!'

Judge Dee then took his leave and strolled back to the main street.

He found a small but fairly clean hostel in one of the side streets, called 'The Eight Immortals.' He rented a room for the night and told the waiter who brought him a pot of hot tea that he would have to leave very early in the morning, to start on the highway as soon as the city gates were open.

After he had drunk two cups, he drew his robe closer about him and lay down on the ramshackle bed for a few hours of sleep.

As the fourth nightwatch was sounded, Judge Dee rose and
rinsed his mouth with the cold tea. Then he straightened his
robes and left the hostel of the Eight Immortals.

A brisk walk through the deserted streets took him to the
main gate of the tribunal, where a sleepy guard admitted him,
looking in astonishment at Judge Dee's strange attire.

Without saying a word the judge went straight to the main
courtyard, where he could vaguely make out the dark forms
of a large number of people, standing silently around his
official palankeen.

Sergeant Hoong lighted a single paper lantern and assisted
the judge in ascending the palankeen. Inside Judge Dee took
off his brown gown, and changed into his official robes.
Having placed the black judge's cap on his head, he lifted up
the curtain and beckoned Ma Joong and Chiao Tai.

His two lieutenants presented an imposing sight. They had
put on the heavy iron mail coat of cavalry captains. Their
heads were covered by a pointed iron helmet. Each carried
two long swords and a large bow and their quivers were full
of arrows.

Judge Dee said to them in a low voice:

'We shall first proceed to the mansion of the retired general,
then to that of the judge and finally to the houses of the two
guildmasters. You two will lead the way on horseback.'

Ma Joong bowed.

'We have wrapped the hooves of our horses in straw,' he
replied. 'There won't be any sound!'

Judge Dee nodded contentedly and at a signal the procession left the tribunal. Silently it moved westwards, rounded the outer wall of the tribunal compound and then went north, till they arrived at the general's mansion.

Sergeant Hoong knocked. Immediately the double doors swung open.

The sergeant saw the general's military palankeen standing ready in the courtyard, surrounded by about thirty of the general's retainers.

Judge Dee's palankeen was carried in. He descended and met the general at the foot of the steps that led to the reception hall.

The general had put on his parade dress for this occasion and although he was over seventy years of age, he was a most imposing figure. He wore a gold-embroidered robe of purple silk and a golden mail-coat. A huge jewel-studded sword hung from his girdle and the coloured pennants of the five divisions which he once commanded in victorious campaigns in Central Asia, spread fanwise from the high point of his golden helmet.

After they had bowed to each other, Judge Dee spoke:

'I deeply regret that I have to inconvenience Your Excellency at such an unusual hour. Your Excellency's presence is urgently needed for the exposure of a foul crime. I pray you to follow carefully the proceedings, so as to be able to deliver testimony in court later.'

The general seemed pleased to join this nightly expedition. He replied in his clipped soldier's voice:

'You are the magistrate here, I follow your orders. Let us be on our way!'

Judge Dee repeated the same formula with the retired judge, and later with the two guildmasters.

When the procession, which now consisted of five palankeens and over a hundred men neared the northern gate, the judge called Ma Joong to the side of his palankeen. He said curtly:

'As soon as we have passed through the city gate, you and Chiao Tai will pass the word that nobody is allowed to detach himself from this procession, on penalty of death. You and Chiao Tai will ride up and down along our flanks. Arrows will be on the bowstring. The first man who tries to leave the ranks is shot on the spot. Now ride ahead and order the military guards to open the gate!'

Soon two soldiers were opening the heavy, iron-studded doors of the northern gate and the procession passed through.

They turned east, to the Temple of Boundless Mercy.

When they arrived at the front gate, Sergeant Hoong knocked on the door. The head of a sleepy monk appeared behind the grated peephole.

Sergeant Hoong barked:

'We are constables of the tribunal, to catch a burglar that has entered your compound. Open the door!'

They heard the crossbar being pushed back and the doors were drawn to a crack. Ma Joong and Chiao Tai, who had tethered their horses outside the gate, now quickly pushed the double gate wide open. They locked two frightened monks in the gatekeeper's lodge, promising that their heads would be chopped off if they made a single sound. Then the entire procession moved into the courtyard. Judge Dee descended from his palankeen and the four witnesses followed suit.

Judge Dee asked them in a low voice to accompany him to the main courtyard; everybody else was to stay where they were. With Tao Gan leading the way and Ma Joong and Chiao Tai bringing up the rear they strode on silently till they had arrived in front of the main hall.

The spacious courtyard was sparsely lighted by the shine of the bronze lanterns which burned all night in front of the sacred statue of the goddess Kwan Yin.

The judge raised his hand. All stood still. After a few moments a slight figure entirely covered by the hooded cloak of a Buddhist nun detached itself from the shadows, and having bowed deeply before the judge, whispered something in his ear.

Judge Dee turned to Tao Gan and said:

'Lead us to the abbot's room!'

Tao Gan ran up the stairs of the terrace and entered the corridor on the right of the hall. He pointed to the closed door at the end.

Judge Dee nodded to Ma Joong. With one thrust of his shoulder the latter pushed the door in, and then stood aside to let the others pass.

They saw a luxurious room, lighted by two large candles. The air was heavy with incense and perfume. The abbot lay snoring on a carved ebony couch, under a quilt of richly-embroidered silk.

'Put that man in chains!' the judge ordered. 'Secure his arms behind his back.'

Ma Joong and Chiao Tai dragged the abbot from his couch, threw him on the floor, and had his arms bound behind his back with a thin chain before he was really awake.

Ma Joong jerked him to his feet and growled:

'Bow before your magistrate!'

The abbot's face was ashen. He seemed to think that he had suddenly been transferred to the Inferno and that the two iron-clad men were the henchmen of the Black Judge of the Nether World.

Judge Dee addressed the witnesses:

'Please observe this man carefully, paying special attention to the crown of his shaven head!'

Then he turned to Sergeant Hoong.

'Run as fast as you can to the constables in the front court-yard,' he commanded. 'Order them to put every monk they can put their hands on in chains. They may light their lanterns now. Tao Gan will show them where the quarters of the monks are located.'

In the twinkle of an eye the courtyard was full of lighted lanterns, bearing in large letters the inscription 'The Tribunal of Poo-yang.' Orders were barked, doors were kicked in. Chains clanked. Screams of terror resounded through the air as the constables let swing their clubs and hit those who resisted with the handles of their heavy whips. Finally a crowd of about sixty frightened monks had been herded together in the centre of the main courtyard.

Judge Dee, who had been surveying this scene from the top of the stairs, now called out:

'Make them kneel in rows of six, facing this terrace!'

When this order had been executed, the judge said:

'Let all those who came here together with us range themselves in orderly fashion along the three sides of this courtyard.'

Then he called Tao Gan and ordered him to lead them to the secluded garden. Turning to the girl in the nun's cloak who had been waiting in front of the main hall, the judge said:

'You will point Apricot's pavilion out to us, Blue Jade!'

Tao Gan opened the garden gate and they walked along the winding footpath. In the flickering light of the lanterns carried by Tao Gan and the girl, the elegant garden seemed like a dream of the Western Paradise.

Blue Jade stopped before a small pavilion in the midst of a miniature bamboo grove.

Judge Dee beckoned the witnesses to come nearer and showed them the unbroken seal on the locked door.

He nodded to Blue Jade. She tore off the seal and opened the lock with her key.

Judge Dee knocked on the door and called out:

'I, the magistrate, am here!'

Then he stepped back.

The red-lacquered door opened and they saw Apricot standing there clad in a thin silk nightrobe, holding a candlestick.

Seeing the group with the general and Judge Wan in front, she hastily turned back and wrapped herself in a hooded cloak. Then all entered the small pavilion and observed the magnificent painting of the goddess hanging on the wall, the large couch with the brocade coverlets and the other luxurious appointments of the room.

The judge bowed respectfully before Apricot and the others followed suit automatically, the pennants of the general's helmet waving in the air.

Then Judge Dee said:

'Now show us the secret entrance!'

Apricot went to the door and turned round one of the many copper knobs that studded its lacquered surface. A narrow panel in the middle of the door swung open.

Tao Gan clapped his hand to his forehead.

'Imagine that even I was fooled by this trick!' he exclaimed incredulously. 'I looked everywhere, except in the most obvious place!'

Turning to Apricot, Judge Dee enquired:

'Are all of the other five pavilions occupied?'

When Apricot nodded, Judge Dee continued:

'Please go with Blue Jade to the guest quarters in the first courtyard and tell the husbands of the ladies concerned to come and unlock the doors of the pavilions and fetch their wives. The husbands shall then go to the main courtyard alone, I wish them to be present when I conduct the preliminary hearing of this case.'

Apricot and Blue Jade left the pavilion. Judge Dee carefully surveyed the room. Pointing to a small table that stood by the side of the couch, he said to the four witnesses:

'Gentlemen, I wish to draw your attention to that small

DISTINGUISHED PERSONS VISIT A TEMPLE PAVILION

ivory box with lip salve there on that table; please remember its position! The general will now seal this box. It will be brought forward in due time as an exhibit.'

While they were waiting for Apricot to return, Tao Gan studied the secret panel in the door. He found that it could be noiselessly operated from both sides by turning round one of the ornamental copper knobs.

Then Apricot returned to report that the occupants of the other five pavilions had been brought to the first courtyard. Their husbands were waiting in front of the main hall.

Judge Dee led his companions to each pavilion in succession. In every one of them Tao Gan located the secret panel without difficulty.

Judge Dee turned to the witnesses.

'Gentlemen,' he said quietly, 'I ask your concurrence in the falsification of one fact, as an act of mercy. I propose to state at the hearing that we found that two of these pavilions, the location of which shall not be specified, had not been provided with a secret entrance. Do you gentlemen agree?'

'The point is very well taken, Magistrate,' the retired judge remarked, 'and shows your consideration for the welfare of the people. I agree, on condition that the true facts shall be recorded in a separate enclosure, for the exclusive use of the juridical authorities.'

After Judge Dee and the others had expressed their approval, Judge Dee said:

'Gentlemen, let us now proceed to the terrace in front of the main hall. I shall there open the preliminary hearing of this case.'

As they stood on the terrace, dawn began to break and its reddish glow spread over the bald heads of the sixty monks kneeling in the courtyard below.

The judge ordered the headman of the constables to have a large table and chairs brought from the refectory of the temple. When the temporary tribunal had been set up, Ma Joong dragged the abbot in front of the bench.

When the abbot, shivering from the cold morning air, had seen the judge, he hissed at him:

'You dog-official, you accepted my bribe!'

'You are mistaken,' the judge said coldly, 'I only borrowed it! Every copper cash of the funds you sent me was used to bring about your own downfall.'

Judge Dee bade the general and the judge to sit down on his right, behind the bench, and the two guildmasters on his left. Apricot and Blue Jade sat down on tabourets which Sergeant Hoong had placed by the side of the bench while he himself remained standing behind the two girls.

The senior scribe and his assistants took up their positions behind a smaller side table. Ma Joong and Chiao Tai stood at attention on the right and left corners of the terrace.

When everyone was in his appointed place Judge Dee surveyed the weird scene for a moment. Not a sound came from the crowd.

Then Judge Dee's stern voice was heard.

'I, the magistrate, open the preliminary hearing of the case against the abbot and an unspecified number of monks of the Temple of Boundless Mercy. The quadruple charge is adultery with married women, rape of married women, defiling of a recognised place of worship, and extortion.'

The judge glanced at the headman and ordered:

'Bring the plaintiff before me!'

Apricot was led in front of the bench where she knelt.

Judge Dee said:

'This is an extraordinary session of this tribunal. I rule that the plaintiff be excused from kneeling!'

Apricot rose and threw back the hood that covered her head.

Judge Dee's stern face softened when he looked at the slight figure, wrapped in her long cloak, standing before him with downcast eyes. He said kindly:

'Let the plaintiff state her name and file her accusation!'

Apricot replied in a faltering voice:

'This insignificant person's family name is Yang and her personal name Apricot, a native of Hunan Province.'

The senior scribe took it down.

The judge leaned back in his chair.

'Proceed!' he ordered.

Eighteenth Chapter: A BEAUTIFUL GIRL DELIVERS STARTLING
TESTIMONY; JUDGE DEE EXPLAINS THE CASE TO HIS
LIEUTENANTS

AT first Apricot spoke rather diffidently, but as she gained
confidence her clear voice rang out over the silent audience.

'Yesterday afternoon,' she began, 'I repaired to this temple
accompanied by my younger sister, Blue Jade. I obtained an
interview with the abbot and begged to be allowed to offer
my prayers to the miraculous statue of our Lady Kwan Yin.
The abbot said that my prayers would be effective only if I
passed the night in this temple, meditating on the boundless
mercy of the goddess. He asked payment for the lodging in
advance and I gave him one bar of gold.

'Yesterday evening the abbot led my sister and myself to a
small pavilion in the back garden. He told me that I should
stay there overnight, while my sister would be accommodated
in the guest quarters of the temple. He said that in order to
safeguard my honour against the possible slander of rumour
mongers, my sister herself should lock the door to my cham-
ber. She did so, impressing her seal on the strip of paper that
was pasted over the lock. The abbot told her to keep the key.

'Alone in the locked pavilion,' continued the girl, 'I first
offered a long prayer in front of the image of Our Lady that is
hanging on the wall. When I felt tired I lay down on the
couch, leaving the candle on the dressing-table burning.

'It must have been past the second nightwatch when I
awoke and found the abbot standing in front of the couch. He
said that he personally guaranteed that my wish would be
granted. Then he blew out the candle and forced me to submit
to his embraces. It so happened that I had left my box of lip

salve standing open on the table by the side of my pillow and unbeknownst to him I marked the top of his shaven head with that red salve. After he had violated me the abbot said: "Now when in due time your wish has been fulfilled, don't forget to send a suitable present to this poor temple! Should I fail to receive this, your worthy husband might learn some unpleasant news!" The next thing I knew he had somehow or other left the pavilion.'

There was considerable shifting and murmuring from the gathering as Apricot went on:

'I remained lying there in the darkness, weeping bitterly. Suddenly a monk was in my room. He said: "Do not cry, your lover has arrived!" Disregarding my protests and entreaties, he also possessed me. But although my distress was great, I still managed to mark him as I had marked the abbot.

'Determined to collect evidence in order to be able to avenge these atrocious deeds when a suitable opportunity would present itself, I pretended to like this monk, who seemed to be a rather stupid man. I lighted the candle with a glowing coal from the tea stove. Now teasing, then flattering him I coaxed him into showing me the secret of the hidden panel in the door.

'When he had left, a third monk visited me, but I pretended to be ill. While pushing him away, however, I also marked him with my lip salve.

'An hour ago my sister knocked and told me that the magistrate of this district had arrived for an investigation. I asked her to report at once that I wished to file an accusation.'

Judge Dee spoke in a stern voice:

'I request the witnesses to verify the mark on the head of the first accused!'

The general and his companions rose.

The early rays of the morning sun clearly showed the red patch on the crown of the abbot's shaven head.

A BUDDHIST ABBOT SURPRISES A GUEST

Judge Dee ordered the headman of the constables to walk along the rows of kneeling monks and bring before him those whose head was marked by a similar patch.

Soon the constables dragged two monks up the stairs and pressed them to their knees alongside the abbot. The red marks on their heads were there for all to see.

Judge Dee proclaimed:

'The guilt of these three criminals has been established beyond all possible doubt. The plaintiff may stand back!

'I shall hear this case once more during the afternoon session of this tribunal in the city. Then I shall recapitulate all evidence collected. I shall question all other monks of this temple under torture to determine who else is guilty.'

At that moment a very old monk who was kneeling in the first row raised his head, and called out in a trembling voice:

'I pray Your Honour to hear me!'

The judge gave a sign to the headman and the old monk was led before the bench.

'Your Honour,' he stammered, 'this ignorant monk begs to state that his name is Complete Enlightenment and that he is the rightful abbot of this Temple of Boundless Mercy. That man over there who calls himself abbot is nothing but an intruder, who has not even been ordained a priest. Some years ago he came to my temple and intimidated me into yielding the place to him. Later, when I protested against his foul behaviour to the ladies who repaired to this temple for worship, he had me locked up in a cell in the back courtyard. I have been kept a prisoner there until Your Honour's constables broke the door open an hour ago.'

The judge raised his hand and ordered the headman:

'Report on this!'

'This old monk,' the headman of the constables announced, 'was indeed found in a small cell that had been barred and locked on the outside. There was a small grated spyhole in the door and we heard him calling us in a weak voice. I had the door rammed in. He offered no resistance but asked to be brought before Your Excellency.'

Judge Dee nodded slowly and said to the old monk:

'Proceed!'

'One of my two disciples,' the monk continued, 'who originally inhabited this temple with me, was poisoned by the abbot when he threatened to report him to the high priest of our sect. The other, who is present here before Your Honour's tribunal, pretended to have turned against me. He spied upon the abbot and his henchmen, secretly reporting to me all he discovered. Unfortunately he did not succeed in collecting any evidence. The abbot kept his nefarious doings secret to all except his own group of favourite satellites. Thus I ordered my disciple to bide his time and not to report to the authorities, since that would only make the abbot kill us and thus destroy the last chance to expose this awful desecration of this holy abode. He, however, will be able to point out to Your Honour those renegades who joined with the abbot in his lecherous deeds.

'The other monks are either true believers or just lazy persons who were attracted by the luxurious and easy life in this temple. I pray Your Honour to be allowed to intercede on their behalf.'

On a sign of the judge, the constables took the chains off the old abbot who led the headman to another elderly monk. He walked with the headman along the rows of kneeling monks pointing out seventeen young fellows, who were immediately dragged in front of the bench.

Made to kneel down they began screaming and cursing, some shouting that Spiritual Virtue had compelled them to violate the ladies. Others begged for mercy, some loudly demanded to confess their crimes.

'Silence!' barked Judge Dee.

The constables' whips and clubs descended on the heads and shoulders of the monks till their shouts had changed into suppressed moans.

When order had been restored Judge Dee said:

'The other monks will be freed from their chains. They will immediately resume their religious duties, under the direction of His Reverence Complete Enlightenment.'

When the courtyard had been cleared, the crowd of spectators, by now augmented by people from the northern suburb who had come to see what the commotion in the temple meant, pressed forward to the stairs of the terrace, muttering curses against the monks.

'Stand back in an orderly manner, and listen to your magistrate!' Judge Dee shouted.

'The despicable criminals assembled here have been gnawing like rats at the roots of our peaceful society and thus are guilty of a crime against the State. For has not our peerless Sage, Master Confucius himself, said that the family is the foundation of the State? They violated decent married women who came here in a devout spirit to pray to the goddess. Women who were defenceless because of their responsibility for the honour of their family and the legitimacy of their offspring.

'Fortunately, however, these villains did not dare add a secret entrance to all of the six pavilions; two were found to be without. Since I am not an impious man and since I profoundly believe in the infinite grace and mercy of the Powers on High, I wish it to be clearly understood that the fact that a lady passed the night in this temple does not necessarily mean that the child subsequently born to her is illegitimate.

'As to these criminals, I shall interrogate them during the afternoon session in the tribunal and there they shall be given an opportunity to speak for themselves and confess their crimes.'

Turning to the head of the constables Judge Dee added:

JUDGE DEE DISMISSES A WICKED MONK

'Since our jail is too small for accommodating these rascals you will temporarily place them in the stockade outside the east wall of the tribunal. Convey them there with the utmost despatch!'

As Spiritual Virtue was being led away he shouted at the judge:

'You miserable fool, know that soon you will be kneeling before me in chains and it will be I who pass judgement on you!'

Judge Dee smiled coldly.

The constables lined the twenty men up in two rows of ten, bound them together securely with heavy chains and then drove them on prodding them with their clubs.

Judge Dee ordered Sergeant Hoong to conduct Apricot and Blue Jade to the front courtyard and send them back to the tribunal in his own palankeen.

Then the judge called Chiao Tai.

'When the news of these events has spread through the town,' he observed, 'I fear that an angry mob will try to attack these monks. Ride as fast as you can to the garrison headquarters and tell the commander to send a company of lance knights and mounted archers to the stockade immediately. They are to form a double cordon round the palissade. Their headquarters are not far from the tribunal so the soldiers should be there before the prisoners.'

As Chiao Tai hurried away to execute this order the general remarked:

'A wise precaution, Magistrate!'

'Gentlemen,' Judge Dee said to the general and the three other witnesses, 'I regret that I have to intrude still further on your valuable time. This temple is a treasure house of gold and silver. We cannot leave here before everything has been inventoried and sealed in your presence. I anticipate that the higher authorities will order all the property of this temple confiscated, and the tribunal will have to append a complete list of all assets to the official report on this case.

'I assume that the almoner of this temple has an inventory, but all items will have to be verified and that will take several hours. I propose, therefore, that we first repair to the refectory to take breakfast.'

Judge Dee sent a constable to the kitchen to give the necessary orders. All left the terrace and walked to the large refectory on the second courtyard. The crowd of spectators filed to the first courtyard, angrily cursing the monks.

Judge Dee excused himself to the general and the three other witnesses for not acting as their host. To save time he wanted to give further instructions to his lieutenants while they ate.

While the general, the retired judge and the two guild-masters engaged in a polite contest as to who should preside over their table, Judge Dee chose a smaller table somewhat apart from the others and there sat down with Sergeant Hoong, Ma Joong and Tao Gan.

Two novices placed bowls with rice gruel and pickled vegetables before them. The small group ate in silence until the novices were out of earshot.

Then the judge said with a wry smile:

'I fear that during the past weeks I must have been a difficult master for all of you and especially for you, Sergeant! Now, however, you shall hear my explanation.'

Judge Dee finished the gruel, put his spoon on the table and began:

'It must have hurt you, Sergeant, when you saw me accept that wretched abbot's bribe. Three bars of gold and three bars of silver! The fact is that although at that time I had not yet decided on a definite course of action, I knew that sooner or later I would be in need of funds. You know that I have no income except my official salary and I did not dare to take money from the comptroller of the tribunal for fear that the abbot's spies would discover that I was contemplating some action.

'As it turned out this bribe was exactly sufficient to pay expenses for setting my trap. Two gold bars were used for redeeming the two girls from the house that owned them. The third I gave to Apricot, to be used in persuading the abbot to let her stay in the temple for one night. One bar of silver I gave to the steward of my distinguished colleague Lo, the magistrate of Chin-hwa, as commission for arranging this transaction and to cover the costs of conveying the two girls to Poo-yang. I gave the second bar of silver to my wife to buy the girls new dresses. The rest was used to purchase their cloaks and for the rent of the two luxurious palankeens in which they proceeded to this temple yesterday afternoon. Thus you can dismiss that worry from your mind, Sergeant.'

The judge noted the look of relief on the faces of his assistants. He smiled patiently and continued:

'I selected these two girls in Chin-hwa because I recognised in them those virtues that make our peasant class the very backbone of our glorious Empire, virtues that even the exercise of an unfortunate profession cannot substantially affect. I was confident that if they assisted me in the execution of my plan, they would certainly be successful.

'The girls themselves, and also my family, thought that I had bought them as my concubines. I did not dare to confide my secret to anyone, not even to my First Lady. As I said before, the abbot may well have had spies among the servants in my mansion and I could not afford the slightest risk of the secret leaking out. I had to wait till the two girls adapted themselves to their new mode of life and until they could play the role of a distinguished lady and her maidservant, before I could execute my plan.

'Thanks to the untiring efforts of my First Lady, Apricot

made unusually quick progress and yesterday I decided to act.'

The judge picked up some vegetables with his chopsticks.

'Yesterday, after I left you, Sergeant,' he went on, 'I went directly to their courtyard and told the girls of my suspicions regarding the Temple of Boundless Mercy. I asked Apricot whether she would consent to play her role, adding that since I had an alternative plan that did not involve their co-operation she was completely free to refuse. Apricot, however, agreed immediately. She indignantly said she would never forgive herself if she let this chance pass to save other women from the lusts of those depraved monks.

'Then I told them to put on the best dresses my wife had given them, and conceal these by wrapping themselves in the long hooded cloak of Buddhist nuns. They were to leave the tribunal secretly by the back-door and rent two of the best palankeens in the market-place. When they arrived at the temple, Apricot was to tell the abbot that she was the concubine of an exalted personage in the capital, so exalted indeed that his name could not be disclosed; that his First Lady was exceedingly jealous of her, and that she feared further that her master's feelings for her were cooling. Threatened with being expelled from that mansion, she had come to the Temple of Boundless Mercy as a last resort. Her lord was childless and if she could present him with a son, her position would be safe.'

Here Judge Dee paused for a moment. His assistants had hardly touched their food.

'Now this was a plausible story,' the judge went on, 'but since I knew the abbot to be an extremely shrewd man, I still feared that he would refuse her because Apricot would not give him her real name and more personal details. So I instructed her to appeal to both his greed and his base lusts. She was to offer him the bar of gold and show him her beauty, giving him to understand by the means well known to every woman that she thought him a handsome man.

'Finally I told Apricot what to do during her vigil. I did not rule out the possibility that after all everything rested on the miraculous powers of the statue of the goddess, especially since I had been greatly impressed by Tao Gan's failure to locate a secret entrance to the pavilion.'

Tao Gan looked embarrassed. He hastily buried his face in his bowl of gruel. Judge Dee smiled indulgently and continued:

'So I told Apricot that should a real saint appear before her in mid-air, she was to prostrate herself on the floor and humbly tell the complete truth, stating that I, the magistrate, bore full responsibility for her being there under false pretences. If, however, a common mortal should enter her room, she was to try to find out by what means he had effected his entrance— thereafter she was to act as circumstances dictated. But I gave her a small box of red lip salve and instructed her to mark the head of the man who embraced her.

'At the end of the fourth nightwatch Blue Jade would secretly slip out of the guest quarters, and knock twice on the door of Apricot's pavilion. If she was answered by four knocks she would know that my suspicions had been groundless, three knocks meant that there had been foul play.

'The rest you know.'

Ma Joong and Tao Gan clapped their hands excitedly, but the Sergeant was looking worried.

After some hesitation, Sergeant Hoong said:

'The other day, when Your Honour gave me what I then thought to be the final statement on the problem of the Temple of Boundless Mercy, Your Honour made a remark that still greatly worries me. Namely that even if convincing evidence against the monks could be found, and their confessions obtained, the Buddhist church would intervene and protect them, and have them set free long before the case would have been closed. How can this problem be solved?'

Judge Dee knotted his heavy eyebrows, and pensively tugged his beard.

Just at that moment the clatter of hooves was heard outside in the courtyard. Chiao Tai came rushing into the refectory.

He quickly looked about and seeing the group he came running to their table, his brow covered with sweat.

'Your Honour,' he panted excitedly, 'I only found four foot soldiers in the garrison headquarters! The rest of the garrison left yesterday for Chin-hwa on emergency orders of His Excellency the Governor. When I passed the stockade on the way back here, I saw a furious crowd of several hundred people ramming the palissade. The constables had fled inside the tribunal!'

'This is a most unfortunate coincidence!' exclaimed Judge Dee. 'Let us hasten back to the city!'

He hurriedly explained the situation to the general and put him in charge of concluding affairs in the temple, assisted by the master of the Guild of Goldsmiths. Judge Dee asked the retired Judge Wan and the master of the Carpenters' Guild to accompany him.

Judge Dee ascended the general's military palankeen with Sergeant Hoong. The old judge and the guildmaster disappeared into theirs while Ma Joong and Chiao Tai leaped on their horses. They raced back to the city as fast as the bearers could go.

The main street was teeming with an excited crowd, which broke out in wild cheers as they saw Judge Dee in the open palankeen. On all sides people shouted 'Long live our Magistrate!' 'Thousand years to His Excellency Judge Dee!'

As they approached the tribunal, however, they found fewer people about and when they rounded the north-east corner of the compound an ominous silence hung over the deserted streets.

The palissade had been broken down in several places. Inside were the mutilated remains of the twenty criminals, stoned and trampled to a horrible death by the maddened crowd.

JUDGE DEE did not descend from his palankeen. One glance was sufficient to indicate that nothing could be done. A mass of mangled bodies and torn limbs covered with blood and mud made it unnecessary to look for any signs of life. Judge Dee ordered the palankeen bearers to proceed to the main gate of the tribunal.

The guards opened the double gate and the palankeens of Judge Dee and his companions disappeared into the main courtyard.

Eight frightened constables emerged and dropped to their knees by the side of Judge Dee's palankeen knocking their heads on the flagstones. One of them began to recite an elaborate apology, but the judge cut the explanation short.

'You need not apologise,' he said, 'the eight of you could never have held the crowd back. That was the task of the mounted soldiers whom I called but who failed to come.'

Judge Dee and his two lieutenants, the retired Judge Wan and Guildmaster Ling descended from their palankeens, and proceeded to Judge Dee's private office. On the desk lay a pile of documents that had arrived during his absence.

Judge Dee picked up a large envelope bearing the seal of the Governor of Kiangsu Province.

'This,' he said to Judge Wan, 'will be the official communication regarding the calling up of our garrison. I beg you to verify this!'

Judge Wan broke the seal and after a glance at the contents he nodded and handed it back to Judge Dee.

'This letter,' Judge Dee observed, 'must have arrived yesterday evening after I had left the tribunal on an urgent, secret investigation. I passed the night in a small hostel called "The Eight Immortals" in the northern quarter of this city.

'I came back to the tribunal before dawn but had to leave immediately for the Temple of Boundless Mercy. I barely had time to change my clothes and did not even enter this office.

'I would appreciate if, as a matter of form, you and Master Ling would interrogate the servants of my mansion, the manager of the Eight Immortals hostel, and the soldier who brought the governor's message. I want to include your testimony in my report on this case, lest it be said that the death of those unfortunate criminals was caused by negligence on my part.'

Judge Wan nodded and replied:

'Recently I received a letter from an old friend of mine in the capital from which I understand that the Buddhist church has become quite influential in Government circles. I am sure that the high dignitaries of the church will study this report on the Temple of Boundless Mercy as sedulously as if it were their favourite sutra. If they can find a flaw they will certainly pounce on it and try to discredit you with the government.'

'The exposure of those villainous monks,' the guildmaster said, 'has brought joy and relief to all of us here in Poo-yang and I can assure Your Honour that the people are full of gratitude. I regret all the more that the crowd, in their indignation, behaved in such a lawless manner. I apologise humbly for the behaviour of my fellow citizens!'

Judge Dee thanked them. The two witnesses took their leave to verify matters as the judge had requested.

Judge Dee immediately took up his writing brush and drafted a stern warning addressed to the people of Poo-yang. He sharply denounced the massacre of the monks, stressing that the punishment of criminals is the exclusive right and duty of the State. He added that any person engaging in further acts of violence would be executed on the spot.

Since all the scribes and clerks were still in the temple, Judge Dee ordered Tao Gan to prepare five copies in large characters. He himself wrote out five others in his bold calligraphy. Having impressed on these proclamations the large red seal of the tribunal, the judge told Sergeant Hoong to have the placards posted on the gate of the tribunal and other central points in the town. He also ordered the sergeant to have the remains of the twenty monks placed in baskets for a later cremation.

When the sergeant had left to attend to those matters, Judge Dee spoke to Ma Joong and Chiao Tai:

'Violence often breeds violence. If we don't take measures immediately, further disorders may arise. Lawless elements may loot the shops; with the garrison away it will be difficult to curb them once they break loose. I shall again go out in the general's palankeen and show myself in the main streets to prevent disorder. You two will ride by my side, with your bows ready to shoot on the spot anyone who tries to create disorder.'

First they went to the temple of the tutelary deity of the city. The procession consisted only of Judge Dee in his palankeen, with Ma Joong and Chiao Tai riding by his side, and two constables in front and behind. The judge, clad in his full official dress, was there for all to see as he sat in the open palankeen. A subdued crowd respectfully made way for him. The people did not cheer. They seemed to be ashamed of the violence that had been committed.

Judge Dee burned incense in the temple and in an earnest prayer offered his apologies to the deity, begging him to forgive the defilement of the town. For the tutelary deity does not like the earth within the city he presides over to be polluted with blood. It is for that reason that the execution ground is always located outside the city gates.

From there Judge Dee proceeded westward to the Temple of Confucius and there offered incense before the tablets of the Immortal Sage and his illustrious disciples. Thereafter he went north, passed the park outside the northern wall of the tribunal compound and offered also a prayer in the Temple of the War God.

The people in the streets were very quiet. They had read the placards and there were no signs of unrest. The fury of the crowd had spent itself with the massacre of the monks.

Having thus satisfied himself that there was no fear of further disorder, Judge Dee returned to the tribunal.

Soon the general came back from the Temple of Boundless Mercy, and with him the entire personnel of the tribunal.

The general handed the judge the inventory. He reported that all funds and valuables, including the golden sacrificial vessels, had been placed in the treasure house of the temple and that the doors were now sealed. The general had taken the liberty of sending for spears and swords from his own armoury and issued these to his retainers and the constables. He had left twenty of his men and ten constables guarding the temple. The old general was in high spirits and seemed to enjoy thoroughly this break in the dull routine of retired life.

Judge Wan and Guildmaster Ling came in to report that they had verified that it had been impossible for Judge Dee to take cognisance of the communication regarding the calling up of the garrison.

Then all proceeded to the large reception hall where refreshments were served.

When the constables had placed extra tables and chairs, all sat down to work. Under Judge Dee's direction a detailed report on the events of that day was drafted.

Whenever necessary the scribes took down special statements of witnesses. Once Apricot and Blue Jade were summoned from the judge's mansion to deliver a full statement and affix their thumb-marks. Judge Dee added a special clause reporting that it had been impossible to find the culprits who had actually killed the monks in a crowd of several hundred people; that since the provocation had been great, and since no further disorder had ensued, he respectfully recommended that no punitive measures be taken against the citizens of Poo-yang.

Night had fallen when, at last, the draft of the report together with its various enclosures had been completed. Judge Dee invited the old general, the retired judge and the two guildmasters to join him at the evening meal.

The indefatigable general seemed inclined to accept, but Judge Wan and the two others begged to be excused since they felt tired after such a strenuous day. Thus the general had to decline the invitation too and all took their leave.

Judge Dee personally conducted them to their palankeens and again expressed his gratitude for their valuable assistance.

Then the judge changed into an informal robe and retired to his own quarters.

In the main hall of his mansion he found his First Lady presiding over a festive dish with his Second and Third Ladies as well as Apricot and Blue Jade gathered round it.

They all rose and welcomed the judge. He sat down at the head of the table and while tasting the steaming dishes enjoyed the harmonious atmosphere of his home that he had been missing so much during the past weeks.

When the dishes had been cleared away and tea was being served by the steward, Judge Dee said to Apricot and Blue Jade:

'This afternoon, while drawing up the report on this case for the higher authorities, I inserted a recommendation to the effect that four bars of gold should be taken from the confiscated funds of the Temple of Boundless Mercy and presented to each of you as a small reward for your assistance in solving this case.

'Pending the approval of this proposal, I shall send by courier an official letter to the magistrate of your native district requesting that he make enquiries about your family. Perhaps August Heaven has granted that your parents are still alive. And should they have passed away, other members of your family will certainly be located to receive you. I shall have you conducted there as soon as a military transport leaves for Hunan Province.'

Judge Dee smiled kindly at the two girls and went on:

'You shall have a letter of introduction to the local authorities, recommending you to their care. With the reward of the government you will be able to purchase some land or open a shop. No doubt your family will in due time arrange a suitable marriage for you.'

Apricot and Blue Jade knelt bowing their heads to the floor several times in expression of gratitude.

Judge Dee rose and took leave of his ladies.

On the way back to the tribunal Judge Dee passed the open corridor that led through the garden to the front gate of his mansion. Suddenly he heard light footsteps behind him. Turning round, he saw Apricot standing there alone, her eyes downcast.

She bowed deeply but did not speak.

'Well, Apricot,' Judge Dee said kindly, 'if there is anything else I can do, please don't hesitate to speak!'

'My lord,' Apricot said softly, 'it is true that one's heart always longs for one's native place. Yet, since a propitious fate has placed my sister and myself under Your Honour's protection, both of us feel extremely reluctant to leave this mansion which has become dear to us. And since Your Honour's First Lady kindly said that it would gratify her if——'

Judge Dee raised his hand and said with a smile:

'That meetings end in separation is the way of this world! You will soon realise that you are happier as the first wife of an honest farmer of your own village rather than as the fourth or fifth wife of a district magistrate. Pending the closing of this case you and your sister will honour my mansion as guests.'

Having thus spoken Judge Dee bowed and persuaded himself that the drops he had seen glistening on Apricot's cheek were a trick of the moonlight.

As he entered the main courtyard, Judge Dee noticed that all the rooms of the chancery were still brilliantly lighted. There the scribes and the clerks were still busy writing out the report that had been drafted that afternoon.

In his private office the judge found his four lieutenants. They were listening to the headman of the constables who, on the order of Sergeant Hoong, had made the round of the watchposts near Lin Fan's mansion. It appeared, however, that nothing had happened there during their absence.

Judge Dee dismissed the headman and, having seated himself behind his desk, looked through the other official documents that had come in. Putting three letters apart he said to Sergeant Hoong:

'These are the reports from three military posts along the canal. They stopped and searched several junks bearing the markings of Lin Fan's firm, but found nothing but bona fide cargo. It seems that we are too late for obtaining proof of Lin Fan's smuggling.'

The judge then disposed of the rest of the correspondence, jotting down directions for the scribe in the margin of each document with his vermilion brush.

Then he drank a cup of tea and settled back in his arm-chair.

'Last night,' he said to Ma Joong, 'I went in disguise to the Temple of Transcendental Wisdom and paid a visit to your friend Sheng Pa. I had a close look at that deserted temple. It seems that something queer is going on inside. I heard some strange sounds.'

Ma Joong glanced doubtfully at Sergeant Hoong, and Chiao Tai looked uncomfortable. Tao Gan slowly pulled at the three hairs that grew from the mole on his left cheek. No one said a word.

Their manifest lack of enthusiasm did not perturb the judge. 'That temple,' he continued, 'has excited my curiosity. This morning we had ample experience with a Buddhist temple. Why should we not supplement that tonight with a sample of a Taoist sanctuary?'

Ma Joong smiled bleakly. Rubbing his big hands on his knees he said:

'Your Honour, I dare say that in a single combat I fear no man in the Empire. But as to mixing with the denizens of the other world——'

'I am not,' Judge Dee interrupted him, 'an incredulous man and I would be the last to deny that on occasion phenomena of the Nether World are found in the daily life of common mortals. On the other hand I am firmly convinced that he whose conscience is clear need fear neither ghosts nor goblins. Justice reigns supreme in both worlds, the seen and the unseen.

'Moreover, I shall not hide from you, my loyal friends, that the events of today and the period of waiting preceding them, have not left me undisturbed. I expect that an investigation in that Taoist temple will rest my mind.'

Sergeant Hoong tugged thoughtfully at his beard. He observed:

'If we go there, Your Honour, what about Sheng Pa and his gang? I take it that our visit will have to be a secret one.'

'I have thought of that,' Judge Dee replied. 'You, Tao Gan, will now go to the warden of that quarter. Tell him to go to the Temple of Transcendental Wisdom and inform Sheng Pa that he must leave that place immediately. Those fellows are shy of the authorities and they will have disappeared before the warden has finished talking! But tell the headman anyway to go there also with ten constables, in case the warden needs assistance.

'In the meantime we shall change into inconspicuous robes and go to the neighbourhood in an ordinary palankeen, as soon as Tao Gan has returned. I shall take nobody but the four of you. But don't forget to bring four paper lanterns and a good supply of candles with you!'

Tao Gan went to the quarters of the guards and ordered the headman to collect ten constables.

Tightening his girdle, the headman remarked with a broad smile to the others:

'Isn't it curious how soon a magistrate will improve if he has an experienced headman like me? Look, when His Excellency arrived here he immediately went all out for that vulgar murder in Half Moon Street, where there was not one single copper cash to be earned. Soon after, however, he became interested in the Buddhist temple and that place looks like the abode of the God of Wealth himself! I anticipate with pleasure more work there, when the decision of the higher authorities has come in.'

'I thought,' a constable said nastily, 'that your inspection of the watchpost near Lin Fan's mansion this afternoon was not unprofitable either!'

'That,' the headman sternly rebuked him, 'was just an exchange of amenities between two gentlemen. Mr Lin Fan's steward wished to express his appreciation of my courteous attitude.'

'That steward's voice,' another constable observed, 'had a remarkably silvery ring.'

With a sigh the headman extracted one silver piece from his girdle and threw it to the constable, who caught it dexterously.

'I am not a stingy man,' the headman said, 'and you may divide that among yourselves. Since you rascals keep an eye on everything you may as well hear the whole story. The steward presented me with a few silver pieces, asking if tomorrow I could take for him a letter to a friend. I replied that I would certainly do so if I were there tomorrow. Since tomorrow I shall not be there, I shall not be able to accept that letter. Thus I don't disobey His Excellency's orders, I don't offend a gentleman by declining a courteous gift and I don't depart from the standard of rigid honesty I have set for myself.'

The constables agreed that that was an eminently reasonable attitude. All left the guard house to join Tao Gan.

Twentieth Chapter: AN EMPTY TAOIST TEMPLE POSES MANY
A VEXING PROBLEM; A DESERTED COURTYARD DELIVERS UP
ITS GRUESOME SECRET

◆◆◆

WHEN the second nightwatch was being sounded Tao Gan
came back. The judge drank a cup of tea, then changed into
a simple blue robe and put a black skull cap on his head.
Accompanied by his four lieutenants he left the tribunal by a
small side gate.

They rented sedan chairs in the street and had themselves
carried to the crossing near the Temple of Transcendental
Wisdom. There they paid off the bearers and continued on
foot.

In the yard in front of the temple it was pitch dark, and very
still. Evidently the warden and the constables had done their
job well, Sheng Pa and his vagabonds had left.

Judge Dee said to Tao Gan in an undertone:
'You'll force the lock of the side door, on the left of the
main gate. Don't make more noise than is strictly necessary!'

Tao Gan squatted down and wrapped his neckcloth round
his lantern. When he had struck his flint and lighted it, only
one thin ray shone through, sufficient for guiding his steps as
he went up the broad stairs.

When he had located the locked side gate he carefully
scrutinised it by the light of his lantern. His failure to discover
the secret panel in the Temple of Boundless Mercy had
wounded his pride, he was determined to execute this order
quickly and expertly. He took a set of thin iron hooks from
his sleeve and set to work on the lock. Soon he could open it
and take down the crossbar. When he gave the door a gentle
push it swung open. There was no second crossbar on the

inside. He hurriedly went down the steps to report to Judge Dee that they could enter the temple.

All of them climbed up the stairs.

Judge Dee waited a few moments in front of the gate, listening intently for sounds within. But everything remained silent as the grave. Then they stole inside, the judge leading the way.

Judge Dee whispered to Sergeant Hoong to light his lantern. As he held it high they saw that they were in the large front hall of the temple. On the right they noticed the inside of the triple front gate, provided with heavy crossbars. Evidently the side door through which they had just come in was the only means by which one could enter without breaking down the thick doors of the main gate.

On the left stood an altar, almost ten feet high, carrying three enormous gilded statues of the Taoist Triad. One could see their hands raised in benediction, their shoulders and heads remained hidden in the darkness on high.

Judge Dee stooped and scrutinised the floor. The wooden boards were covered with a thick layer of dust, showing only the tiny traces left by rats.

He beckoned his companions and walked round the altar, into a dark corridor. When Sergeant Hoong raised his lantern, Ma Joong uttered an oath. The light shone on a severed woman's head with distorted features and dripping with blood. It was held up by a claw-like hand clutching its hair.

Tao Gan and Chiao Tai stood stock-still in horrified silence. But Judge Dee remarked in a calm voice:

'Don't get excited! As is usual in a Taoist temple, the walls of this corridor show a panorama of the Ten Courts of Hell, with all its horrors! It is live men we should be afraid of!'

Despite Judge Dee's reassuring words his lieutenants were deeply shocked by the fearful scenes an ancient artist had sculptured in wood along both walls of the corridor. They were life-size, luridly coloured representations of the punishments meted out to the souls of the wicked in the Taoist Nether World. Here blue and red devils were sawing people asunder, impaling them on swords, or removing their entrails with iron forks. There a number of unfortunates were thrown into cauldrons of boiling oil or had their eyes plucked out by infernal birds of prey.

Having traversed this corridor of horrors, the judge slowly pushed a double door open. They looked out on the first courtyard. The moon had come out, its rays shone on a neglected garden. A bell tower stood in the centre, near a lotus pond of fanciful shape. The tower consisted of a stone platform of about twenty feet square, and raised about six feet above the ground. Four thick red-lacquered pillars supported a graceful pointed roof, decked with green-glazed tiles. The large bronze bell, ordinarily suspended from the cross-beams under the roof had now been let down on the platform, as is usually done when a temple is vacated, in order to preserve it from damage. This bell was about ten feet high, the outside was covered by intricate ornamental designs.

Judge Dee silently surveyed this peaceful scene. Then he led his assistants along the open corridor that went round the courtyard.

The rows of small rooms along this corridor were completely empty, the floors were covered with dust. When the temple was still in use these rooms had served for receiving guests and for reading the holy books.

The gate at the back led to the second courtyard, surrounded by the empty cells of the monks. At the back there was a large, open kitchen.

This seemed to be all there was to see in the Temple of Transcendental Wisdom.

By the side of the kitchen Judge Dee noticed a narrow door.

'I assume,' he said, 'that this is the back door of the compound. We might as well open it and see which street runs behind this temple.'

He gave a sign to Tao Gan, who quickly opened the rusty padlock that secured the heavy iron crossbar.

They saw to their amazement that there was a third courtyard, about twice as large as the others. It was paved with flagstones and surrounded by high, two-storied buildings. They seemed completely deserted, a deep silence reigned. There were signs, however, that this courtyard had been inhabited till recently, no weeds grew among the flagstones, and the buildings seemed in good repair.

'This is strange indeed!' Sergeant Hoong exclaimed. 'This third courtyard seems quite superfluous. What could the monks have used it for?'

Just as they were debating this question a cloud obscured the moon and all went dark.

Sergeant Hoong and Tao Gan quickly started to relight their lanterns. Suddenly the silence was broken. From the farther end of the courtyard came the sound of a door falling shut.

Judge Dee hurriedly took the Sergeant's lantern and ran across the courtyard. There he found a heavy wooden door. It opened noiselessly on well-oiled hinges. Holding his lantern high the judge saw a narrow corridor. There was a faint sound of hurried footsteps, then the thud of a door being slammed shut.

Judge Dee ran inside but found his progress barred by a high, iron door. He quickly scrutinised it, Tao Gan looking over his shoulder. As he righted himself the judge remarked:

'This door is quite new, but I fail to see any lock, and there is no handle or knob for opening it from this side. You'd better have a good look at it, Tao Gan!'

Tao Gan eagerly examined the polished surface of the door inch by inch, then went over the doorposts. But he could locate no sign of the mechanism for opening it.

'If we don't force this door right now, Your Honour,' Ma Joong said excitedly, 'we'll never know what bastard has been spying on us! If we don't catch him now he'll escape!'

Judge Dee slowly shook his head. He rapped the smooth iron surface with his knuckles, then said:

'Barring a heavy battering-ram we can never force this formidable door. Let's inspect those buildings!'

They left the corridor and surveyed the dark buildings surrounding the courtyard. Judge Dee selected a door at random and pushed it. It was unlocked. They entered a large room, empty but for the mats that covered the floor. After a quick glance around Judge Dee walked over to the ladder standing against the back-wall. He ascended and pushed the trapdoor in the ceiling up. Climbing through he found himself in a spacious loft.

When his four lieutenants had joined him, they all curiously looked around. The loft was in reality a long hall, thick wooden pillars supported the high ceiling.

Judge Dee said, astonished:

'Has any one of you ever seen a similar arrangement in a Taoist or Buddhist temple?'

Sergeant Hoong slowly pulled his frayed beard.

'Perhaps,' he observed, 'this temple possessed formerly a very large library. Then they could have used this loft for storing the books.'

'In that case,' Tao Gan put in, 'one would expect some traces of bookshelves along the walls. As it is, this loft rather seems a kind of warehouse for storing goods.'

Ma Joong shook his head. He asked:

'What would a Taoist temple do with a warehouse? Look at these thick mats that cover the floor. I think Chiao Tai will agree with me that this is an armoury, used for practising sword and spear fighting.'

Chiao Tai had been examining the walls. Now he nodded his head and said:

'Look at these pairs of iron hooks here! They must have been used for putting up long spears. I think, Your Honour, that this place was the headquarters of some secret sect. Its members could practise here the martial arts, without any outsider suspecting these goings on. Those blasted monks must have been in it too, they acted as cover!'

'There is much in what you say,' Judge Dee said pensively. 'Apparently those conspirators stayed on after the monks had left, and cleared out only a few days ago. You see that this loft has been thoroughly cleaned quite recently, there is not a speck of dust on the mats.' He tugged at his whiskers, then added angrily: 'They must have left one or two men behind, including the rascal who takes such an interest in our investigation! It's a pity that I didn't consult the city map before coming out here. Heaven knows where that locked iron door below is leading to!'

'We might try to get on to the roof,' Ma Joong remarked, 'and see what is behind this temple.'

Together with Chiao Tai he opened the heavy shutters of the large window, and looked outside. Craning their heads they could see along the eaves above a row of long iron spikes, pointing downwards. The high wall at the back of the compound concealed effectively whatever building was behind the temple, and it had a similar row of spikes along its top.

As he stepped back Chiao Tai said sadly:

'Nothing doing! We'd need at least some scaling ladders for going up there!'

The judge shrugged his shoulders. He said testily:

'In that case there isn't anything more we can do here. We know at least that the back part of this temple is used for some secret purpose. Heaven forbid that the White Lotus is stirring again and that we get here a repetition of our troubles in Han-yuan!* Well, we'll come back here tomorrow in broad daylight with the necessary equipment, a thorough investigation seems indicated!'

He climbed down the ladder, followed by his assistants.

Before leaving the courtyard Judge Dee whispered to Tao Gan:

'Paste a slip of paper over the locked door! When we come back tomorrow we'll know at least whether that door was opened again after our departure.'

Tao Gan nodded. He took two narrow strips of thin paper from his sleeve. Having moistened them on his tongue, he pasted them across the crevice between the door and its frame, one high up and the other near the floor.

They walked back to the first courtyard.

Arrived at the gate that led to the corridor of horrors, Judge Dee halted in his steps. Turning round he surveyed the neglected garden. The moonlight shone on the large dome of the bronze bell, setting off the fantastic ornamental designs covering its surface. Suddenly the judge felt acutely conscious of danger. He felt the presence of evil in this seemingly peaceful scene. Slowly stroking his beard he tried to analyse this queer feeling of foreboding.

Noticing the questioning look of the Sergeant, Judge Dee said in a preoccupied way:

'Sometimes one hears fearful stories about such heavy temple bells being used for hiding gruesome crimes. Since we are here, we might as well have a look under that bell, and make sure that nothing is hidden there.'

As they walked back to the raised platform Ma Joong remarked:

'Those bells are cast in bronze several inches thick. In order to tilt it we'll need to apply leverage.'

* See "The Chinese Lake Murders."

221

'If you and Chiao Tai go to the front hall,' Judge Dee said, 'you'll doubtless find there some of those heavy iron spears and tridents the Taoist monks use for exorcising evil spirits. We might use those for tilting the bell.'

While Ma Joong and Chiao Tai ran back, Judge Dee and the two others picked their way through the thick undergrowth till they found the flight of steps leading up to the bell tower platform. As they stood in the narrow space between the circumference of the bell and the edge of the platform, Tao Gan pointed to the roof and observed:

'When the baldpates left, they took away the pulleys used for raising the bell. But we might manage to tilt it with those spears Your Honour spoke of.'

Judge Dee nodded absent-mindedly. He felt increasingly ill at ease.

Ma Joong and Chiao Tai climbed up on the platform. Each carried a long iron spear. They took off their upper robes, then rammed the points of the spears under the rim of the bell. They put their shoulders under the shafts and succeeded in raising the bell the fraction of an inch.

'Push stones underneath!' Ma Joong panted at Tao Gan.

When he had inserted two small stones under the rim, Ma Joong and Chiao Tai could push their spears farther under the bell. Again they applied leverage, aided by the judge and Tao Gan. When the bell had been lifted about three feet, Judge Dee said to Sergeant Hoong:

'Roll that stone barrel seat underneath!'

The Sergeant quickly overturned the stone seat that was standing on the corner of the platform, and rolled it towards the bell. There were still a few inches lacking. Judge Dee let go of the spear and took off his upper robes. Then he again put his shoulder under the shaft.

They made a final effort. The muscles on Ma Joong's and

222

A WEIRD DISCOVERY UNDER A BELL

Chiao Tai's thick necks swelled. Then the Sergeant could push the stone barrel under the raised rim.

They threw the spears down and wiped the sweat from their faces. At that moment the moon disappeared again behind the clouds. Sergeant Hoong quickly took a candle from his sleeve and lighted it. He peered under the bell. He gasped.

Judge Dee quickly stooped and looked. The space under the bell was covered with dust and dirt. In the middle a human skeleton was stretched out on the floor.

The judge hurriedly took the lantern from Chiao Tai, dropped down on his belly and crawled under the bell. Ma Joong, Chiao Tai and the Sergeant followed his example. When Tao Gan wanted to crawl inside also, Judge Dee barked at him:

'There isn't enough room. You stay outside and watch!'

The four men squatted down by the side of the skeleton. Termites and worms had left nothing but the bare bones. The wrists and ankles had been shackled with a heavy chain that was now a mass of rust.

The judge examined the bones, paying special attention to the skull. But there was no sign of violence. He only noticed that the bone of the left upper arm had been broken at one time, and that the fracture had set badly.

Looking at his assistants Judge Dee said bitterly:

'This unfortunate man was evidently still alive when he was imprisoned here. He was left to die a horrible death of starvation.'

The Sergeant had been stirring the thick layer of dust covering the cervical vertebræ. Suddenly he pointed at a glittering round object.

'Look!' he exclaimed, 'that seems a small golden locket!'

Judge Dee carefully picked it up. It was a round medallion.

He rubbed it clean with his sleeve, and held it close to the lantern.

Its outside was plain, but inside there was engraved the character 'Lin.'

'So it was that bastard Lin Fan who left this fellow to die here!' Ma Joong exclaimed. 'He must have dropped that locket when he was pushing his victim underneath the bell!'

'Then this man is Liang Ko-fa!' Sergeant Hoong said slowly.

Hearing this astounding news Tao Gan crawled under the bell too. All five of them stood there close together under the tilted bronze dome, looking down at the skeleton at their feet.

'Yes,' Judge Dee said in a toneless voice, 'it was Lin Fan who committed this vile murder. As the crow flies this temple is not far from Lin Fan's mansion. Doubtless the two compounds have a common back wall, they are connected by that heavy iron door.'

'That third courtyard,' Tao Gan said quickly, 'must have been used by Lin Fan for storing his smuggled salt! The secret sect must have left there much earlier, together with the monks.'

Judge Dee nodded.

'We have obtained valuable evidence,' he said. 'Tomorrow I shall open the case against Lin Fan.'

Suddenly the stone barrel was jerked away. With a dull crash the bronze bell settled down over the five men.

Twenty-first Chapter: THE JUDGE AND HIS FOUR MEN FALL
INTO A WEIRD TRAP; A DANGEROUS CRIMINAL IS ARRESTED
IN HIS OWN MANSION

ALL burst out in angry exclamations. Ma Joong and Chiao
Tai cursed violently, they groped frantically with their
fingers along the smooth inside of the bronze dome. Tao Gan
started to lament loudly, cursing his foolish mistake.

'Silence!' barked Judge Dee. 'Time is short, listen carefully!
We could never raise this accursed bell here from the inside.
There's only one possible method for getting out from here.
We must try to displace this bell a few feet by pushing it.
When one part of it is over the edge of the platform, there'll
be an opening through which we might climb down.'

'Won't the corner pillars be in the way?' Ma Joong asked
hoarsely.

'I don't know,' the judge replied curtly. 'But even a small
opening will serve at least to save us from being suffocated.
Put the lights out, the smoke spoils the little air we have.
Don't talk, strip and set to work!'

Judge Dee threw his cap on the floor and stripped naked.
Scraping about with his right foot till he had got a hold in a
groove between the stones, he bent his back and pushed the
bell.

The others followed his example.

Soon the air became close and breathing became increasingly
difficult. But at last the bell moved a little. It was but for the
fraction of an inch. But now they had proof that their task
was not impossible and they redoubled their efforts.

None of the five men ever knew how long they toiled in
their bronze prison. Perspiration streamed down their naked

bodies. Their breath came in gasps, the foul air scorched their lungs.

Sergeant Hoong's force gave out first. He collapsed on the floor just when a desperate effort had pushed the bell a few inches over the edge of the platform.

A small crescent-shaped opening appeared at their feet and a waft of fresh air entered their prison.

Judge Dee dragged the Sergeant to the opening so that he could catch the fresh air. Then they concentrated all their strength on one more effort.

The bell moved further over the edge. There was now an opening large enough for a child to crawl through. They pushed and pushed with all their remaining strength, but in vain. Apparently the bell had become stuck against one of the pillars.

Suddenly Tao Gan squatted and let his legs down through the opening. He made a determined effort to get through. The rough stone edge cut a deep gash all along his back, but he would not give up. Finally he managed to get his shoulders free and he dropped down among the undergrowth.

After a few moments a spear was passed through the opening. Now Ma Joong and Chiao Tai could make the bell move round a bit, and soon the opening was large enough for letting Sergeant Hoong down through it. Then Judge Dee and the two others followed.

They sank down among the shrubs, completely exhausted.

But soon Judge Dee rose again and went over to where the Sergeant was lying. When he had felt his heart he said to Ma Joong and Chiao Tai:

'Let's carry the sergeant to the lotus pond and moisten his face and breast. Don't let him get up before he has completely recovered!'

As he turned round the judge saw Tao Gan kneeling behind him, and knocking his forehead on the ground.

'Rise, my man!' Judge Dee said. 'Let this be a lesson for you! You have seen now for yourself what'll happen if you don't execute my orders—which as a rule are not given without a good reason. Come along now and help me to verify how our prospective murderer succeeded in wrenching that stone barrel out from under the bell.'

Clad only in his loincloth Judge Dee climbed on to the platform, followed by a very submissive Tao Gan.

Once there they soon realised how it had been done. Their assailant had taken one of the spears they had used for tilting the bell, and laid it behind the barrel. Then he had pushed it further till its point had landed against the nearest pillar. Using this spear as a lever, he could wrench the stone loose.

Having verified this point, the judge and Tao Gan picked up their lanterns and went to the third courtyard.

When they examined the iron back door, they saw that the strips of paper, which Tao Gan has pasted on, were broken.

'This,' said Judge Dee, 'clearly proves that Lin Fan is the criminal. He opened this door from inside and secretly followed us to the first courtyard. He spied on us while we were tilting the bell and when he saw that all of us had crept inside he realised that this was his chance to get rid of us for ever.'

The judge glanced about him.

'Let us now go back,' he said, 'and see how Sergeant Hoong is getting along.'

They found that the sergeant had regained consciousness. When he saw the judge he wanted to get up. But Judge Dee firmly ordered him to stay where he was. He felt the sergeant's pulse and said kindly:

'There is nothing for you to do just now, Sergeant. Stay where you are and rest here till the constables arrive!'

The judge turned to Tao Gan.

'Run to the warden of this quarter and order him to come

here with his men. He is to send a man to the tribunal on horseback to summon twenty of my constables. They are to come here immediately, bringing two sedan chairs. When you have transmitted these orders, Tao Gan, you run as fast as you can to the nearest pharmacy. You are bleeding all over.'

Tao Gan rushed away. In the meantime Ma Joong had collected Judge Dee's cap and robes from beneath the bell. He had shaken the garments free of dust and dirt. Now he was holding them up for the judge to put on.

Judge Dee shook his head.

To Ma Joong's amazement he put on only his undergarment and rolled up the sleeves, baring his muscular forearms. He tucked its slip under his girdle. Parting his long beard, he made it into two strands. He threw them over his shoulders and then knotted both ends together behind his neck.

Ma Joong eyed the judge critically and decided that although he had some excess fat on him he would be an unpleasant customer in a hand-to-hand fight.

While the judge completed his preparations by tying his hair up with a handkerchief, he said to Ma Joong:

'I hope I am not a vindictive man. But this Lin Fan tried to kill all of us in a most cruel manner. Had we not succeeded in pushing this bell over the edge of the platform, another sensational disappearance would have been added to the records of Poo-yang. I am not going to deny myself the pleasure of arresting Lin Fan with my own hands. I hope that he puts up some resistance!'

The judge added, turning to Chiao Tai:

'You will stay here with the sergeant. When the constables arrive they shall haul the bronze bell into its original position. The bones shall be collected and placed in a casket. Then you will sift carefully the dirt of the area under the bell and search for more clues.'

Together with Ma Joong he left the temple by the side gate.

After walking through many narrow streets, Ma Joong located the front gate of Lin Fan's mansion. Four sleepy constables stood guard there.

While Judge Dee remained in the background Ma Joong advanced and whispered his instructions into the ear of the eldest constable.

He nodded and knocked on the gate. When the peephole opened, the constable barked at the gatekeeper:

'Open the gate and be quick about it! A burglar has entered your compound. What would happen to this mansion, you lazy dog, if we constables were not always so vigilant? Open up, before the thief makes off with your savings!'

As soon as the gatekeeper had opened the double gate, Ma Joong leaped forward and gripped him by the throat. He clapped his hand over the man's mouth till the constables had trussed him up effectively and gagged him with a piece of oil-cloth.

Then Judge Dee and Ma Joong rushed inside.

The courtyards seemed deserted. Nobody appeared to stop them.

In the third courtyard Lin Fan's steward suddenly emerged from the shadows. Judge Dee barked at him:

'You are arrested on the orders of the tribunal!'

The steward's hand shot to his girdle and a long knife suddenly glittered in the moonlight.

Ma Joong prepared to jump on him, but he was not quick enough. The judge had already crashed a sweeping blow to the steward's heart, and the man fell backwards with a gasp. The judge aimed an accurate kick under his chin. The steward's head snapped back and crashed on the flagstones. He lay quite still.

'Well done!' Ma Joong whispered.

While Ma Joong picked up the steward's knife Judge Dee ran to the back courtyard. Only one paper window reflected a yellow light. Ma Joong caught up with the judge just as he kicked the door open.

They saw a small but elegant bedroom, lighted by a silk lantern on a carved blackwood stand. On the right stood a bedstead of the same material, on the left an elaborately-carved dressing-table with two burning candles.

Lin Fan, clad in a thin nightrobe of white silk, was sitting in front of the table, his back to the door.

Judge Dee pulled him round roughly.

Lin Fan looked at the judge in speechless terror. He made no move to fight. His face was pale and drawn and his forehead showed a deep gash. He had been applying a medicinal salve to this gash when the judge entered. His left shoulder was bare and showed some ugly bruises.

Much disappointed at seeing his adversary thus disabled, Judge Dee said gruffly:

'Lin Fan, you are under arrest. Stand up! You shall be taken to the tribunal at once!'

Lin Fan did not speak.

He rose slowly from his chair. Ma Joong, standing in the middle of the room, unwound a thin chain from his waist for binding Lin Fan.

Suddenly Lin Fan's right hand shot out to a silk cord that hung on the left side of the dressing-table. Judge Dee lashed out and landed a ferocious blow under Lin Fan's chin which made the latter's back crash against the wall. Lin Fan did not release his grip on the cord and as he sank unconscious to the floor his weight pulled it.

Judge Dee heard an oath behind him and turned round just in time to see Ma Joong toppling over. A trapdoor had opened under his feet.

The judge clutched his collar, thus saving him from dropping into the dark hole beneath. He pulled him up.

The trapdoor measured four feet square. It had swung down

on its hinges, revealing a steep stone stairway leading into darkness.

'You were lucky, Ma Joong,' Judge Dee observed. 'If you had been standing in the middle of this treacherous thing you would have broken your legs on those stairs!'

Examining the dressing-table, the judge found a second silk cord on the right. He pulled. Slowly the trapdoor rose. Then a click, and the floor seemed perfectly normal again.

'I don't like to hit a wounded man,' said Judge Dee, indicating Lin Fan's prostrate form, 'but if I had not knocked him down who knows what other tricks he would have attempted.'

'It was a good clean blow, Your Honour,' Ma Joong said with hearty approval. 'I wonder, though, how he got that nasty gash on his head and those bruises on his shoulder. Apparently he has had some rough handling earlier today!'

'That we shall find out in due time,' Judge Dee said. 'You will now securely bind Lin Fan and also his steward. Then fetch the constables from the front gate and search the entire mansion. Arrest any other servants you may find and convey all of them to the tribunal. I shall investigate this secret passage further.'

Ma Joong stooped over Lin Fan. The judge opened the trapdoor again by pulling the cord. He took a lighted candle from the dressing-table and went down.

Having descended a dozen of the steep steps, Judge Dee found himself in a narrow passage.

Holding his candle high, he saw a stone platform on the left. Black, murky water was lapping over two broad steps under a low stone archway in the wall. On the right the passage ended with a large iron door which had a complicated lock.

He climbed up again till his head and shoulders were on a level with the floor and called to Ma Joong:

'There is a locked door down here that must be the same as

the one we tried to open a few hours ago! The bales of salt were transported from the storehouse in the third courtyard of the temple along an underground water passage, that must lead to the river, inside or outside the watergate. Search the sleeves of Lin Fan's upper gown for a set of keys so that I can open that door!'

Ma Joong went through an embroidered robe that hung on the bedstead. He pulled out two keys of intricate design and handed them to Judge Dee.

The judge descended again and tried them in the lock. The heavy iron door swung open, revealing the third courtyard of the Temple of Transcendental Wisdom bathed in the soft moonlight.

Judge Dee called a farewell to Ma Joong and stepped out into the cool night air. He heard the far-off shouts of his constables.

••

JUDGE DEE slowly walked on to the first courtyard.

It was brightly illuminated now by dozens of large paper
lanterns bearing the inscription 'The Tribunal of Poo-yang.'

Under the supervision of Sergeant Hoong and Chiao Tai
the constables were busy adding pulleys to the cross beam of
the bell tower.

When he saw the judge, Sergeant Hoong hurriedly came
over to enquire about further developments.

Judge Dee noticed with satisfaction that the sergeant looked
none the worse for his adventure under the bronze bell.

The judge described Lin Fan's arrest and the secret passage
connecting his mansion with the temple.

While the sergeant assisted the judge in putting on his
robes, Judge Dee said to Chiao Tai:

'Go to the farm of Lin Fan with five constables! There you
will find the four constables who took over from you. Arrest
all inhabitants of the farm. Also the people on the junk that is
lying moored to the jetty. It is a long night for you, Chiao
Tai, but I want all of Lin Fan's henchmen safely under lock
and key!'

Chiao Tai answered cheerfully that he liked the excitement.
He immediately began selecting five sturdy men from among
the constables.

Judge Dee walked over to the bell tower.

The pulleys had been put in place. The heavy bell was slowly
hauled up by strong cables till it hung in its normal position
about three feet above the floor.

For a few moments Judge Dee surveyed the trampled area underneath. The bones had been scattered during the frantic half hour they spent trying to escape from their bronze prison.

'Chiao Tai has given you my instructions,' he said to the headman of the constables. 'I repeat that after you have collected the bones, the dirt and dust under the bell must be sifted with the greatest care. You may find other important clues. Thereafter you will help to search Lin Fan's mansion. Leave four constables on guard duty. Report to me tomorrow morning!'

Then Judge Dee and Sergeant Hoong left the Temple of Transcendental Wisdom. Their sedan chairs awaited them in the yard. They were carried back to the tribunal.

The next morning introduced a fine autumn day.

Judge Dee issued orders to the archivist to search in the land register for material relating to the Temple of Transcendental Wisdom and Lin Fan's mansion. Thereafter he had a late breakfast in the garden behind his private office, attended by Sergeant Hoong.

When the judge was once more seated at his desk and tea had been served, Ma Joong and Chiao Tai entered.

Judge Dee ordered the clerk to bring them a cup of tea also and then asked Ma Joong:

'Well, was there any difficulty in apprehending Lin Fan's men?'

'All went very smoothly,' Ma Joong said with a smile. 'I found the steward lying unconscious where Your Honour had knocked him down. I turned him and Lin Fan over to the constables. Then we searched the entire mansion for others but found only one man, a burly ruffian who started to act a bit rough. With a little persuasion, however, he soon let himself be trussed up nicely. Thus we have four prisoners: Lin Fan, his steward, his henchman, and the old gatekeeper.'

'I have brought in one prisoner,' Chiao Tai added. 'It

turned out that three people were living on the farm. All of them are simple Cantonese peasants. On the junk we found five men, that is to say the captain and four boatmen. The boatmen are just stupid sailors, but the captain has all the marks of a hardened criminal. I placed the peasants and the sailors in custody at the warden's house, but the captain I had taken to our jail here.'

Judge Dee nodded.

'Call the headman of the constables!' he ordered the clerk. 'Then go to Mrs Liang's house and tell her that I wish to see her as soon as possible.'

The headman respectfully greeted the judge and then remained standing in front of the desk. He seemed tired, but he had an unmistakably smug look on his face.

'In accordance with Your Honour's instructions,' he began importantly, 'we have collected the bones of Liang Ko-fa and placed them in a basket now in the tribunal. We carefully sieved the dirt under the bell but discovered nothing. Then, under my personal supervision, the entire mansion of Lin Fan was thoroughly inspected and the rooms sealed. Finally I myself examined the water passage under the trapdoor.

'I discovered a small flat-bottomed boat moored under the archway. I took a torch and poled it all along the passage. It ends in the river, just outside the watergate. There I found another stone arch in the river bank, hidden under the over-hanging bushes. This arch is so low that the boat could not pass underneath, but if one jumped into the water, one could easily wade through.'

Caressing his whiskers, Judge Dee gave the headman a sour look.

'You, my friend,' he said, 'showed remarkable zeal so late in the night! I regret that your exploration of the water passage did not yield any hidden treasure. I take it, however, that in Lin Fan's mansion there were a few small things lying about that you could transfer to your capacious sleeves. But restrain yourself, my man, lest some day you find yourself in trouble. You may go now!'

The headman hurriedly took his leave.

'That greedy rascal,' Judge Dee said to his lieutenants, 'brought to light at least how the steward succeeded in leaving the city the other day without attracting the attention of the guards on the watergate. He evidently went by this underground passage and waded under the archway into the river.'

As he spoke the archivist came in. He bowed and placed a sheaf of documents before the judge saying:

'Following Your Honour's instructions early this morning, I searched the files of the land registration. I located these documents relating to Mr Lin Fan's possessions.'

'The first document,' he continued soberly, 'is dated five years ago and records Mr Lin Fan's purchase of the mansion, the temple, and the farm. All three belonged originally to Mr Ma, the landowner who now lives outside the eastern city gate.

'This temple had been the headquarters of a secret, unorthodox sect, which had been suspended by the authorities. Mr Ma's mother firmly believed in Taoist magic. She installed six priests in the temple and had them read masses for her dead husband. In the deep of night she had the monks perform magical séances, during which the souls of the dead were called up and she could converse with them by means of the planchette. She had a passage built between the two compounds so that she could visit the temple at any time.

'Six years ago the old lady died. Mr Ma closed the mansion but allowed the priests to stay in the temple on the understanding that they kept it in good repair. The priests could provide their own living by reading masses and selling amulets to the devout.'

The archivist paused and cleared his throat. Then he continued:

'Five years ago Mr Lin made enquiries about a site in the north-west corner of the city. Shortly after that he purchased the mansion, the temple and the farm, paying a good price. This is the deed of sale. Your Honour will find a detailed ground plan attached.'

The judge glanced through the deed and then unfolded the map. Calling his lieutenants to his desk, he said:

'One can well imagine that Lin Fan was prepared to pay a high price! This property was eminently suited for his smuggling plans.'

Judge Dee's long finger traced across the map.

'You see on this map,' he said, 'that at the time of the purchase the passage between the two compounds consisted of an open stairway; the iron door and the secret trapdoor were later added by Lin Fan. I don't see any indication of the underground water passage. For that we shall have to refer to older maps.'

'The second document,' the head of the archives continued, 'is dated two years ago. It is an official communication signed by Lin Fan, addressed to this tribunal He reports that he has found out that the monks do not keep their vows and lead a dissolute life, engaging in drinking and gambling; that he has therefore ordered them to vacate the temple and that he requests that the compound be sealed by the authorities.'

'That,' Judge Dee observed, 'must have been when Lin Fan discovered that Mrs Liang was on his track! I assume that when he told the monks to leave he gave them a good reward. It is impossible to trace such vagrant monks, so we shall never know what part they took in Lin Fan's secret activities, or whether they knew about the murder under the bell.' Addressing the archivist he added: 'I shall keep these documents here for reference. You'll now find me an old map of this city that shows the situation about one hundred years ago.'

When the head of the archives had gone, a clerk came in with a sealed letter. He respectfully handed it to the judge adding that it had been delivered by a captain from the garrison headquarters.

Judge Dee broke the seal and glanced through the contents. He handed it to Sergeant Hoong saying:

'This is the official notification that our garrison has returned to the city this morning and has resumed its duties.'

He settled back in his arm-chair and ordered a fresh pot of hot tea. 'Let Tao Gan come here also,' he added. 'I want to discuss with all of you how to initiate the case against Lin Fan.'

After Tao Gan had come in, all sipped a cup of hot tea. Just when Judge Dee put his cup down the headman came in and announced that Mrs Liang had arrived.

The judge shot a quick look at his lieutenants.

'This will be a difficult interview!' he muttered.

Mrs Liang seemed much better than the last time Judge Dee had seen her. Her hair was neatly done up and there was an alert look in her eyes.

When Sergeant Hoong had made her sit down in a comfortable arm-chair in front of the desk, Judge Dee said gravely:

'Madam, I have at last found sufficient evidence for arresting Lin Fan. At the same time I discovered another murder committed by him, here in Poo-yang.'

'Did you find Liang Ko-fa's body?' the old lady exclaimed.

'Whether it was your grandson, Madam, I can't say yet,' Judge Dee replied. 'Only a skeleton was left, and there was nothing to identify it.'

'It must be his!' Mrs Liang cried out. 'Lin Fan planned to kill him as soon as he learned that we had traced him to Poo-yang! Let me tell you that when we escaped from the burning redoubt, a falling roof-beam struck Liang Ko-fa's left arm. I had the broken bone set as soon as we were safe, but it never healed properly.'

239

The judge looked at her thoughtfully, slowly caressing his side-whiskers. Then he said:

'I regret to inform you, Madam, that the skeleton did indeed show a badly-healed fracture of the bone of the left upper arm.'

'I knew that Lin Fan murdered my grandson!' Mrs Liang wailed. She started trembling all over, tears came flowing down her hollow cheeks. Sergeant Hoong quickly gave her a cup of hot tea.

Judge Dee waited till she had composed herself. Then he spoke:

'You may rest assured, Madam, that this murder shall now be avenged. I hate to cause you more distress, but I must ask you a few more questions. The records you gave me state that when you and Liang Ko-fa had escaped from the burning redoubt, you found shelter with a distant relative. Could you give me a more detailed account of how you managed to elude the attacking ruffians, and how you made your way to that relative?'

Mrs Liang looked at the judge with a vacant stare. Suddenly she started to sob convulsively.

'It . . . it was so horrible!' she brought out with difficulty. 'I don't . . . I don't want to think of it . . . I——' Her voice trailed off.

Judge Dee gave a sign to the sergeant. He put his arm round Mrs Liang's shoulders and led her away.

'It's no use!' the judge said resignedly.

Tao Gan pulled at the three long hairs on his left cheek. Then he asked curiously:

'Why are those details of Mrs Liang's flight from the burning redoubt important, Your Honour?'

'There are a few points,' Judge Dee answered, 'that puzzle me. But we can discuss that later. Let's now see first what action we can take against Lin Fan. He is an extremely astute scoundrel, we'll have to formulate our charge with the utmost care.'

'It seems to me, Your Honour,' Sergeant Hoong said, 'that the murder of Liang Ko-fa provides the best approach. That's the most serious charge, if we can convict him on that we needn't bother about his attack on us or about his smuggling!'

The three others nodded their approval, but the judge made no comment. He seemed deep in thought. At last he said:

'Lin Fan had ample time to obliterate the traces of his salt smuggling. I don't think we could assemble sufficient evidence for getting him on that charge. Besides, even if I could make him confess to the smuggling, he'll slip through our fingers. For cases of infringing on the State monopoly are beyond my jurisdiction, they can be dealt with only by the Provincial Court. And that gives Lin Fan time and opportunity to mobilise his friends and relatives on his behalf, and have them distribute bribes wherever they can.

'Further, his attempt at trapping us under the bell is, of course, assault with murderous intent. And on an Imperial official to boot! I must look up the Code, if memory serves such an assault is even termed a crime against the State. Perhaps there's a good opening there.'

He pensively tugged at his moustache.

'But doesn't the murder of Liang Ko-fa provide a much better way of attack?' Tao Gan asked.

Judge Dee slowly shook his head.

'Not with the evidence we have at our disposal now,' he answered. 'We don't know when and how that murder was committed. The records state that Lin Fan closed the temple because of the dissolute behaviour of the monks. He may give a very plausible explanation of the murder, saying, for instance, that Liang Ko-fa while spying on him struck up an acquaintance with the monks. And that it was presumably they who killed him after a gambling quarrel and concealed his body under the bell.'

Ma Joong looked unhappy.

'Since we know,' he said impatiently, 'that Lin Fan is guilty of Heaven knows how many crimes, why bother about legal technicalities? Let's put him in the screws and see whether he won't confess!'

'You forget,' Judge Dee said, 'that Lin Fan is an elderly man. If we subject him to severe torture, he may well die on our hands, and then we would be in serious trouble. No, our only hope is to get more direct proof. During the afternoon session of the tribunal I shall first hear Lin Fan's steward, and the captain of his boat. They are sturdy fellows, if necessary we shall question them with legal severities.

'Now you, Ma Joong, will go with Sergeant Hoong and Tao Gan to the Lin mansion, and institute a thorough search for incriminating documents or other clues. Also——'

Suddenly the door burst open and the warden of the jail came rushing in. He seemed very upset.

He knelt in front of Judge Dee's desk and knocked his forehead on the floor several times in succession.

'Speak up, man!' the judge shouted angrily. 'What has happened?'

'This unworthy person deserves to die!' the warden wailed. 'Early this morning Lin Fan's steward engaged one of my stupid guards in conversation, and the blockhead told him that Lin Fan had been arrested and would be tried for murder. Just now when I inspected the jail I found the steward dead.'

Judge Dee crashed his fist on the table.

'You dogshead!' he barked, 'didn't you search the prisoner for hidden poison and didn't you take his belt away from him?'

'All routine precautions were taken, Your Excellency!' the warden cried. 'The fellow bit his tongue through and bled to death!'

The judge heaved a deep sigh. Then he said in a calmer voice:

'Well, you could not help it. That man is a ruffian of unusual courage, and if such a man decides to kill himself there is little one can do to prevent it. Go back to the jail and have the junk captain chained hands and feet to the wall. Also put a wooden gag between his teeth. I can't afford to lose another witness!'

When the warden had taken his leave, the archivist came back. He unrolled a long scroll, yellowed by age. It was a pictorial map of Poo-yang, painted one hundred and fifty years before.

Pointing to the north-west section of the city Judge Dee said with satisfaction:

'The water passage is clearly marked here! At that time it was an open watercourse, feeding an artificial lake on the site now occupied by the Taoist temple. Later it was covered up, and Lin Fan's mansion was built over it. Lin Fan must have accidentally discovered this subterranean waterway, and found that the house was even more suitable for his smuggling than he had surmised!'

The judge rolled up the map again. Looking at his assistants he said gravely:

'Better be on your way now! I do hope that you find some clues in Lin Fan's mansion, for we sorely need them!'

Sergeant Hoong, Ma Joong and Tao Gan quickly took their leave, but Chiao Tai made no move to depart. He had taken no part in the discussion, but he had been listening intently to every word said. Pensively pulling at his small moustache he now spoke up:

'If I may speak frankly, Your Honour, I received the impression that Your Honour is loath to discuss the murder of Liang Ko-fa.'

Judge Dee shot him a quick look.

'Your impression is correct, Chiao Tai!' he replied calmly. 'I consider discussion of that murder premature. I have a theory about it, but so fantastic that I can hardly believe it. Some time I shall explain it to you and the others. But not now.'

He took a document up from his desk and started reading it. Chiao Tai rose and took his leave.

As soon as the judge was alone he threw the paper on the table. He took from his drawer the thick roll with documents relating to the case Liang *versus* Lin. He started reading it, his forehead creased in a deep frown.

Twenty-third Chapter: A THOROUGH SEARCH IS INSTITUTED
IN A LIBRARY; A CRAB RESTAURANT YIELDS AN IMPORTANT
CLUE

WHEN Sergeant Hoong and his two companions had arrived
at the Lin mansion, they directly went to the library in the
second courtyard. It was a pleasant room with large windows
giving on to an elegant landscape garden.

Tao Gan went immediately to the massive desk of carved
blackwood in front of the window on the right. He looked
casually at the costly set of writing implements standing on its
polished top. Ma Joong tried to pull out the drawer in the
middle. But it would not open although no lock was visible.

'Wait a moment, brother!' Tao Gan said. 'I have been in
Canton, I know the tricks of the cabinet-workers there!'

He ran his sensitive finger-tips along the carving that
decorated the front part of the drawer. He soon found the
hidden spring. As he pulled the drawer out they saw that it
was packed with thick wads of documents.

Tao Gan piled them up on the desk.

'That's your affair, Sergeant!' he said cheerfully.

While the sergeant seated himself in the cushioned arm-
chair in front of the desk, Tao Gan asked Ma Joong to help
him push the heavy couch away from the back wall. He
scrutinised the wall inch by inch. Then they removed the
books from the high shelves, and started examining them.

For a long time there was no sound save the rustling of
papers and the muttered curses of Ma Joong.

At last Sergeant Hoong leaned back in his chair.

'Nothing but straight business correspondence!' he announced disgustedly. 'We'll take the whole lot back to the

245

tribunal for further study, perhaps there are some letters that contain veiled allusions to the smuggling. How are you two getting along?'

Tao Gan shook his head.

'Nothing doing!' he said sourly. 'Let's go on to the bastard's bedroom!'

They sauntered to the back courtyard and entered the room with the trapdoor.

There Tao Gan soon discovered a secret panel in the wall behind Lin Fan's bedstead. But it revealed only the closed door of an iron safe with a most complicated lock. Tao Gan worked on it for a considerable time, but finally gave up.

'We must make Lin Fan tell us how to open it,' he said with a shrug. 'Let's have another look at the corridor and the third courtyard of the temple. That's where the scoundrel stored his salt bags, perhaps some of their contents spilled there.'

Revisiting it in daylight they saw even better than the night before how carefully the place had been cleaned. The mats were swept clean, and the stone flags of the corridor had been gone over with a stiff broom, there was not a speck of dust in the grooves, let alone grains of salt.

The three friends went back to the house in low spirits. They searched the other rooms of the mansion, but without success. They were empty, the furniture had been removed when the womenfolk and the servants left for the south.

Noon was approaching, they felt tired and hungry.

'Last week,' Tao Gan said, 'when I was on guard duty here, one of the constables told me there is a small crab restaurant near the fish-market. They stuff the shells with minced crab-meat mixed with pork and onions, and then steam them. That's a local speciality and said to be delicious!'

'You make my mouth water!' Ma Joong growled. 'Let's hurry!'

The restaurant proved a small two-storied building that

bore the elegant name of 'Kingfisher Pavilion.' A long strip of red cloth hung from the eaves, proclaiming in large characters that choice liquor from the north and south was obtainable there.

When they pulled aside the door-screen they saw a small kitchen. The air was thick with an appetising smell of frying meat and onions. A fat man with naked torso was standing behind an enormous iron pot, armed with a long bamboo ladle. On top of the pot stood a bamboo frame, loaded with piles of stuffed crab shells that were being steamed there. At his side a youngster was busy chopping meat on a large block.

The fat man smiled broadly and shouted:

'Please go upstairs, Excellencies! We shall serve you this very moment!'

Sergeant Hoong ordered three dozen stuffed crabs and three large jugs of wine. Then they climbed the rickety stairs.

When he was half-way up Ma Joong heard a loud noise coming from above. Turning to the Sergeant who was coming up after him he said:

'It seems that there's quite a party going on upstairs!'

But they found the room empty but for one large man who was sitting at the table in front of the window, with his back to them. Bent over the table he was vigorously sucking crab shells, with a prodigious amount of noise. He wore a black damask jacket over his broad shoulders.

Ma Joong motioned to the others to stay behind. He walked up to the table and laid his hand on the fat man's shoulder, saying gruffly:

'It's a long time since we met, brother!'

The man quickly looked up. He had a large, round face, its lower half was completely covered by a thick, greasy beard. He gave Ma Joong a baleful look. Then he turned to his food again, sadly shaking his large head. Idly picking with his forefinger among the empty shells on the table he said with a sigh:

'People like you, brother, make a man lose trust in his fellow beings. The other day I treated you like a friend. Now they say you are a runner of the tribunal. I suspect that it was you who had me and my men chased away from our comfortable quarters in that temple. Use humanity as a yardstick, my friend, and reflect on your behaviour!'

'Come on,' Ma Joong said, 'let there be no ill feeling! Everybody in this world has his allotted task, and mine happens to be to run around in this city for His Excellency the Judge.'

'So the rumour is true!' the fat man said mournfully. 'No, brother, I lost my affection for you. Leave an honest citizen alone while he meditates on the small portions the greedy owner of this dismal inn chooses to dish up.'

'Well,' Ma Joong said jovially, 'as to small portions, if you would favour another dozen stuffed crabs, I and my friends shall be very pleased if you would join us in our meal!'

Sheng Pa slowly wiped his fingers on his beard. After a while he said:

'Well, it shan't be said of me that I can't let bygones be bygones. It will be an honour to meet your friends.'

He rose and Ma Joong introduced him ceremoniously to Sergeant Hoong and Tao Gan. Ma Joong selected a square table and insisted that Sheng Pa take the place of honour with his back against the wall. The Sergeant and Tao Gan sat down on either side of him, and Ma Joong took the seat opposite. He shouted down the stairs for more food and wine.

When the servant had gone down again, and the first round drunk, Ma Joong said:

'I see with pleasure, brother, that you have at last found yourself a nice jacket! That must have cost you a pretty penny, people don't give away stuff of that quality! You must have become a wealthy man!'

Sheng Pa looked uncomfortable. He mumbled something

about the approaching winter, then hastily buried his face in his wine cup.

Ma Joong suddenly rose and knocked the wine cup from his hand. Pushing the table against the wall he barked:

'Speak up, you rascal! Where did you get that jacket?'

Sheng Pa quickly looked left and right. He was pinned against the wall by the table edge pressing into his tremendous paunch, and with Sergeant Hoong and Tao Gan on either side of him there was no means of escape. He heaved a deep sigh and slowly started to loosen his jacket.

'I should have known,' he growled, 'that nobody can expect to eat in peace with you running dogs of the tribunal! Here, take this wretched jacket! This old man shall freeze to death in the coming winter, and little will you people care!'

Seeing Sheng Pa so amenable, Ma Joong sat down again and poured out a cup of wine. He pushed it over to the fat man and said:

'Nothing is farther from me than to inconvenience you, brother. But I must know how you got that black jacket.'

Sheng Pa looked very doubtful. He pensively scratched his hairy chest. Sergeant Hoong now joined the conversation.

'You are a man of the world,' he said affably, 'and you have a rich and varied experience. You doubtless know that it's a wise policy for people in your position to be on good terms with the tribunal. And why shouldn't you? Brother, as a counsellor of the Beggars' Guild you belong, so to speak, to the city administration! Why, I consider you as a colleague!'

Sheng Pa emptied his cup, and Tao Gan quickly refilled it for him. Then he said sadly:

'When pressed hard by both threats and flattery, there is nothing left for a defenceless old man but to tell the simple truth.'

He emptied his cup in one draught, then went on:

'Last night the warden comes and tells us to clear out of the temple yard at once. Did he give us a reason? No! But obedient citizens as we are, we leave. But an hour or so later I come back, for I buried a few strings of cash in a corner of that yard, as an emergency fund, and I feel I shouldn't leave those there.

'I know that yard as the palm of my hand, so I don't need any light. Just when I put the strings in my belt, I see a man coming out of the side gate. I think that must be a low ruffian, for what honest citizen rushes about in the middle of the night?'

Sheng Pa looked expectantly at his companions. When no one made an encouraging comment, he went on resignedly:

'I trip that man up when he comes down the stairs. Heavens, what a mean crook! He scrambles up and pulls a knife on me! In self-defence I knock him down. Do I strip him naked and steal all his possessions? No! I have my principles. So I only take his jacket, meaning to bring it to the warden this afternoon while reporting this case of assault. Then I leave that place, hoping and trusting that the proper authorities will deal with the ruffian in their own good time. That is the whole, unvarnished truth!'

Sergeant Hoong nodded. He said:

'You acted like a good citizen, brother! Now we shan't speak of the cash you found in that jacket, such small things are not mentioned among gentlemen. But what about the personal belongings you found in the sleeves?'

Sheng Pa promptly handed the jacket to the Sergeant.

'Everything you find inside is yours!' he said generously.

Sergeant Hoong went through both sleeves. They were completely empty. But when he ran his fingers along the seam, he felt a small object. He put his hand inside and brought out a small square seal of jade. He showed it to his two friends. They saw that four characters were engraved on it, reading: 'Lin Fan's true seal.'

The Sergeant put it in his sleeve and handed the jacket back to Sheng Pa.

'Keep it,' he said. 'As you said correctly, the man you took it from is a mean criminal. You'll have to go back with us to the tribunal as a witness, but I assure you that you have nothing to fear. Now let us get at those crabs before they grow cold!'

They all fell to with gusto and the piles of empty crab shells rose on the table with astounding speed.

When they had finished Sergeant Hoong paid the bill. Sheng Pa wangled from the owner a ten per cent reduction. Restaurant keepers always give special prices to officials of the Beggars' Guild, for else crowds of repulsive-looking beggars would assemble in front of their door and scare away customers.

Back at the tribunal they took Sheng Pa straight to Judge Dee's private office.

When Sheng Pa saw the judge sitting behind his desk, he raised his hands in astonishment.

'May August Heaven preserve Poo-yang!' he exclaimed horrified. 'Now a fortune-teller has been appointed magistrate over us!'

Sergeant Hoong quickly explained the truth to him. Sheng Pa hastily knelt down in front of the desk.

When the sergeant had handed Lin Fan's seal to the judge and reported what had happened, Judge Dee was exceedingly pleased. He whispered to Tao Gan:

'That's how Lin Fan got wounded! He was attacked by this fat rascal just after he had trapped us under the bell!' To Sheng Pa he said: 'You have made yourself very useful, my man! Now listen carefully. You shall be present during the afternoon session of this tribunal. A certain person shall be brought forward and I shall confront you with him. If that should be

251

the man you fought with last night, you'll say so. Now you can go and rest awhile in the guard house.'

When Sheng Pa had taken his leave, Judge Dee said to his lieutenants:

'Now that I have this additional evidence, I think I can lay a trap for Lin Fan! Since he is a dangerous opponent, we shall place him in as disadvantageous a position as possible. He is not accustomed to being treated as an ordinary criminal, so that is exactly the way we shall treat him! If he loses his temper, I am confident that he'll fall into my trap!'

Sergeant Hoong looked doubtful.

'Wouldn't it be better first to force that safe in his bedroom, Your Honour?' he asked. 'And I also think we should first hear that captain.'

The judge shook his head.

'I know what I am doing,' he replied. 'For this session I only need half a dozen mats from the loft behind the temple. Tell the headman to go now and get them, Sergeant!'

His three assistants looked at each other in blank amazement. But Judge Dee vouchsafed no explanation. After an awkward pause Tao Gan asked:

'But what about the murder charge, Your Honour? We could confront Lin Fan with his own golden locket, found right on the spot!'

Judge Dee's face fell. Knitting his bushy eyebrows, he remained deep in thought for a while. Then he said slowly:

'To tell you the truth, I really don't know what to do about that locket. Let's wait and see what develops during the hearing of Lin Fan.'

The judge unrolled a document on his desk and started reading. Sergeant Hoong gave a sign to Ma Joong and Tao Gan. They silently left the office.

Twenty-fourth Chapter: A WILY CRIMINAL IS CAUGHT BY A CLEVER STRATAGEM; FOUR STATESMEN ENGAGE IN AFTER-DINNER CONVERSATION

THAT afternoon a large crowd of spectators had assembled in the court-hall. The news of the night's commotion in the Temple of Transcendental Wisdom and of the arrest of the wealthy Cantonese merchant had spread already through the town, and the citizens of Poo-yang were eager to know what this was all about.

Judge Dee ascended the dais and called the roll. Then he filled out a form for the warden of the jail. Soon Lin Fan was brought in between two constables. An oil plaster had been pasted over the wound on his forehead.

He did not kneel. He looked sourly at the judge and opened his mouth to say something. The headman immediately hit him on the head with his club and two constables pressed him roughly down on his knees.

'State your name and profession!' ordered Judge Dee.

'I demand to know——' Lin Fan began.

The headman hit him in the face with the handle of his whip.

'Speak respectfully, and answer His Excellency's questions, you dogshead!' he barked at him.

The plaster had become loose, and the wound on Lin Fan's forehead started to bleed profusely. Chafing with rage he brought out:

'This person is called Lin Fan, a merchant from the city of Canton. I demand to know why I was arrested!'

The headman lifted his whip, but Judge Dee shook his head. He said coldly:

'We'll come to that presently. First tell me whether you have seen this object before.'

While speaking the judge pushed the golden locket, found under the bell, over the edge of the bench. It clattered down on the stone floor, in front of Lin Fan.

He gave it a casual look, then suddenly took it up eagerly and examined it in the palm of his hand. He clutched it to his breast.

'This belongs to——' he burst out. But he quickly caught himself up. 'It belongs to me!' he said firmly. 'Who gave it to you?'

'It's the privilege of this court to formulate questions,' the judge replied. He gave a sign to the headman who quickly snatched the locket from Lin Fan's hands and replaced it on the bench. Lin Fan rose, his face livid with fury. He screamed:

'Give it back to me!'

'Kneel down, Lin Fan!' Judge Dee barked. 'I shall now answer your first question.' As Lin Fan slowly knelt again, the judge continued: 'You asked why you were arrested. I, the magistrate, tell you that you are guilty of infringement of the State monopoly. You smuggled salt.'

Lin Fan seemed to regain his composure.

'That's a lie!' he said coldly.

'The wretch is guilty of contempt of court!' Judge Dee shouted. 'Give him ten lashes with the heavy whip!'

Two constables tore Lin Fan's robe down and threw him with his face on the floor. The whip swished through the air.

Lin Fan was wholly unaccustomed to corporal punishment. His screams rose to heaven as the whip tore into his flesh. When the headman dragged him up his face was grey and his breathing came in gasps.

When he had stopped groaning Judge Dee said:

'I have a reliable witness, Lin Fan, who will testify to your smuggling. It won't be easy to extract the testimony from him, but a few lashes with the heavy whip will doubtless make him talk!'

Lin Fan looked up at the judge with bloodshot eyes. He still seemed half dazed. Sergeant Hoong shot a questioning look at Ma Joong and Chiao Tai. They shook their heads. They didn't have the faintest idea about whom the judge was talking. Tao Gan looked dumbfounded.

Judge Dee gave a sign to the headman. He left the hall, followed by two constables.

Deep silence reigned. The eyes of all the spectators were glued on the side door through which the headman had disappeared.

When he came back, he was carrying a roll of black oil-paper. The two constables walked behind him, staggering under heavy rolls of reed mats. An astonished murmur rose from the crowd.

The headman spread the oil-paper out on the floor in front of the bench. The constables unrolled the mats on top of it. As the judge nodded, the three men took their whips and started beating the mats with all their might.

The judge watched them calmly, slowly stroking his long beard.

At last he raised his hand. The three men stopped and wiped the sweat from their brows.

'These mats,' Judge Dee announced, 'were taken up from the floor in a secret storehouse at the back of Lin Fan's mansion. We shall now see what testimony they present to this court!'

The headman rolled the mats up again. Then he took up the oil-paper at one end, motioning the two constables to lift the other side. When they had shaken the sheet to and fro for some time, a small quantity of grey powder had gathered in its centre. The headman scooped up a bit on the point of his sword and presented it to the judge.

Judge Dee touched it with his moistened finger. He tasted it and nodded contentedly.

'Lin Fan,' he said, 'you thought you had obliterated all traces of your smuggling. But you did not realise that however carefully you had the mats swept, a very small quantity of the salt had penetrated into the fibre. It isn't much, but it is enough to prove that you are guilty!'

Loud cheers rose from the crowd.

'Silence!' shouted the judge. He continued to Lin Fan:

'Moreover, there is a second charge pending against you, Lin Fan! Last night you assaulted me and my lieutenants while we were engaged in an investigation of the Temple of Transcendental Wisdom. Confess your crime!'

'Last night,' Lin Fan replied sullenly, 'I was in my mansion nursing a wound received while stumbling in the dark courtyard. I have no idea what Your Honour is talking about!'

'Bring the witness Sheng Pa before me!' shouted the judge at the headman.

Sheng Pa advanced gingerly to the dais, pushed by the constables.

When Lin Fan saw Sheng Pa clad in the black damask jacket, he quickly averted his face.

'Do you know this man?' Judge Dee asked Sheng Pa.

The fat man slowly looked Lin Fan up and down, tugging at his greasy beard. Then he announced ponderously:

'This, Your Honour, is indeed the mean dogshead who attacked me last night in front of the temple.'

'That's a lie!' Lin Fan shouted angrily. 'It was that scoundrel who assaulted me!'

'This witness,' Judge Dee said calmly, 'had hidden himself in the first courtyard of the temple. He saw how you spied there on me and my lieutenants. And when we were standing under the bronze bell, he saw clearly how you took up the iron spear and wrenched the stone barrel away.'

Judge Dee gave a sign to the headman to lead Sheng Pa away. Then he leaned back in his chair and continued in a conversational tone:

'You see now, Lin Fan, that you can't deny having assaulted me. When I have punished you for that crime, I shall have you forwarded to the Provincial Court, to answer the charge of infringement on the State monopoly!'

When he heard these last words, an evil gleam came into Lin Fan's eyes. He remained silent for a while, licking his bleeding lips. He heaved a deep sigh. Then he began in a low voice:

'Your Honour, I now realise that there is no use in denying my guilt. That I assaulted Your Honour was a foolish and mischievous prank, for which I here offer my sincere apologies. The fact is, however, that during the last days I had felt very annoyed at the vexatious measures the tribunal had been taking against me. When last night I heard voices in the temple compound and went to investigate, I saw Your Honour and his assistants standing under the bell. I gave way to a wicked impulse to teach Your Honour a lesson, and wrenched the stone barrel away. Then I rushed back to summon my steward and the servants to liberate Your Honour. I planned to apologise then to you, and explain that I had thought you and your lieutenants were marauders. But when I reached the iron connecting door I found to my consternation that it had slammed shut. In great fear that Your Honour would suffocate under the bell, I ran to the front gate of the temple meaning to go back to my house through the street. But on the front steps I was knocked down by that wretched footpad. When I had regained consciousness I ran home as quickly as I could. I ordered my steward to go at once and set Your Honour free. I myself stayed behind for a few moments to put a salve on my head-wound. When Your Honour suddenly appeared in my bedroom in a . . . slightly unusual attire,

I thought you were another intruder trying to intimidate me. This is the complete truth.

'I repeat that I deeply regret my childish prank that so easily could have turned into a fearful tragedy, and I shall gladly undergo the punishment prescribed by the law.'

'Well,' Judge Dee said indifferently, 'I am glad that you confessed at last. You'll now listen to the scribe as he reads out your statement.'

The senior scribe read out aloud Lin Fan's confession. Judge Dee seemed to have lost interest in the proceedings. He leaned back in his chair, idly caressing his side-whiskers.

When the scribe had finished, the judge asked the formal question:

'Do you agree that this is your true confession?'

'I agree!' Lin Fan answered in a firm voice. The headman presented the document to him, and Lin Fan impressed his thumb-mark on it.

Suddenly Judge Dee leaned forward.

'Lin Fan, Lin Fan!' he said in a terrible voice, 'for many years you have eluded the law, but now the law has caught up with you and you shall perish! Just now you have signed your own death warrant.

'You know very well that the punishment for assault is eighty blows with the bamboo, and you hoped you could ensure that it would be soft blows by bribing my constables. Thereafter, when brought before the Provincial Court, you knew that your powerful friends would start action on your behalf, and that you would probably be let off with a heavy fine.

'Now I, the magistrate, tell you that you will never appear before the Provincial Court! Your head, Lin Fan, will fall on the execution ground, outside the south gate of the city of Poo-yang!'

Lin Fan lifted his head and stared at the judge with unbelieving eyes.

'The Code states,' Judge Dee continued, 'that high treason, parricide and crimes against the State shall be punished with the extreme penalty in one of its more severe forms. Mark those words "crimes against the State," Lin Fan! For elsewhere the Code observes that assaulting an official in the execution of his duty is equivalent to a crime against the State. I don't hesitate to admit that it is doubtful whether the lawmaker intended these two passages to be read in connection with each other. But in this particular case I, the magistrate, choose to interpret the law according to its letter.

'The charge of a crime against the State is the most serious one that can be made, and must be reported by courier directly to the Metropolitan Court. No one shall be able to interfere on your behalf. Justice will take its course, a course which in your case ends in an ignominious death.'

Judge Dee let his gavel descend on the bench.

'Since you, Lin Fan, of your own free will confessed to having assaulted your magistrate, I pronounce you guilty of a crime against the State, and propose for you the extreme penalty!'

Lin Fan rose tottering to his feet. The headman quickly draped his robe again over his bleeding back. For a man condemned to death is treated with courtesy.

Suddenly a soft but very clear voice spoke up by the side of the dais:

'Lin Fan, look at me!'

Judge Dee leaned forward. Mrs Liang was standing there, stiffly erect. The load of the years seemed to have fallen from her, she seemed suddenly much younger.

A long shudder shook Lin Fan's body. He wiped the blood from his face. Then his still eyes grew very wide, his lips started moving but no sound came forth.

Mrs Liang slowly lifted her hand and pointed accusingly at Lin Fan.

'You murdered——' she began. 'You murdered your——'
Suddenly her voice trailed off. She bent her head. Wringing
her hands she began again in a faltering voice: 'You murdered
your——'

She slowly shook her head. She lifted her tear-stained face
and gave Lin Fan a long look. Then she started to sway on her
feet.

Lin Fan stepped up to her but the headman was too quick
for him. He grabbed him and pinned his arms behind his back.
As two constables dragged him away, Mrs Liang fell down in
a swoon.

Judge Dee let his gavel descend on the bench and declared
the session closed.

Ten days after this session of the tribunal in Poo-yang, the
Grand Secretary of State happened to entertain three guests at
an informal dinner in the main hall of his palace in the Imperial
capital.

Late autumn was changing into early winter. The triple
doors of the spacious hall were open so that the guests could
enjoy the view of the palace garden where a lotus lake
glittered in the moonlight. Large bronze braziers heaped with
glowing coals stood near the dining-table.

All four were men of over sixty, grown grey in the service
of the State.

They were gathered around a table of carved blackwood,
loaded with rare delicacies in dishes of the finest porcelain. A
dozen servants were attending upon them, supervised by the
intendant of the Palace, who saw to it that the cups of solid
gold were never empty.

The Secretary had given the place of honour to the President
of the Metropolitan Court, a heavy man of imposing mien
with long, grey side-whiskers. On his other side he had the
Imperial Master of Ceremonies, a thin man with a slight stoop,

acquired by being every day in the Imperial Presence. Opposite sat a tall greybeard with piercing eyes. This was the Imperial Censor Kwang, feared all over the Empire because of his uncompromising honesty and his fierce sense of justice.

The dinner was nearing its end, they were lingering over their last cup of wine. The official matters which the Secretary had wanted to discuss with his friends had been disposed of during the dinner, now they engaged in desultory conversation.

The Secretary let his silvery beard glide through his thin fingers and said to the President:

'The scandalous affair in that Buddhist temple in Poo-yang has deeply shocked His Imperial Majesty. Four days in succession His Holiness the Chief Abbot has been pleading the cause of his church before the Throne, but in vain.

'I may tell you in strict confidence that the Throne will announce tomorrow that the Chief Abbot has been relieved of his duties as a member of the Grand Council. At the same time it will be announced that Buddhist institutions shall no longer be exempt from taxation. This, my friends, signifies that the Buddhist clique shall not meddle any more in national affairs!'

The President nodded and said:

'Sometimes a lucky chance permits a petty official to perform unwittingly a great service to the State. The local magistrate, a certain Dee, acted very rashly indeed in attacking that large and wealthy monastery. With the situation as it was till recently, the entire Buddhist clique would have risen in anger and that magistrate would have perished before he could have closed the case. But it so happened that on that very day the garrison was away, and the angry mob killed the monks. That fellow Dee doesn't realise that this lucky coincidence saved his career, if not his very life!'

'I am glad, President,' the Censor spoke, 'that you mention

that magistrate Dee, for that reminds me of something. I still have on my desk the reports of two other cases solved by that same man. One was a rape-murder committed by a vagrant ruffian, quite a simple case that needs no comment. The other concerned a wealthy merchant from Canton. Here I found myself in complete disagreement with his verdict, based on nothing but a legal trick. Since, however, the report has been initialled by you and your colleagues of the Court, I presume there were special circumstances. I would appreciate it if you would kindly enlighten me.'

The President put down his wine cup. He said with a smile:

'That, my friend, is a long story! Many years ago I sat as junior judge in the Provincial Court of Kwantung. At that time the presiding judge was that despicable Fang, who later was beheaded here in the capital for embezzling Government funds. I saw that merchant escape the just punishment for an atrocious crime by paying a heavy bribe. Thereafter he committed other sordid crimes, including a ninefold murder.

'That magistrate of Poo-yang knew that he had to dispose of the case quickly, for he knew the influence those wealthy Cantonese merchants have in Government circles. He did not try, therefore, to formulate a major charge but managed to make the criminal confess to a minor offence, but one that could be construed as a crime against the State. Since we thought it most fitting that a man who during more than twenty years had been cheating the law was finally caught by a legal technicality, we unanimously decided to uphold the magistrate's verdict.'

'Quite,' the Censor said. 'Now I understand. I shall initial the report first thing tomorrow morning.'

The Master of Ceremonies had been listening with interest to this conversation. Now he said:

'I am not an expert in judicial affairs, but I understand that this magistrate Dee solved two cases which proved of national importance. One made a breach in the power of the Buddhist clique, the other strengthened the Government's position with those haughty Cantonese merchants. Should that man not be promoted to a higher office in order to give him more scope for exercising his talents?'

The Secretary slowly shook his head.

'That magistrate,' he said, 'is probably barely forty years old, a long official career lies before him. In the ensuing years he'll have ample opportunity to prove his zeal and ability. If promotion comes too late, it embitters; if too soon, it gives rise to exorbitant expectations. In the interest of our civil service both extremes should be avoided.'

'I quite agree,' the President said. 'On the other hand that magistrate might well be granted some token of official approval, just as an encouragement. Perhaps the Master of Ceremonies will favour us with suggesting a suitable gesture.'

The Master of Ceremonies pensively stroked his beard. Then he said:

'Since His Imperial Majesty has graciously consented to take a personal interest in the case of that Buddhist Temple, I shall be glad to petition the Throne tomorrow to grant that magistrate Dee an Imperial Inscription. Not, of course, the August Handwriting itself, but a copy of some suitable text, engraved on an ornamental board.'

'That,' the Secretary exclaimed with approval, 'exactly meets the requirements of the case! How delicate is your judgement in these matters!'

The Master of Ceremonies permitted himself one of his rare smiles.

'Rites and Ceremonies,' he observed, 'keep our complicated government machinery in the correct balance. For many years I have been engaged in weighing against each other praise and blame, censure and recognition, as carefully as a goldsmith weighs his gold. One grain of difference would be sufficient for tipping the beam.'

They rose and left the table.

Led by the Grand Secretary of State they descended the broad stairs for a stroll around the lotus lake.

Twenty-fifth Chapter: TWO CRIMINALS ARE EXECUTED
OUTSIDE THE SOUTHERN GATE; JUDGE DEE KNEELS DOWN
BEFORE AN IMPERIAL INSCRIPTION

++

WHEN the final verdict on the three cases arrived from the
capital, Judge Dee's four assistants had a dull and frustrating
fortnight behind them.

Ever since the sensational session when Lin Fan was convicted, the judge had been in a morose mood, silently brooding
over a problem the four men could only guess at. Instead of
leisurely reviewing the case with them as was his wont after he
had obtained a criminal's confession, Judge Dee had only
expressed his appreciation of their loyal service, then immediately buried himself in the routine affairs of the district
administration.

The special messenger from the capital arrived in the
afternoon. Tao Gan, who was auditing the accounts of the
tribunal in the chancery, signed the receipt for the bulky
envelope, and took it to Judge Dee's private office.

Sergeant Hoong sat waiting there for the judge with some
documents to be signed, and Ma Joong and Chiao Tai were
keeping him company.

Tao Gan showed them the large seal of the Metropolitan
Court on the envelope, then he threw it on the desk saying
happily:

'This'll be the final verdict on our three cases, brothers!
Now the judge'll cheer up a bit!'

'I don't think,' the sergeant said, 'that our judge is worrying
about the higher authorities approving his conduct of the
cases. He never said a word to me about what is weighing on

his mind, but I believe it's something very personal, something he is trying in vain to puzzle out for himself.'

'Well,' Ma Joong put in, 'I know one person who'll suddenly recover as soon as the judge has pronounced his final verdict! And that's the old lady, Mrs Liang! Of course our dear Board of Finance will help itself to a generous chunk of Lin Fan's property, but what'll be assigned to Mrs Liang should still make her one of the richest women in the land!'

'She deserves it!' Chiao Tai remarked. 'It was sad to see her collapse the other day, the very hour of her triumph! Evidently the excitement was too much for her, it seems she has not been able to leave her bed these last two weeks.'

At that moment Judge Dee came in and all rose quickly. He curtly greeted his lieutenants, then opened the sealed envelope Sergeant Hoong handed to him.

Glancing through its contents he said:

'The higher authorities have approved my verdicts in the three capital cases we dealt with. A terrible fate awaits Lin Fan. In my opinion simple decapitation would have met the case. But we must abide by the official decision.'

Then the judge read the enclosure, which bore the seal of the Board of Rites and Ceremonies. Having passed the documents to Sergeant Hoong, Judge Dee bowed respectfully in the direction of the capital.

'A signal honour has been bestowed upon this tribunal,' he said. 'His Imperial Majesty has deigned to grant an ornamental board, bearing the engraved copy of an inscription originally written by the Vermilion Brush. As soon as this Imperial favour arrives, Sergeant, you'll see to it that it is immediately suspended in the place of honour, over the dais in the court-hall!'

Brushing aside the congratulations of his men, the judge continued:

'I shall pronounce the sentences tomorrow morning in a

special session two hours before dawn, as usual. Give the necessary instructions to the personnel, Sergeant, and inform the garrison commander that I want a military escort here at the appointed time for conveying the criminals to the execution ground.'

Judge Dee thought for a while, tugging at his beard. Then he sighed and opened the dossier on the district finances that Sergeant Hoong had placed on his desk for his signature.

Tao Gan pulled at Sergeant Hoong's sleeve. Ma Joong and Chiao Tai nodded encouragingly. The sergeant cleared his throat, then he addressed the judge:

'All of us, Your Honour, have been wondering about Lin Fan's murder of Liang Ko-fa. Would Your Honour, now that the case will be officially closed tomorrow morning, favour us with an explanation?'

Judge Dee looked up.

'Tomorrow, directly after the execution of the criminals,' he replied curtly. Then he turned again to his reading.

The next morning, long before the appointed hour, the citizens of Poo-yang had been streaming to the tribunal through the dark streets. Now a dense crowd was waiting patiently in front of the main gate.

At last the constables threw the large double doors open and the throng entered the court-hall, lighted by dozens of large candles placed along the walls. A murmur of subdued conversation rose from the crowd. Many cast apprehensive eyes on the giant who stood motionless behind the headman of the constables. He carried a long, two-handed sword on his broad shoulders.

Most of the spectators had come because they were eager to hear the final verdict on the three cases that had occurred in their midst. Some of the elder people, however, had come with a heavy heart. They knew how serious a view the Government took of sedition, and the massacre of the monks could easily be interpreted as such. They feared that the central authorities would have decided on punitive measures against their district.

Three deep sounds of the large bronze gong boomed through the tribunal.

The screen behind the dais was pulled aside and Judge Dee appeared, followed by his four assistants. A scarlet pelerine hung over his shoulders, signifying that he would deliver capital sentences.

Judge Dee seated himself and called the roll. Then Hwang San was led before the bench.

During the period of waiting in jail his wounds had healed. He had been given the last meal of roast, and he seemed resigned to his fate.

As he knelt in front of the bench, Judge Dee unrolled a document and read aloud:

'The criminal Hwang San shall be decapitated on the execution ground. His body shall be cut into pieces and thrown to the dogs. His head shall be exposed on the city gate three days, as a warning example.'

Hwang San's arms were bound behind his back. The constables attached a long white signboard to his shoulders, on which his name, his crime and his punishment were written in large characters. Then he was led away.

The senior scribe handed Judge Dee another document. Unrolling it he ordered the headman:

'Bring before me His Reverence Complete Enlightenment, and the two Yang sisters!'

The headman led the old abbot forward. He wore the purple robe with the yellow seams indicating his ecclesiastical rank. Laying the crooked staff of red lacquer on which he supported himself on the floor, he slowly knelt.

Apricot and Blue Jade were led in by Judge Dee's steward. They wore green robes with long trailing sleeves, and their hair was bound up with a band of embroidered silk, the coiffure of unmarried girls. The crowd stared with admiration at these two beautiful girls.

Judge Dee spoke:

'I shall now read the verdict in the case of the Temple of Boundless Mercy.

'The Government have decided that the entire property of the said temple shall be confiscated. Except for the main hall and one side hall, the entire temple compound shall be razed to the ground within a period of seven days from the date of the present.

'His Reverence Complete Enlightenment is allowed to continue serving the goddess, assisted by not more than four monks.

'Since the judicial investigation has proved that two of the six pavilions in the said temple compound were not provided with a secret entrance, it is herewith stated that the fact that a woman conceived during her stay in the temple is to be taken as due only to the infinite grace of the Goddess Kwan Yin and shall never be construed as casting doubt on the legitimacy of the child subsequently born.

'Four bars of gold shall be taken from the treasury of the temple and conferred as a reward on the girl Yang, called Apricot, and her sister. The magistrate of their native district has been ordered to add in the district register a remark to the entry regarding the Yang family reading "Well deserved of the State." As a consequence of this official recommendation the said Yang family shall be exempt from all taxes for a period of fifty years.'

Here Judge Dee paused a moment. Stroking his beard he surveyed the audience. Then he went on slowly, stressing each word:

'The Imperial Government note with profound displeasure that the citizens of Poo-yang have dared to infringe on the prerogative of the State and have wantonly attacked and foully murdered twenty monks, thus preventing the law from taking its normal course. The entire city is held responsible for this outrage. The Government originally contemplated severe punitive measures. Having taken cognisance, however, of the special circumstances of the case, and of the recommendation for leniency proffered by the magistrate of Poo-yang, the Government have decided that, in this particular case and as an exception, mercy shall prevail over justice. The Government confine themselves to a severe warning.'

A murmur of gratitude rose from the crowd. Some started to cheer the judge.

'Silence!' Judge Dee called out in a thunderous voice.

As the judge slowly rolled up the document the old abbot and the two girls knocked their foreheads on the floor several times in succession to express their gratitude. Then they were led away.

Judge Dee gave a sign to the headman. Lin Fan was led before the bench by two constables.

He had aged considerably during the period of waiting in jail. His small eyes were sunk deeply in his emaciated face. When he saw the scarlet pelerine on Judge Dee's shoulders and the forbidding shape of the executioner, he started to tremble so violently that the constables had to assist him in kneeling before the dais.

Folding his arms in his sleeves Judge Dee straightened himself in his arm-chair and then read slowly:

'The criminal Lin Fan has been found guilty of a crime against the State, for which the law prescribes the extreme penalty in one of its more severe forms. Accordingly the said criminal Lin shall be executed by the process of being quartered alive.'

Lin Fan uttered a hoarse cry. He collapsed on the floor. While the headman started to revive him by burning vinegar under his nose, the judge continued:

'All movable and immovable property of the said criminal Lin, and all his liquid and vested assets are confiscated by the State. When the transfer has been completed, one-half of the said property shall be given to Mrs Liang née Ou-yang, as a compensation for the manifold wrongs that her house suffered at the hands of the criminal Lin Fan.'

Judge Dee paused and surveyed the hall. Mrs Liang did not seem to be among the audience.

'This,' he concluded, 'is the official verdict on the case of the State *versus* Lin Fan. Since the criminal shall die and blood money be paid to the house of Liang, this also closes the case Liang *versus* Lin.'

He rapped his gavel and closed the session.

As Judge Dee left the dais to return to his private office, the spectators burst out in loud cheers. Then everyone tried to get outside and into the street as quickly as possible, in order to accompany the cart of the condemned to the execution ground.

The open cart stood ready in front of the main gate, surrounded by lance knights from the garrison headquarters. Eight constables brought Lin Fan and Hwang San outside, and made them stand side by side in the cart.

'Make way, make way!' shouted the guards.

Judge Dee's palankeen was carried out, preceded by a group of constables marching in rows of four. A similar group brought up the rear. They were followed by the cart of the condemned, surrounded by the soldiers. The procession set into movement, headed for the southern city gate.

Arrived on the execution ground the judge descended from his palankeen and the garrison commander, resplendent in his shiny armour, led him to the temporary dais which had been erected during the night. Judge Dee seated himself behind the bench, and his four lieutenants took up their places by his side.

The executioner's two assistants made Lin Fan and Hwang San descend from the cart. The soldiers dismounted and drew a cordon round them, their halberds glittered in the red glow of dawn.

A large crowd thronged around the cordon. They looked with awe at four heavy plough buffaloes that were standing there, quietly eating the cut grass that a peasant was feeding them.

On a sign of the judge the two assistants made Hwang San kneel. They removed the placard from his back and loosened his collar. The executioner lifted his heavy sword and looked up at the judge. As Judge Dee nodded the sword swung down on Hwang San's neck.

He fell on his face through the force of the blow, but his head was only partly severed from his body. Either his bones were exceptionally thick, or the executioner had failed to take accurate aim.

A murmur rose from the crowd. Ma Joong whispered to Sergeant Hoong:

'The fellow was right! Till his very last moment the poor bastard has bad luck!'

The two assistants jerked Hwang San up and now the executioner struck such a ferocious blow that the head flew through the air and crazily rolled several feet from the bleeding body.

The executioner lifted the head up in front of the bench, and Judge Dee marked its forehead with his vermilion brush. Then it was thrown into a basket, later to be nailed by its hair to the city gate.

Lin Fan was led to the centre of the execution ground. The assistants cut the ropes that held his hands. When he saw the four buffaloes he uttered a piercing scream and started to grapple with the men. But the executioner gripped his neck and threw him on the ground. His assistants attached thick ropes to his wrists and ankles.

The executioner beckoned to the old peasant. He led the

four buffaloes to the centre. Judge Dee bent over to the commander and whispered something to him. The commander barked an order, and the soldiers formed a closed square round the group in the centre so that the crowd could not see the gruesome scene that would be enacted there. They looked at the judge, sitting up on the raised platform.

Deep silence reigned on the execution ground. One could faintly hear a cock crow on a distant farm.

Judge Dee nodded.

Suddenly they heard Lin Fan scream wildly. Then his screams turned into deep groans.

There was the soft whistling peasants use to coax buffaloes on. This sound, reminding one of a peaceful scene on the rice-fields, now made the crowd shudder with intense horror.

Lin Fan's screams again rent the air, now mixed with a madman's laughter. There was a dry sound, as if a tree was splitting apart.

The soldiers resumed their original position. The spectators saw the executioner cut off Lin Fan's head from his mangled body. He presented it to the judge who marked its forehead with his brush. Later it would be exposed on the city gate, together with the head of Hwang San.

The executioner handed the old peasant a silver piece, as is customary. But he spat and refused that unlucky money, although it is not often that silver passes over the palm of a peasant's hand.

Gongs were sounded, the soldiers presented their arms and Judge Dee left the dais. His lieutenants noticed that his face was ashen, sweat pearled on his brow despite the cold morning air.

Judge Dee ascended his palankeen and was carried to the temple of the tutelary deity of Poo-yang, where he burned incense and prayed. Then he went back to the tribunal.

Upon entering his private office he found his four assistants waiting for him. The judge silently motioned to Sergeant

273

Hoong, who quickly poured out a cup of hot tea for him. As he sipped it slowly, suddenly the door opened and the headman came in.

'Your Honour!' he said excitedly. 'Mrs Liang has committed suicide by swallowing poison!'

There were loud exclamations from Judge Dee's lieutenants, but the judge didn't seem surprised. He ordered the headman to go there with the coroner, and have the latter draw up a death certificate, stating that Mrs Liang committed suicide while of unsound mind. Then the judge leaned back in his chair and said in a toneless voice:

'Thus at long last the case Liang *versus* Lin has now been concluded. The last living member of the house of Lin died on the execution ground, the only surviving member of the Liang clan committed suicide. For nearly thirty years the feud dragged on, a dreadful chain of murder, rape, arson and base deceit. And this is the end. All are dead.'

The judge stared straight ahead of him. His four assistants looked at him with wide eyes. No one dared to speak.

Suddenly the judge roused himself. He folded his arms in his sleeves and began in a matter-of-fact voice:

'When I studied this case I was at once struck by a curious inconsistency. I knew that Lin Fan was a ruthless criminal, I knew that Mrs Liang was his main opponent. I knew that Lin had done his utmost to destroy her—but only until she came to Poo-yang. I asked myself: why didn't he kill her here? Until recently Lin Fan had all his henchmen with him here, he could have had her murdered easily, and make it appear as if it had been an accident. He didn't hesitate to kill here Liang Ko-fa, he didn't hesitate one moment when he thought he could murder me and the four of you. But he didn't lift a finger against Mrs Liang—after she had come to Poo-yang. I was greatly puzzled by this. Then the golden locket we found under the bronze bell supplied a clue.

'Since the locket was marked with the surname Lin, all of you assumed that it was Lin Fan's. But such lockets are worn by a cord round the neck, on the bare skin under the clothes. If the cord breaks, the locket will drop in the bosom. Lin Fan couldn't have lost it. Since it was found near the skeleton's neck I concluded it belonged to the murdered man. Lin Fan didn't see it because his victim wore it under his clothes. It came to light only when the termites had devoured the clothes, and the cord it had been attached with to the man's neck. I suspected that the skeleton was not that of Liang Ko-fa, but of a person bearing the same surname as his murderer.'

Judge Dee paused and quickly emptied his tea-cup. Then he went on:

'I reread my own notes on the case and found a second indication that the murdered man was someone else. Liang Ko-fa must have been about thirty years old when he came to Poo-yang. The person Mrs Liang registered under this name was indeed stated to be thirty years old, but the warden told Tao Gan that he seemed rather a youngster of about twenty.

'Then I began to suspect Mrs Liang. I thought she might well be another woman, resembling Mrs Liang and knowing everything about the old feud. A woman who hated Lin Fan as much as Mrs Liang, but a woman whom Lin Fan didn't want or didn't dare to harm. I again studied the records of the feud she had given me, and tried to find a woman and a youngster that could have posed as Mrs Liang and her grandson. Then I formed a theory which at first I considered utterly fantastic, but which was confirmed by the facts that subsequently came to light.

'You'll remember that the records state that soon after Lin Fan had raped Mrs Liang Hoong, his own wife disappeared. It was surmised that Lin Fan had murdered her. But no evidence was given and the body was never found. I now knew that Lin Fan did not kill her. She left him. She had been deeply in love with him, so deeply that she could perhaps have forgiven him for his murdering her brother, and causing the death of her father. For a woman shall follow and obey her husband. But when her husband fell in love with her sister-in-law, her love changed into hatred, the terrible hatred of a woman scorned.

'Having resolved to leave her husband and take revenge on him, what was more natural than that she would secretly approach her old mother, Mrs Liang, and offer to join her in her attempts to bring Lin Fan to ruin? Mrs Lin had dealt her husband already a cruel blow by leaving him. For, strange as it may seem to you, my friends, Lin Fan loved her dearly. His desire for Mrs Liang Hoong had only been a perverse whim, that did not affect his love for his wife—the only restraint this hard and cruel man ever knew.

'After he had lost her, Lin Fan's evil nature asserted itself, he became ever more violent in his persecution of the Liang family. Finally he had them killed in the old fortress. All perished there, including old Mrs Liang, and her grandson Liang Ko-fa.'

Tao Gan began to speak, but Judge Dee raised his hand.

'Mrs Lin,' he went on, 'continued where her old mother had left off. Being completely in her mother's confidence, and being naturally conversant with all the affairs of the Liang family, it was not difficult for her to pose as Mrs Liang. I presume there was a family likeness, she only had to make herself look older than she was. Moreover, her mother must have been expecting new attacks by Lin Fan, and entrusted to her daughter all documents relating to the feud for safe keeping, before she went to the old fortress.

'Soon thereafter Mrs Lin must have revealed to Lin Fan her identity. This blow hit him even harder than the first. His wife had not perished, she had left him, and she had declared herself his sworn enemy. He could not denounce her personation—

what man with any pride left would admit that his own wife had turned against him? Besides, he loved her. The only thing he could do was to hide himself from her. Thus he fled here to Poo-yang, and when she continued to harass him, he prepared to flee again to somewhere else.

'Mrs Lin had told Lin Fan the truth about herself, but she had lied to him about the youngster who was with her. She told Lin Fan it was Liang Ko-fa. This brings me to the most unbelievable, the most inhuman part of this dark, inhuman tragedy. Mrs Lin's lie was part of a fiendish scheme more repulsive in its subtle cruelty than any of Lin Fan's own barbarous crimes. The youngster was her own son, begotten by Lin Fan.'

Now all four men started to speak, but again the judge silenced them by raising his hand.

'When Lin Fan raped Mrs Liang Hoong, he didn't know that his wife, after all those years of frustration, had just become pregnant. I wouldn't presume, my friends, that I can gauge the deepest secrets of a woman's soul. But I take it that Lin Fan going to another woman just at the time which Mrs Lin considered as the climax of their married love, inspired her with that maniacal and inhuman hatred. I say inhuman, because she sacrificed her own son in order to be able to deal Lin Fan, after she would have succeeded in ruining him, one last, shattering blow. She would tell him that he had murdered his own son.

'Doubtless she had convinced the youngster that he was indeed Liang Ko-fa, by telling him, for instance, that the young children had been exchanged in order to protect him better against Lin Fan's attacks. But she made him wear the locket that Lin Fan had given her on their wedding day.

'I am telling you this fearful tale as I could finally complete it for myself during my hearing of Lin Fan. Till then it was but a vague theory. The first confirmation was Lin Fan's reaction when I showed him the locket; he nearly said that it belonged to his wife. The second and final confirmation came during those brief, pathetic moments when man and wife stood facing each other before my bench. Mrs Lin's supreme moment had at last arrived, the goal she had been working for so assiduously had been reached: her husband was ruined, he would perish on the execution ground. Now the time had come to deal him the blow that would break his heart. Raising her hand in accusation she began: "You murdered your——" But then she found she couldn't bring out those last two words that would complete the terrible sentence "You murdered your own son." When she saw her husband standing there covered with blood, at last defeated, all her hatred suddenly left her. She saw only the husband she had loved. When, overcome by emotion, she started swaying on her feet, Lin Fan rushed towards her. Not to attack her, as the headman and everyone else thought. I saw the look in his eyes, I know that he only wanted to support her, to prevent her from falling and hurting herself on the stone floor.

'That is all. You'll now understand the difficult position I found myself in, already before I heard Lin Fan. I had arrested him, and I had to convict him quickly, and without utilising his murdering his son. It would have taken months to prove Mrs Lin's usurping Mrs Liang's identity. Therefore I had to try to trap Lin Fan and make him confess his assault on us.

'But his confession didn't solve my quandary. The central authorities would certainly assign a major part of Lin Fan's confiscated property to the supposed Mrs Liang. I could never allow the pseudo Mrs Liang to obtain that property which rightfully belonged to the State. I was waiting for her to approach me, for she must have suspected that I knew the truth when I started questioning her about details of the flight from the burning redoubt. When she didn't come, I feared I would be obliged to take legal action against her. Now also that problem is solved. Mrs Lin decided to kill herself. But she waited because she wished to die on the same day and the same hour as her husband. And now Heaven shall judge her.'

Deep silence reigned in the room.

Judge Dee shivered. Pulling his robes closer he said:

'Winter is approaching, there's a chill in the air. On your way out, Sergeant, you might tell the clerks to prepare a brazier.'

When his four assistants had left, Judge Dee rose. He went over to the side-table with the cap-mirror to take off his winged judge's cap. The mirror reflected his haggard, tortured face.

Automatically he folded the cap up and placed it in the drawer of the mirror stand. He put on his house cap, and started pacing the floor, his hands behind his back.

He tried desperately to compose his mind. But as soon as he had succeeded in diverting his troubled thoughts from the horrors he had just related, there rose before his mind's eye the gruesome sight of the mangled bodies of the twenty monks, and the mad laughter of Lin Fan as his limbs were torn apart began to ring again in his ears. He asked himself in despair how August Heaven could will such inhuman suffering, such sickening bloodshed.

Torn by doubt he stood still in front of his desk, he buried his face in his hands.

When he lowered his hands his eye fell on the letter from the Board of Rites and Ceremonies. With a forlorn sigh he remembered his duty to verify whether the clerks had placed the board in the proper place.

He pulled aside the screen that separated his private office from the court-hall. Walking past the dais he stepped down into the hall, and turned round.

He saw the bench covered with scarlet cloth, and his empty arm-chair. He saw behind it the screen with the large embroidered unicorn, the symbol of perspicacity. And as he looked higher, he saw on the wall above the canopy over the dais, the horizontal board with the Imperial Words.

When he read them he felt deeply moved. He knelt on the bare flagstones. All alone in the cold, empty hall he remained so for a long time, in earnest and humble prayer.

High up above him the morning sun coming through the windows shone on four large gilded characters, written in the Emperor's faultless calligraphy:

'Justice outweighs human life.'

JUDGE DEE KNEELS BEFORE AN IMPERIAL INSCRIPTION

POSTSCRIPT

A FEATURE all old Chinese detective stories have in common is that the role of detective is always played by the magistrate of the district where the crime occurred.

This official is in charge of the entire administration of the district under his jurisdiction, usually comprising one walled city and the countryside around it for fifty miles or so. The magistrate's duties are manifold. He is fully responsible for the collection of taxes, the registration of births, deaths and marriages, keeping up to date the land registration, the maintenance of the peace, etc., while as presiding judge of the local tribunal he is charged with the apprehension and punishing of criminals and the hearing of all civil and criminal cases. Since the magistrate thus supervises practically every phase of the daily life of the people, he is commonly referred to as the 'father-and-mother official.'

The magistrate is a permanently overworked official. He lives with his family in separate quarters right inside the compound of the tribunal, and as a rule spends his every waking hour upon his official duties.

The district magistrate is at the bottom of the colossal pyramidal structure of ancient Chinese government organisation. He must report to the prefect, who supervises twenty or more districts. The prefect reports to the provincial governor, who is responsible for a dozen or so prefectures. The governor in his turn reports to the central authorities in the capital, with the Emperor at the top.

Every citizen in the Empire, whether rich or poor and regardless of his social background, could enter official life and become a district magistrate by passing the literary examinations. In this respect the Chinese system was already a rather democratic one at a time when Europe was still under feudal rule.

A magistrate's term of office was usually three years. Thereafter he was transferred to another district, to be in due time promoted to prefect. Promotion was selective, being based solely on actual performance; less gifted men often spent the greater part of their lives as district magistrate.

In exercising his general duties the magistrate was assisted by the permanent personnel of the tribunal, such as the constables, the scribes, the warden of the jail, the coroner, the guards and the runners. Those, however, only perform their routine duties. They are not concerned with the detection of crimes.

This task is performed by the magistrate himself, assisted by three or four trusted helpers; these he selects at the beginning of his career and they accompany him to whatever post he goes. These assistants are placed over the other personnel of the tribunal. They have no local connections and are therefore less liable to let themselves be influenced in their work by personal considerations. For the same reason it is a fixed rule that no official shall ever be appointed magistrate in his own native district.

The present novel gives a general idea of ancient Chinese court procedure. The illustrations facing p. 50 and 280 show the arrangement of the court-hall. When the court is in session, the judge sits behind the bench, with his assistants and the scribes standing by his side. The bench is a high table covered with a piece of red cloth that hangs down in front from the top of the table to the floor of the raised dais.

On this bench one always sees the same implements: an inkstone for rubbing black and vermilion ink, two writing brushes, and a number of thin bamboo spills in a tubular holder. These staves are used to mark the number of blows that a criminal receives. If the constables are to give ten blows, the judge will take ten markers and throw them on the floor in front of the dais. The headman of the constables will put apart one marker for every blow.

One will also see on top of the bench the large square seal of the tribunal, and the gavel. The latter is not shaped like a hammer as in the West. It is an oblong piece of hardwood about one foot long. In Chinese it is significantly called *ching-t'ang-mu* 'Wood that frightens the hall.'

The constables stand facing each other in front of the dais, in two rows on left and right. Both plaintiff and accused must kneel between these two rows on the bare flagstones and remain so during the entire session. They have no lawyers to assist them, they may call no witnesses, and their position is generally not an enviable one. The entire court procedure was in fact intended to act as a deterrent, impressing the people with the awful consequences of getting involved with the law. As a rule there were every day three sessions of the tribunal, in the morning, at noon, and in the afternoon.

It is a fundamental principle of Chinese law that no criminal can be pronounced guilty unless he has confessed to his crime. To prevent hardened criminals from escaping punishment by refusing to confess even when confronted with irrefutable evidence, the law allows the application of legal severities, such as beating with whip and bamboo, and placing hands and ankles in screws. Next to these authorised means of torture magistrates often applied more severe kinds. If, however, an accused should receive permanent bodily harm or die under such severe torture, the magistrate and the entire personnel of his tribunal were punished, often with the extreme penalty. Most judges, therefore, depended more upon their shrewd psychological insight and their knowledge of their fellow men than on the application of severe torture.

All in all the ancient Chinese system worked reasonably well. Sharp control by the higher authorities prevented excesses, and public opinion acted as another curb on wicked or irresponsible magistrates. Capital sentences had to be ratified by the Throne and every accused could appeal to the higher judicial instances, going up as far as the Emperor himself. Moreover, the magistrate was not allowed to interrogate the accused in private, all his hearings of a case, including the preliminary examination, had to be conducted in the public sessions of the tribunal. A careful record was kept of all proceedings and these reports had to be forwarded to the higher authorities for their inspection.

The reader may wonder how it was possible that the scribes accurately noted down the court proceedings without the use of shorthand. The answer is that the Chinese literary language in itself is a kind of shorthand. It is possible, for instance, to reduce to four written ideographs a sentence that counts say twenty or more words in the colloquial. Moreover there exist several systems of running handwriting, where characters consisting of ten or more brush strokes can be reduced to one scrawl. While serving in China I myself often had Chinese clerks make notes of complicated Chinese conversations and found their record of astonishing accuracy.

I may remark in passing that the old Chinese written language did not as a rule have any punctuation and that in Chinese there is no difference between capitals and small type. The falsification mentioned in the fourteenth chapter would, of course, be impossible in most alphabetical systems of writing.

'Judge Dee' is one of the great ancient Chinese detectives. He was a historical person, one of the well-known statesmen of the T'ang dynasty. His full name was Ti Jen-chieh, and he lived from A.D. 630 till 700. In his younger years, while serving as magistrate in the provinces, he acquired fame because of the many difficult criminal cases which he solved. It is chiefly because of his reputation as a detector of crimes that later Chinese fiction has made him the hero of a number of crime stories which have only very slight foundation in historical fact, if any.

Later he became a Minister of the Imperial Court and through his wise counsels exercised a beneficial influence on affairs of State; it was because of his energetic protests that the Empress Wu who was then in power abandoned her plans to appoint to the Throne a favourite instead of the rightful Heir Apparent.

In most Chinese detective novels the magistrate is at the same time engaged in the solving of three or more totally different cases. This interesting feature I have retained in the present novel, writing up the three plots so as to form one continuous story. In my opinion Chinese crime novels in this respect are more realistic than ours. A district had quite a numerous population, it is only logical that often several criminal cases had to be dealt with at the same time.

I have followed Chinese tradition in inserting near the end of the book a kind of survey of the cases by neutral observers (twenty-third chapter), and I also added a description of the execution of the criminals. Chinese sense of justice demands that the punishment meted out to the criminal should be set forth in full detail. At the same time, Chinese readers want to see at the end of the book the meritorious magistrate promoted and all other deserving persons suitably rewarded. This trait I reproduced in a more or less subdued way: Judge Dee receives an official commendation in the form of an Imperial inscription, and the Yang girls a gift in money.

I have adopted the custom of Chinese Ming writers to describe in their novels men and life as during the sixteenth century, although the scene of their stories is often laid several centuries earlier. The same applies to the illustrations, which reproduce customs and costumes of the Ming period rather than those of the T'ang dynasty. Note that at that time the Chinese did not smoke, neither tobacco nor opium, and did not wear the pigtail—which was imposed on them only after A.D. 1644 by the Manchu conquerors. The men wore their hair long and done up in a topknot. Both outdoors and inside the house they wore caps.

The posthumous marriage mentioned in the thirteenth chapter was fairly common in China. It occurred most often in the case of *chih-fu*, or the marriage of unborn children. Two friends would decide that their children would eventually marry each other. Frequently, if one of the two children died before having reached marriageable age, it was married to the surviving partner posthumously. In case of the bridegroom surviving this was a mere matter of form. The polygamic system allowed him to marry one or more other wives, but in the family register the dead child-bride remained recorded as the one and only First Wife.

In the present novel the Buddhist clergy is placed in a very un-favourable light. In this respect also I followed Chinese tradition. The writers of ancient novels were mostly members of the literary class who as orthodox Confucianists had a prejudice against Buddhism. In many ancient Chinese crime stories the villain is a Buddhist monk.

I also adopted the Chinese custom of beginning a crime novel with a brief introductory story where the main events of the novel itself are alluded to in veiled terms. And I also retained the Chinese-style chapter headings in two parallel sentences.

The plot of the 'Rape Murder in Half Moon Street' is derived from one of the most famous cases ascribed to Pao-kung, 'Judge Pao' (full name Pao Ch'eng), a well-known statesman who lived during the Sung period; he was born in 999 and died in 1062. Much later, during the Ming dynasty, cases allegedly solved by him were written up by an anonymous author in a collection of crime stories called *Lung-t'u-kung-an*, or in other editions, *Pao-kung-an*. The case utilised in the present novel is called in the original *O-mi-t'o-fo-chiang-ho*. This brief story gives but a bare outline, while the way in which the magistrate discovers the truth is not very satisfactory. He makes the criminal confess by letting his agents act the part of ghosts of the underworld, a popular motive in Chinese detective novels. I preferred to substitute a more logical solution, giving 'Judge Dee' some scope for exercising his deductive talent.

'The Secret of the Buddhist Temple' is based on a story entitled *Wang-ta-yin huo-fen Pao-lien-ssu*, 'Magistrate Wang burns the Pao-lien Temple.' This is the thirty-ninth tale in a seventeenth-century collection of crime and mystery stories, published under the title of *Hsing-shih-heng-yen*, 'Constant Words for Rousing the World.' This collection was compiled by the Ming scholar Feng Meng-lung (died 1646); he was a prolific writer who in addition to two similar collections published also a number of plays, novels and scholarly treatises. I retained all main features of the plot, including the introduction of the two prostitutes. The original, however, ends with the magistrate burning down the monastery and summarily executing the monks, an arbitrary procedure that is not allowed under the ancient Chinese Penal Code. I substituted a more complicated solution, utilising the attempts of the Buddhist church to dominate the government, which during the T'ang dynasty at one time constituted quite a problem. It is not inapposite to let 'Judge Dee' play the leading role in this story. It is an historic fact that at one time in his career he had a large number of temples where evil practices prevailed destroyed.

The essence of the 'Case of the Skeleton under the Bell' was suggested by the famous old Chinese crime novel *Chiu-ming-ch'i-yuan*, 'The Strange Feud of the Nine Murders.' This novel is based on a ninefold murder which actually took place in Canton, round the year 1725. In the original the case is solved in the regular way in court. I gave it a more sensational ending, borrowing the motif of the bronze temple bell, which occurs at least once in every collection of crime and mystery stories of the Ming and Ch'ing periods

The flogging of the mats utilised in the twenty-fourth chapter was suggested by the following story: 'When Li Hui of the Later Wei Dynasty (A.D. 386–534) served as Prefect of Yung-chou, a salt carrier and a wood carrier quarrelled about a lamb-skin, each claiming it as the very one he used to wear on his back. Li Hui ordered one of his officers: "Question this skin under torture, then you will know its owner." All the officers were dumbfounded. Li Hui had the lamb-skin placed on a mat, and had it beaten with a stick; then grains of salt came out of it. He showed them to the contestants, and the wood carrier confessed' (c.f. R. H. van Gulik, *T'ang-yin-pi-shih*, 'Parallel Cases from under the Pear-tree,' a thirteenth-century manual of Jurisprudence and Detection, Sinica Leidensia, Vol. X, Leiden, 1956).

I thought that a more or less detailed account of the feud between the two families as given in the thirteenth chapter of the present novel would be of some interest to the Western reader. The Chinese are by nature a very forbearing people, most controversies are settled out of court by compromise. On occasion, however, virulent feuds will arise between families, clans or other groups, and then these are carried on relentlessly till their bitter end. The case Liang *versus* Lin is a good example of such a feud. Similar instances sometimes occurred among Chinese immigrant communities abroad. I mention the 'tong wars' in the United States, and the internecine fights of the 'Kongsi's' or Chinese secret societies in the former Netherlands East Indies in the end of the nineteenth, and the early years of the twentieth century.

R. H. v. G.